COLLISION
COURSE

By the Author

Lake Effect Snow

Collision Course

Visit us at www.boldstrokesbooks.com

COLLISION COURSE

by

C.P. Rowlands

2010

COLLISION COURSE

ISBN 10: 1-60282-133-X
ISBN 13: 978-1-60282-133-0

THIS TRADE PAPERBACK ORIGINAL IS PUBLISHED BY
BOLD STROKES BOOKS, INC.
P.O. BOX 249
VALLEY FALLS, NY 12185

FIRST BOLD STROKES PRINTING: JANUARY 2010

CREDITS
EDITORS: CINDY CRESAP AND STACIA SEAMAN
PRODUCTION DESIGN: STACIA SEAMAN
COVER DESIGN BY SHERI (GRAPHICARTIST2020@HOTMAIL.COM)

Acknowledgments

Special thanks to Jennifer Knight, who saw something in this story. To Rad, for offering the contract and also for always being there, within minutes, when I had a question. Also, thanks to Vic Oldham for a read-through and suggestions.

To my only beta reader, Nikki, who didn't let me down, ever. Not once.

My fellow authors were a brick wall for me, and I thank you all.

Finally, there is only one Cindy Cresap in the world, and this book would not be here without her insight, enormous help, and humor. I'm not sure why, but she never threatened my life. At least that I'm aware of. She is absolutely irreplaceable.

Dedication

For Gloria—For all the summers.

PROLOGUE

"Niki! Whoa!" Brie yelled. Niki had just turned left instead of right. "Aren't we going to the lake?"

"I've got something to show you first, baby. I'm so excited I can't wait another day." Niki revved the powerful red BMW convertible up a notch and cut a corner very close. Brie grabbed the armrest and braced herself against the dashboard.

"Damn! Slow down. Please?"

Niki gave her a wild, high-flying grin and slowed the car. "I'm sorry, I'm just so hyped I can barely stand it." She pulled over to the curb in an area close to the center of Milwaukee. "Look, Brie." She sat on the top of the seat and held her arms out. "This is it."

Brie ran her hands through her windblown hair and looked around. "What?" she said. They were in one of the most run-down sections of the city. Almost all of the houses on her side of the street were deserted and in terrible shape: Windows were either broken out or boarded up. One was partially burned. A house across the street still had crime scene tape wrapped across the porch.

Niki didn't seem to notice, and her energy never faltered. "This is it. Century! The next project I'm taking on for the Willis Foundation!"

Brie took another look around. "You're going to be…here? You know about the…crime rate here?" She was more than flabbergasted. She was a little frightened.

Niki slid back into her seat and turned toward Brie. "Baby, you know the story. Grandad started the Willis Foundation right after the Second World War. This was the first land he bought in Milwaukee. Fifteen acres." She gestured in the air. "Brie, our house is done. I've finished the design of the sports complex on the lake. This"—she gestured again—"will be the next project. I get to finish Grandad's and Dad's dream."

"You and what army of bodyguards, Niki Willis?" Brie exclaimed. "Listen, I'll quit teaching and learn to shoot. I'll come out here every day with you." She turned for another look at the burned house and then swiveled back to Niki. "I'll be—" She stopped when she saw the pure happiness and love on Niki's face. Niki started the car and this time drove toward Lake Michigan.

"Where are your shoes, honey?" Brie said. "It's against the law to drive barefoot."

"At home, by the back door." Niki grinned as she turned the car off the pavement and onto the beach. She downshifted as they moved onto the sand. She navigated the car carefully around several dunes and rolled to a stop close to the water's edge. The sand crunched under the wheels as she backed the car to a safer spot. Brie adjusted the volume of the music while Niki stretched for the small bucket in the backseat, humming off key.

Brie shook her head at the murdered tune. "Don't give up your day job, honey." Their laughter mixed with the music from the car and drifted out over Lake Michigan. The air still held the sharpness of a cool morning as it faded to afternoon summer warmth. Niki handed Brie a glass.

"To us and life. Our life," Niki said and stood on the driver's seat. One hand gripped the steering wheel and the other held the glass. "This is the best day of my life. Happy anniversary, Brie."

Brie looked up at Niki's small, lithe frame, backlit by the sun. Curly black hair almost touched the white T-shirt. The well-worn jeans were clean. Brie grabbed the windshield for balance, holding her glass to Niki's, and laughed. "We're going to fall over, you know." The sound of crystal clinking blended into the music as they drank and leaned in for a long kiss.

Brie took a quick breath as Niki's fingers slipped inside her braless dress. Her breasts hardened against the touch. It had been like this from the first. "Niki! God, yes."

"Thirteen years, Brie. I've loved you from the moment I saw you."

Brie's stomach muscles twitched as Niki caressed the skin, then moved lower. She gasped. "Put the top up and seats down, now."

"Here," Niki said and handed her the glass. She jumped over the car door onto the sand. "Set the glasses down, honey."

The desire Brie saw on Niki's face made her heart race as she sat down and secured the glasses in the cup holders. "That noise? Is that the waves?" Brie said over her shoulder.

A dirt bike roared from behind a dune and the smell of hot exhaust flooded the air. Niki started to turn as a gunshot echoed and she fell. The next shots hit Brie. The sharp crack of the shattered windshield and her screams echoed together across the water. Seagulls, startled into flight, wheeled between Brie's eyes and the sun.

CHAPTER ONE

Two years later

A light wind cooled Brie's face and she looked up from her book, suddenly aware of the sounds around her. Tree branches scraped above her, their dry leaves adding a little harmony. Kids behind her played soccer and their laughter floated past her.

Her foggy mind drifted. This Milwaukee park next to Lake Michigan had been hers forever. She'd always found it odd that she'd grown up, moved away, then ended up living in the same neighborhood she'd started out in. When she and Niki had bought the house across the street from this park, she felt as if she'd traveled in a circle.

The noise from the soccer game caught her attention again. She'd played soccer here too, learned to skate and ride bikes as well. The breeze swept through the elm, oak, and pine trees in front of her.

The last of the yellow wild lilies nodded in the light wind. She and Niki had planted those five years ago in the middle of a dark, moonless night. They had brought them from their nearby house in a wheelbarrow with flashlights. Then they had planted wild daisies and tiger lilies on the other side. Those flowers, like many in her own yard, had been dug up in the woods in northern Wisconsin. It was illegal to dig up wildflowers in this state and carried a hefty fine if you were caught. The park had left them alone and probably assumed some good citizen had donated them from a local nursery.

Niki, always stretching boundaries. The day they'd been shot, she'd been driving barefoot. Brie tilted her head at the yellow lilies. *Our flowers, baby.*

Several children ran past her, startling her. Brie adjusted the open textbook in her lap, a book she had written for her own class. She tried to concentrate on the words but the printed page blurred, and she rubbed her damp eyes. Were these tears ever going to stop? Disgusted, she tossed her apple core into her brown sandwich bag just as a gust of wind carried the paper sack off the bench. She bent to retrieve it and a skateboard rolled dangerously close to her head.

"Hey," she yelled at the glimpse of red shorts and cropped white T-shirt disappearing quickly over the hill, out of her vision. "Darned kids," she said to no one in particular as her heart raced. "Darned everything," she added, standing and brushing sandwich crumbs off her short black skirt.

"Brie," someone called and she saw her sister Valerie walking toward her.

"How'd you know I was here?" Brie said.

"That blond hair of yours is like a laser, and you're not exactly short."

"Like you?" Brie said but smiled. At almost five-eight, Brie was easy to spot in most crowds. "Did you come directly from the hospital?" She looked at Val's blue scrubs.

"Mom has the boys, and I wanted to see you so I came by on my way to pick them up." They began to walk toward Brie's house. "I stopped by your house first. Your yard looks gorgeous. Niki's flowers."

"I mowed this morning," Brie said. "She'd have loved those blue ones. I think they're called blue wood asters and I can't ever tell anyone where we got them. I remember planting them." She looked at her house, smelling the freshly cut grass, and cleared her throat as her eyes threatened to fill again.

"Okay, illegal but lovely." Val grinned, but the roar of a dirt bike rose above her words. Brie stepped back in a panic…right into the path of a skateboarder. There was a sharp pain and suddenly she was on the rough concrete of the sidewalk.

A woman's worried voice said, "Are you all right? Omigosh, I am so sorry."

Brie's eyes locked on the red shorts and tanned skin. Children talked excitedly in the background. Was someone hurt?

"Did the bike hit someone?" Brie heard her words slur and closed her eyes as strong arms gathered and lifted her.

"A bike? No. There wasn't a bike. Hang on. Your sister's bringing her car." The warm arms holding her increased their grip and she was deposited on the front seat of Val's big SUV.

"Thank you," Brie mumbled and looked up into gray eyes. Deep *concerned* gray eyes with long black lashes.

"Don't move." Val used her nurse voice as the car seat reclined. "I'm driving you to Urgent Care."

"What happened? I heard a dirt bike."

"No, there wasn't a bike," Val said. She moved away but Brie heard her talking to someone. The SUV moved and Brie's eyes opened to the ceiling of Val's car. "Did someone get hurt?" she asked.

"You, dufus. You got hurt. Someone on a skateboard ran into you."

"What's next?" Brie said softly. She rubbed her eyes against the lurking tears.

"Weren't you on duty at Omni last night? Have you been to bed yet?" Val asked.

"I slept when I came home, got up, mowed the yard, and went back to sleep." Brie saw a big smear of blood on the palm of her hand. "Where did this blood come from?"

"You were down and out like a stone." Val parked the car in the Urgent Care lot and examined the blood on Brie's hand.

"I didn't get a good look at that kid, but his mother was with him."

Val threw her head back and laughed. "Oh, brother. That was no kid that hit you, cookie, and that's probably her blood on your hand." She was quiet for a moment, still holding Brie's hand. "Honey, when did you get so thin? You're melting away."

"It's your imagination," Brie said. "I weigh the same as last week."

"Your eyes look older than our mother's." Val sighed and took the keys out of the ignition.

Brie turned her head away. "My eyes weigh the same too. I'm making progress. I'm past spontaneous weeping in public places. Well, almost." Her side began to ache and she shifted against the pain. "Don't you think we should go inside?"

CHAPTER TWO

"Watch out," someone yelled. Jordan stopped instinctively, avoiding a load of bricks moving by. She had rushed to the construction site, late. If she wasn't careful, she was going to have another accident.

"Must be my day," she said, jamming the hard hat farther down on her head. She adjusted the tool belt on her hips. She hurried through the partially framed house, looking for her uncle. Finally she saw him, standing over a table with blueprints.

"Sorry I'm late. I had to drop the kids off and change clothes," she said. "Where are we?" She bent over the table to have a look at the plans.

Her uncle, John Kelly, shifted an unlit cigar in his mouth and took a hard look at her. He stubbed a big meaty finger on the blueprint. "We're here, and what the hell happened to your eye?"

"I was working with Tyler on the skateboard in the park earlier today and ran into someone," she said absently, concentrating on the papers in front of her.

"You're going to have a shiner. Here, look at me." He tilted her chin and turned her head for a more thorough look. "Have you been fighting? Skateboard, my ass. It's going to be a beauty…and you've got a cut."

"It *was* a skateboard. I was on it and this woman just stepped right in front of me."

"Your mom's going to kill me. She'll never believe you didn't get it here. I want you over at Urgent Care as soon as we finish, and I mean it." He laid a brick on the blueprints to keep them from blowing away in the wind. "We won't need your expertise until Friday, so you've got a few more days to put ice on that baby."

Jordan groaned. She'd just dropped Tyler and Jenna off at her mother's and she didn't want to go back. "Can't you find something for me to do here, at least until after dinner?" They grinned at each other. It'd been this way since her dad had died.

"Your daddy would make you go," John said, his grin widening.

Jordan sighed. She'd go. Her father and John had begun this firm the year she was born. Three years ago she'd come into Kelly Construction as a full partner, but she still had to take orders from John.

"Wait," John said. "There is one thing. Go upstairs and look at the framing on the bathroom in the master bedroom. Take a measurement, will you? I just walked by there and I don't think that southwest corner is right. Something's off."

Jordan took the steps, two at a time. The breeze whistled through the wood on the second story as her boots echoed on the floor. She loved this phase of building. Everything smelled good and the possibilities were everywhere. She stopped, bracing herself in a framed window, looking out at Lake Michigan. She was going to be stiff after the collision in the park. Gently, she pulled on her back and arm muscles, then pushed forward, easy and slow. If she'd been paying attention, none of this would have happened. She'd been looking at that house again, the English cottage on the edge of the park, and that woman had stepped right into her, then fallen like a rock. Had she fainted? *Women. Always fainting or screaming.* She'd never understand her own kind. *Well, they also don't pay attention, Jordan.*

A sudden wind sliced pain across her cheek and eye. "Ow," she said softly, kicking her boots against the wood. She didn't look at women very often, but this one was unusual. *Different*, she thought. When she'd picked her up, Jordan had immediately thought of a wounded animal. She hadn't weighed anything.

Jordan pushed on her muscles one more time. It had all happened so fast that she hadn't even caught the woman's name, but something about her had hung in her mind all the way to work. "Huh," she said, thinking of the anatomy drawings that hung on her studio wall. The woman's stomach had been firm with just a hint of feminine hips. It was that graceful bone structure that she always noticed.

The wind kicked up some dust in the yard below and she turned.

"My God, this house is huge," she said, then laughed at herself. Every time she walked through this house she said the same thing. She went into the master bedroom, took out her tape measure, and began to compute the framing on the southwest corner.

"Crap!" John was right. "Who the hell did this?" They had left off about one-fourth of the studs. She stood, looking at the corner. No, they hadn't left it off. They had just stopped and not finished. She turned to go back to John and then decided to talk to her foreman instead. Bix would have this up and done before the day was finished.

CHAPTER THREE

Urgent Care was quiet for a change as Val and Brie walked inside, the cool air swirling around them.

"What's going on?" Brie said. "I can't believe there's no one in here." All the chairs were empty and a custodian was maneuvering a floor polisher down the middle of the gray tile. The screech of the small motor hurt her ears and she frowned down at the floor. It felt as if everything irritated her these days.

Both Val and Brie knew the nurse behind the desk. "Hi, Linda." Val pointed at Brie. "This one got hit by a skateboarder in the park across from her house."

Linda leaned on the counter and looked at Brie. "Still losing weight?"

"No."

"Don't want to talk about it?"

"Right."

"We should get together. You take some of mine and we'll both look better." She pulled a form off the desk. "Tell me what happened."

"Val and I were walking toward my house and I got hit by a skateboarder in the park. My left side hurts. I need someone to look at it. Perhaps an x-ray?"

"We can do that." Linda typed information into the computer, printed the paper, and shoved it across the counter. "You know where to sign."

Brie bent, scribbling her name on the form.

"Do you still like the volunteer work you're doing for Omni Ambulance?" Linda asked.

"I feel as if I'm always in training, but it's interesting. I still like it." Brie handed her the form.

"Nice job the other night. The accident you and Sean brought in," Linda said, taking a thorough look at Brie.

"Just a shame. Kids drinking and lost control, slid into that tree. We had a terrible time getting them out of there."

"Are you up to date on shots?" Linda tapped several computer keys and looked at the information. "If you don't quit losing weight, there won't be anywhere left to give you a shot."

Brie didn't answer. She simply turned and walked to a chair, sitting carefully. Her side was beginning to hurt again. "I have to call Mom," Val said and walked out the front doors, dialing her cell phone. Her blue hospital scrubs made a whispering sound as she walked away.

"Come on, I'll get this started," Linda said. Brie followed and tightened her jaw. God. She hated the chemical smell of hospitals. It always made her think of Niki's death and the three months she'd spent in the hospital recovering from her own injuries.

Brie tried to get comfortable on the hard examination room bed as she and Val waited for the doctor. There was a bruise the size of a watermelon just above her left hip. She traced what she could remember. She'd been talking to Val, smelled the freshly mown grass in her own yard, the noise of the dirt bike, pain, and then…what? All she could think of was red shorts and a caring voice. Wait, there *was* something else. A hint of a woman's sweet sweat. She'd loved that on Niki. The slick skin, touching it with her tongue, the salty taste. She turned her head and looked at her.

"What did you say when I called that kamikaze skateboarder a kid?"

"Hardly a kid. She was a full-grown woman."

"Oh." A *woman* had hit her? But she'd heard children talking.

"There were children there?"

"Two of them. A little blond girl, about six or seven, and a dark-haired boy, maybe ten, looked like his mother."

"A young woman, then?"

"Mid-thirties, probably. Good looking, about your height. Nice muscles."

"Okay," Brie said a little playfully. "That's why you were laughing. I missed a good-looking woman?"

"You may be down, but I'm hoping your eyes haven't died."

Don't count on it, she thought but said instead, "Classes start soon. I have to defend that paper I wrote several years ago, before the shooting. It's due by this January and I've been working on it."

Val's face brightened. "I remember your first year teaching at the university. Niki threw that great party for you, the 'I am so proud of you' party. You were twenty-four and I was twenty-two, just out of nursing school. I got the job at St. Luke's three weeks later. That was the night Harold asked me to marry him." She gave Brie a brilliant smile. What Brie didn't say was that it was also the night that Niki had asked her to move in with her. She stared hard at the ceiling, willing herself not to cry again.

"I've taught at Sparta for fifteen years," Brie said and changed the subject. "Thanks for driving me over. Did you happen to see my book, the one I was reading in the park?" Val shook her head as Dr. Michael Wolfe pulled the curtains aside.

"Brie," he said, smiling and then nodding at Val. "The O'Malley girls."

"Don't even start with me." Brie held up a hand. "Someone on a skateboard hit me. Or I hit them."

"The good news first," he said, handing Val the clipboard. His gray hair shone in the big overhead light as he looked down at Brie. "Nothing's broken."

"But?" Brie let the words hang, knowing the other shoe was going to drop.

"You're off duty at Omni, at least until I'm sure your muscles are healed. That's a hell of a bruise. How big was the person who hit you?"

Brie looked at Val. She had no idea.

"A woman, about one-twenty, give or take," Val said and concentrated. "Around five-eight, about the same as Brie. More muscular."

Brie grinned. "Nice eyes and a warm voice. Does that count?"

He thumped her lightly on the forehead. "You. Be quiet."

"The other woman had a cut on her eye and Brie had her blood on her hand. I was so worried about Brie that I kind of ignored her."

Dr. Wolfe frowned at the paperwork and looked at Val. "She was out? Immediately? Let's fill out one more form, just in case. Come with me, Val."

They left and Brie stared at the ceiling. *I was really out? Christ, what's the point?* She heard Dr. Wolfe say something to Val. He'd been her doctor for so long that she thought of him as family. He'd been a godsend when she and Niki were shot.

People talked in the hallway, a man and a woman. She listened carefully and recognized the man speaking. It was a doctor she knew. When the woman spoke, Brie's eyes flew open. It was the skateboard woman. Or at least it sounded like it.

"We're going to do some blood work on you, kid," Dr. Wolfe said, coming back into the room with Val. At just thirty-nine she was a long way from being a kid. Brie looked at both of them and knew they had talked about her weight. "You've had the hep series for your job at Omni and you're up to date on everything else."

"My favorite vampire," she said wryly and let her arm drop, offering a vein.

At that moment, the woman in the cubicle next to them said, "Ouch. That hurts."

"That's the woman that ran into me," Brie said. Dr. Wolfe and Val both looked at her as if she were speaking in tongues. "I'm serious, listen."

Automatically Val and Dr. Wolfe turned to look at the curtains, listening. Brie slid off the other side of the bed and went through the curtains.

"Brieanna." Val caught her just before she parted the curtains next to her own cube. "You can't do that."

"Why not? I think it was my fault. The least I can do is apologize."

"Have you lost your mind? It was an accident." Val turned her around and shuffled her back into the cubicle.

"Fine. I'll wait for her in the lobby." The woman next door complained again. They were quiet, listening. Dr. Wolfe started laughing.

"You're going to get us kicked out of here, Brie. This is not legal, or ethical. If you want to wait in the lobby, fine, but we can't eavesdrop. You're both in the medical field, you know that." He shook his head, grinning. "My nurse will be in and draw the blood. I'll get back to you, Brie, about the blood work. Now get dressed and get out of here. Oh, remember, ice and ibuprofen when needed and see me next Monday, unless I call you sooner." He closed the curtains and left.

Brie pulled on her skirt, slipped into her sandals, and looked at Val, who was poised at the entrance, watching her.

"Cute top. Yellow's a good color on you," Val said, then pointed at the cubicle curtain. "Are you really going to wait for her? At least you might actually *speak* to another woman." She grinned. "That's hopeful."

"Hopeful?" Brie brushed past Val into the hallway. "More like wishful thinking."

CHAPTER FOUR

The Urgent Care lobby was busy. Brie found a quiet spot near the big windows. Should she have sent Val home? Dr. Wolfe had given her ibuprofen but it hadn't kicked in yet, and she wasn't sure she could walk it. Maybe she should call her mother for a ride. She moved to wait near the door and stared out at the parking lot. That woman certainly was taking a long time, but there had been blood. Was the injury serious?

She heard a voice, *the* voice, and swiveled so fast that pain shot up her side. A woman leaned against the desk. Hands propped on elbows held her head up, one leg curled behind the other. Brie shifted carefully to the left and looked. Val was right. She was a nice-looking woman. Supple body in khaki shorts, construction boots, T-shirt, and nicely muscled arms. Dark brown hair highlighted with gold fell over her ears.

For the first time since Niki, Brie took a second look at another woman. A little rush rocked through her. A *real* look.

She waited until the woman finished her paperwork and turned. Brie saw the huge shiner as the woman looked at her.

"Hi," Brie said cautiously. Her eye and the small cut looked terrible.

"Hello," the woman answered. "Didn't expect to see you here. Are you all right?"

"Just a bruise. A big bruise."

"Me too." She smiled, holding her hand out. "Jordan Carter."

"Brieanna O'Malley." Brie took the offered hand and immediately loved the smile. "That looks sore." Without thinking, she gently touched the injured skin. "Oh. I'm sorry."

"No. *I'm* sorry."

"Ugh. Looks like it hurts. All I could remember was your voice, so when I heard you next to me," she gestured down the hallway, "I waited to apologize." Brie stood straighter with some effort. "It was my fault."

"I had to get to the site and the kids had me late already. Otherwise, I'd have followed you here. Did your sister give you the card I left?"

"No. Maybe. I don't remember."

There was a moment of silence and then both spoke at once.

"Do you have a vehicle here?"

"Do you need a ride?"

They laughed and Brie said, "I sent my sister to pick up her kids. Would you give me a ride home? It's less than a mile north."

"My truck's outside," Jordan said and led Brie through the doors. "Do you live close to the park?"

"Across the street, actually," Brie said. She stopped when they got to the big pickup.

"What?" Jordan said. She opened the truck door.

"Normally, I could get into your truck." Brie shook her head. "Right now, with my side, I'll never make it." She took a step back. "Look, thanks, but I'll walk. It's a nice day and not that far."

"You're hurt," Jordan said. "I managed to get you into your sister's SUV, so I think I can get you into this truck." Before Brie could say anything, Jordan picked her up easily and adjusted her in her arms. "Are you on a diet?"

Brie sighed. If one more person mentioned her weight today... "No, I'm not on a diet," she said. Jordan deposited her on the seat and flashed that wonderful smile again. Brie took a breath.

"Do you have dinner plans or someone coming home for a meal tonight?"

Brie leaned into the one warm arm still casually draped around her shoulders. "No."

"Good. I'll take you out for dinner." Jordan jumped back to the ground effortlessly.

Brie smiled as the big diesel motor started up. *Talk about being swept off your feet.*

When they pulled into the restaurant, Brie uttered a surprised, "Oh," and turned to Jordan. "This is the old drive-in where I hung out when I was in high school." A huge pink sign hung above the building: Patrick's, with garish purple and pink flowers all over it.

"I grew up on the north side, so I never knew about this place," Jordan said. "Hope you're not into fine dining. Just great burgers." Wind off Lake Michigan skittered through the truck, lifting her hair. She absently jingled the key ring in her fingers. "A couple of gay guys own this now." She grinned mischievously. "I hide out here."

"What?" Brie said. "Hide out?"

"Oh, before I forget." Jordan leaned across Brie and opened the glove compartment. "I picked this up where we…met." She held up the book Brie had been reading in the park. "Leave it here so we don't forget it when I take you home. Don't move. I'll get you down."

Brie looked forward to those arms around her again and wasn't disappointed. The taut rope holding her together relaxed several inches. Maybe being slammed to the ground knocked something loose?

Once inside, Brie stopped. The entire place was various shades of lavender, accented with light touches of pink and blue, all complemented by coffee-colored browns. Low lights from antique hanging fixtures softened the colors. It was a long way from what it had been when she had been in here as a kid. Jordan led them to an empty booth, sat down against the wall, and stretched her legs out on the faux leather. "I'm starving and I'm buying. It's the least I can do," she said. She examined her hands. "Darn, I'm dirty, Brieanna. I'm sorry. I didn't notice."

Brie sat across from her. Jordan's brown hair was cut with gold. Rich dark oak, Brie thought. Warm, just like her smile.

"It's Brie and it's fine. I asked you for the ride."

"Brie? Like the cheese?" Jordan teased. "Give me a minute to wash up." She was out of the booth and gone before the waitress could lay the menus on the table. Brie picked up a menu and began to study it. She had eaten cereal that morning and should have been hungry, but nothing looked interesting. Her therapist had said loss of appetite was a common indication of depression. "Well, duh," she said to herself.

Jordan came back to the booth and pointed at the menu. "See something you like? I always have the same thing, so I really don't have a clue what's on there." She scrounged in her shorts pocket, pulling out a watch. "Ha. My watch. I thought I left it at home." Then she pulled out a plain gold band and slid it on her finger.

"Is that a wedding ring?" Brie said without thinking.

"What?" Jordan said just as the swinging doors to the kitchen opened to men's loud laughter. Patrick came striding into the dining room. He skidded to a stop when he saw them.

"Brie," he said. He pulled her out of the booth and hugged her. She almost screamed in pain.

"Wait, Patrick," she said, trying to breathe. She felt Jordan's hand on her shoulder.

"What is it? What's wrong?" He released her and she leaned back into Jordan.

"An accident."

"I'm sorry," he said and looked at Jordan. "What the hell happened to your eye?"

"Same accident," she said. "We had some sort of celestial convergence in the park by Brie's house. I was on a skateboard and ran into her."

Brie sat down gingerly and Patrick bent to look into her face. "How've you been, love? We haven't seen you since the memorial… we've been so busy with this." He stepped back for a more thorough look. "My God, you've lost weight. Dinner's on me for both of you, and I mean it. We have George's special tonight and you'll love it." Patrick grinned at them. "You girls look really banged up. Oh no. Don't tell me, you've joined a roller-derby team." He threw his hands up dramatically, laughing at his own words, and then gestured at the room. "How do you like it, Brie? It's ours, George's and mine."

"You quit your job?"

"No, I come here directly after I'm done. We're having a great time with this. Wait until I tell George you're here," he said, striding back through the swinging doors.

"Are you all right?" Jordan asked. She peeked over the booth at the swinging doors. "Roller derby?"

Embarrassed by the fuss, Brie changed the subject. "Do you come here often?" she said and then realized she'd just uttered the world's oldest cliché. She blushed but Jordan didn't appear to notice.

"This has been my little secret, where I can hide from my mother.

She'd never think of looking for me out here. A restaurant on the lake owned by gay guys."

Brie straightened. "I've known both George and Patrick since high school. This is kind of a historic place for all of us." Uncomfortable, she turned the conversation again. "I seem to remember children today."

"My kids, Jenna and Tyler, ages six and ten."

Brie looked down. *Married.* "So you're a mother and…"

Jordan shifted her body and pulled a leather wallet out of her hip pocket. She took out a business card and pushed it across the table. Brie narrowed her eyes. That wasn't typical of a married woman. A man's leather wallet in the hip pocket.

"I'm a finish carpenter for the family construction business," Jordan said, pointing at the card. Kelly Construction was printed in black print over a green shamrock, followed by Jordan Carter, Finish Carpenter above telephone numbers and an e-mail address. "My dad and Uncle John started this before I was born. I've grown up with it."

"Do you like it?"

"Almost as much as breathing and my kids," Jordan said as Patrick appeared at their table again, holding two steaming plates.

"What are you girls drinking?" he said.

"Beer, and I don't care what kind," Jordan answered, scanning the food.

"Me too, and thank George for us. What is this?" Brie asked.

"I'm not telling until you taste it," he said with a wide grin as they both cut into the meat and took a bite.

"It's heaven." Jordan closed her eyes and chewed.

Brie immediately loved it and was shocked to find herself starving as the fragrant food woke her appetite. "This is excellent."

"George's special cut of beef," he said. "See the sauce? He marinates it for hours and then adds those little potatoes with fresh peas, the pearl onions sprinkled over it all. Brie, the salad has the mystery dressing you've always loved."

His eyes were kind. The last time she had eaten George's food had been at a party that she and Niki had hosted and he had catered. Patrick's face said he remembered too.

"This is outrageous, Patrick." Jordan took another bite. "Thanks."

He grinned and looked at Brie with a question on his face before he disappeared into the kitchen. Jordan raised her eyebrows at the look.

"He's just wondering about me," Brie said. "We need to catch up and it's been months." She took another bite, thoroughly enjoying the taste. "Did you say you *hide out* here?"

"Sometimes my mother sends people looking for me, but they haven't found me…yet. This would be the last place they'd look."

"Looking for you?"

Jordan held up a finger, closing her eyes again as she chewed. Brie stopped, entranced, watching the long eyelashes fall on tanned cheeks. Lovely, despite the eye. The enjoyment on Jordan's face was almost sensual and Brie took yet another deep breath.

"Mom has…" Jordan said, interrupting Brie's thoughts. "Mom… has special dinners now and then, and she wants me there. That's why she sends people looking for me."

Brie saw that Jordan didn't want to talk about this, so she went for something less personal.

"Have you been a carpenter for a long time?"

"Okay, long story short. I was an eighth grade schoolteacher for five years, but I swear, even though I enjoyed it, the wood called to me. I know it sounds dopey, maybe even crazy, but sometimes when I'd walk outside after school, I could smell the wood. Finally, when Tyler started school full time, I threw in the towel and went back to construction. My uncle brought me in as a full partner." Jordan looked up and Brie saw a glimpse of pride slide across her face before the smile took over. "My dad's dead and there's just Mom, but she's a piece of work. She's going to blame this eye on the job, and I want at least one more beer before I face her." Her face was suddenly shy, warming Brie's heart. "I've never told anyone about that business with the wood."

Brie held her hand over her chest. "I swear, your secret's safe with me."

"What about you?"

"You're going to laugh. Teacher."

Jordan chuckled. "Where?"

"Sparta," Brie said. She realized her plate was empty and the salad was gone. It had been months since she'd eaten this much, and she was still hungry.

"Sparta? The private university?" Jordan stopped eating, looking interested. "You're a professor?"

"Political theory and history. I've cut back for the last couple years, a sort of sabbatical, so I'm only teaching two courses right now. I also volunteer for Omni as an EMS."

"No wonder you're so…slender. That's intense stuff, all of it."

"No, college isn't intense. I've been doing that for a long time." Brie slid her plate to the side. "I'm just a volunteer at Omni, a learner with the EMS job. However, I've just become fully qualified to drive the ambulance with lights and sirens. I'll probably wreck it the first time out."

"I think that's a lot, Brie. A professor? That book of yours in my truck has your name on the cover."

Brie nodded. "The old publish-or-perish stuff. Sometimes I use my own work as a source." She looked up to see George leaning against the wall watching her, and motioned him over. "What's for dessert, best of the chefs?"

Quiet and intense, George was as small as Patrick was big. Brie had always felt close to him. He came over, resting against the booth.

"You need to put on some weight, Brie. But you know that."

"Find some of that wonderful raspberry torte thing I know you have back there," Brie teased. "That's worth a million calories."

He gave them both a sweet smile and reappeared a few minutes later with the dessert. Brie thought she was going to drool and looked at Jordan. They gave each other wide grins and dug in. Finally, shoving plates away, they both leaned back and sighed.

Jordan exhaled. "What a feast! Truthfully, I've only eaten hamburgers here. Little did I know."

"He is the finest cook I know and an interesting man. You should talk with him. He has fascinating stories."

Jordan looked at the crowd in the restaurant. "Too bad he's gay. You sound like you connect."

"We *do* connect," Brie said and followed Jordan's eyes out across the room.

Jordan leaned across the table with a little knowing smile. "Listen, the men in here have been checking you out. They must fall over like empty beer bottles when you walk by. Those dimples and eyes."

It wasn't the knowing smile that made Brie's breath hitch or her face color. It was the unexpected flash of sensuality in Jordan's eyes. Something deep inside Brie moved.

"I'm sorry. I didn't mean to embarrass you. Just stating the obvious," Jordan said with a puzzled expression. "Anyway, could we do this again? Eat, I mean. It's been a long time since I've met someone that I'm fairly certain has a brain."

Brie nodded. "Sure, I've enjoyed this too." She narrowed her eyes, baiting Jordan a bit. "Or are you just after George's special raspberry torte?"

They both laughed and Brie liked the warmth caught in Jordan's laughter. She took a card out of her purse, handing it across the table. "Here, take this."

Jordan studied it. "Doctor?"

"Well, yes, to teach…"

"That's right, college level."

❖

Brie turned the lights on in her dark house and realized that she'd forgotten to ask about Jordan's husband. Actually, unlike most married women, Jordan hadn't volunteered any information. And what was the business about the wallet? The ring? *Well, I still wear Niki's ring.* Brie wrapped her arms around herself, remembering how good those arms had felt—and that spectacular smile. And then those eyes, with that flash of sensual…experience? "Whew," she said. She whistled a little, heading for the shower.

How long it had been since she'd been out to eat? Just a meal, nothing special. She scrubbed her hair, suds rolling over her face and body as she counted. Over six months, she was sure. She leaned into the water, rinsing. Where had everyone gone to?

Wrapped in an old robe, she went to the kitchen and poured herself a glass of wine, something else she hadn't done in forever. She turned on her office lights and settled at her desk. She actually felt a little energy. It had been absent so long that she hadn't recognized it. Now that she was officially off the Omni volunteer list until next week, she'd have plenty of time to set up an outline for the graduate class that began

Monday. Maybe even a little work on her book, her fiction. In addition to her academic work, Brie had published two historical mysteries and the second book had been a bestseller. She had signed on for a third novel and written over twenty thousand words, but had lost it when she and Niki had been shot. Along with everything else, she thought. Her fingers hovered over the computer keys. She hadn't looked at it since before Niki's murder. She exhaled and opened the file, beginning to read.

Finally, she finished and closed the file. "A beginning, but that's about all." She looked at the calendar. She had to see her editor soon. Twenty-eight thousand words wasn't nearly enough. She could only remember bits and pieces of why she'd started this third book in the series. The story was based on old letters Niki had found in a house she and her father had demolished. She frowned at the computer. She couldn't even remember where the box of letters was. Tomorrow. She'd look for them tomorrow.

Idly, she opened the book she'd been reading earlier in the park and found the paragraph she'd been studying. Seven years ago, when this work had been published, she and Niki had argued over the writing. Niki felt it should have been broken up for more drama. Brie had argued that the work was academic, structured for information, not fiction. She wanted the facts up front, letting the drama lurk under the data. Niki had debated wonderfully, always staying on point, keeping her quick temper in check.

For three days they had quarreled, bickered, and wrangled. Finally, Niki had shoved her down on the bed, talking old politics as she had slowly taken their clothes off and loved her until she'd screamed. Niki had risen up over her, both of them dripping with sweat and sex. "I give up. The writing stays as you want it and I lose the battle," she had said suggestively, sliding her fingers inside again, "but I win the war."

"If you'd asked ten minutes ago, I'd have said yes to anything," Brie had answered, gasping.

The words blurred again and she closed the book. "Damn," she said at the irritating tears. She turned off the lights and went in search of more ibuprofen.

Careful of her painful left side, she reached for the picture on the nightstand. It was a photo of the two of them, leaning into each other,

her arms draped over Niki's shoulders, pulling Niki back into her, Niki's hair curling down toward those wonderful breasts.

"Hi, girl. Missed you today, but what'd you think of her? *Jordan*...a pretty name. A question mark, but maybe a friend? She feels warm and smart but she doesn't feel *married*. Better tell her I don't do men, don't you think? I've totally lost my gaydar. I could have sworn she batted for our team." She laughed a little and then was quiet, thinking. "Niki...it felt good to be held again."

Brie took a deep breath, listening for Niki's distinctive words but, as usual, heard nothing. She replaced the photo on the nightstand and turned over onto her back, hoping for sleep. It found her.

❖

"Yes." Brie pulled in a sudden deep breath as Niki's fingers traced a long, slow, torturous path from her lips to the hollow of her throat, over her collarbone, and around each nipple.

Brie pushed against the hot, smooth skin as Niki whispered, "I need you."

"I'm here, don't stop. There. Yes." Brie gasped as a warm, familiar mouth settled on her breast, tongue teasing the nipple until it hurt and fingers grazed her belly, down inside her thighs. Only Niki could take her here, arouse her so fast that by the time her fingers slid inside, she was fully wet. Tongue and fingers moved in unison and Brie opened her legs wider.

"Yes." She shuddered as the pressure finally exploded, sending her off the bed, grabbing for the familiar body but finding only pillows.

"No," she groaned into the pillow, "Niki, no." Shuddering, she held the pillow tightly as a second, deep orgasm shook her again.

"Dammit, dammit, godammit." She sobbed, holding on to the pillow so hard her fingers hurt and pain shot down her injured side. Finally, her body stopped shaking and she sat up carefully, wiping her wet face. She felt as dark as the room. She pushed off the bed and started toward the bathroom for a shower to clean herself. Even the bed was wet.

The ibuprofen was still on the counter. She took one and stepped into the shower, scrubbed herself with soap, rinsed, and turned the water to cold. It had been at least seven or eight months since the last dream. "Shit." She gritted her teeth against the cold water. Every part of her ached.

CHAPTER FIVE

The late summer day was giving way to night as Jordan parked the big pickup inside the fenced enclosure. John was on his way out but saw her and stopped. They stood together and watched the lights come on in the city.

"What's the word on your eye?" John asked and took a fresh cigar from his pocket.

"I'm good to go. Just looks like the devil. The darned doctor messed with it." She went silent, looking out at the lake.

"And?"

"I met the woman at Urgent Care, the one I hit in the park today on the skateboard, and took her out to eat. Unique. A nice lady, a professor and an EMS volunteer."

"Right up your alley, a professor," he said and smiled.

"I do love books. By the way, do you remember where I hang out when I'm avoiding Mom?"

"Sure, the old drive-in out on Sheridan Road." He took a drag on the cigar and blew out a cloud of blue smoke.

"We went there and had the best dinner I've had in forever. She knows both of the owners, Patrick and George."

John gave a short laugh. "Patrick's a good man. He did the audit on our company last year, and yes, I know he's gay."

"Huh? Oh, yeah, he is. Mom would never think of that place."

When Jordan's dad had died unexpectedly, her mother was left with three children and immediately sought comfort in the church. Jordan, the youngest at seven, was already rebelling against her rigid, church-inclined mother. John and his wife, Nancy, had offered to help out and then just never let her go. She'd lived in their house until she went to college.

"Well, have to go check on my babies," she said with a little laugh. "Wouldn't that tick Tyler off if he knew I called him a baby?"

"Put ice on that eye," John yelled after her. Jordan heard him and waved but didn't turn around.

❖

Jordan drove slowly past her house. The only lights on her mother's side were in the den. She checked out the street and her mother's driveway. No extra cars. Her mother's latest attempt to find her a man hadn't been a bad effort. But interesting? No. Nothing except carving and her kids seemed to catch her mind these days. Well, except for the bright, beautiful woman she had crashed into today. Brie O'Malley was *interesting*.

She walked up the sidewalk to her door and glanced at her dark studio. She hesitated. No. It was too late. Her father had built the studio and this house two years before she was born. When she was small she had played in the studio while he carved. She loved the way the light slanted down from the skylights and through its odd, square windows. The smell of the wood. The sound of rain on its slate roof. But most of all, she loved the carving.

Jordan looked at the house. When her older brothers had grown up, her mother was left here, alone. Several years later, when Jordan's husband, Pete, had been killed, her mother had asked Jordan and the kids to come and live with her. At first, she had resisted, and then it had seemed like the most sensible thing in the world. Her mother was getting older and though she could be aloof, often rigid, she was dependable.

Uncle John had stepped in and remodeled the entire north wing of the house for Jordan. He had added a kitchen, a den, an office, a double garage, and her own entrance. So far, it had worked. As long as they stayed out of each other's way, Jordan thought. The only time they had fought was when she quit teaching school and went into the construction business. However, her mother's dinners and the men had just about driven her wild. She shook her head and unlocked the door.

Once in the house, she checked her children. Jenna was asleep the wonderful way kids sleep. Totally and wholly. Her blond hair was curled against the pillow, blanket up to her ears. Jordan sat on the bed carefully, laying her fingers lightly on the silky hair, Pete's hair. "Good night, baby," she whispered, bending to kiss the warm little cheek.

Tyler was sprawled on his stomach, brown hair hanging over his face and a baseball gripped in his fingers. Jordan gently pried it loose and set it on the desk. She kissed his hair and pulled the door half closed behind her.

With a deep breath, she braced herself to confront her mother. The gray light of the television flickered in the dim room. She coughed so she wouldn't startle her. "Mom?" she said.

Charlotte Kelly was stretched out in a big recliner, the gray in her hair reflecting the light off the television. "Take those boots off, Jordan. I won't tolerate construction dirt in this house. You can do what you want on your side but not mine."

"Sorry, just wanted to let you know I'm home. Thanks. I'll see you tomorrow."

She turned to go but her mother spoke. "Jordan, the kids were wonderful today. We baked cookies. Isn't Jenna beautiful?"

"She's Pete's twin, Mom. Yes, she is."

"How are you doing?" her mother said kindly, something Jordan didn't hear very often. She stopped, mindful of her eye.

"Fine, thanks for asking." She waited, puzzled.

"I'm going to take a trip."

"What?"

"I'm sure you remember that my mother was born in Ireland, close to Dublin. Someone from church is going over there and I'm going too. I'd like to see where my mother was born and the rest of my family that is still there. I'm not getting any younger."

Jordan thought before she answered. This was a loaded statement from her mother. "None of us are, Mom. You should go. When?"

"The end of next week."

"Next week?" Jordan repeated, caught off guard. "Go, Mom. Enjoy. John and Nancy will help with the kids. Is there anything I can do?"

"I talked to Nancy today. I've been thinking of this for a while, picking up things here and there. I'm almost ready and even have my passport."

"I'm glad you're going. Have a good time."

"Thank you." Her mother nodded. "That's all, dear. Have a good night's sleep."

"Mom," Jordan said walked around so her mother could see her fully. "I had an accident in the park today, while I was showing Tyler how to manage that new skateboard. I've got a black eye and thought I should tell you before you saw it and wondered what happened."

"I know. The kids told me. Jenna has the most vivid imagination. She said you hit the woman in the moon. That woman must look like that little picture that hangs on Jenna's bedroom wall?"

Jordan nodded. "I suppose she does." They shared a rare laugh. Jordan bent to see the book her mother held. It was a current mystery, one that she'd just finished, and she looked up, surprised one more time.

"I didn't know you read," she blurted out before she thought.

"Of course I read. I've read all my life."

Jordan bit her tongue. "I'm sorry," she said and left for her own part of the house, feeling foolish. She should have known the kids would have said something about the accident, something she and Uncle John hadn't thought of.

She took a bottle of cold water from the refrigerator, grabbed a package of frozen peas, and settled down into the dark kitchen. Holding the peas against her eye, she watched the big full moon hanging over the lake and thought about her mother.

She pulled a pad of paper from the desk in the kitchen and rummaged for a pen. The frozen peas melted on the table while she did a quick sketch of Brie O'Malley by the bright light of the moon. On her way to the shower, she tossed the paper and pen on her bed. *Something about her body.*

She downed two aspirin, then checked the kids one last time. Finally, she crawled in under the covers, braced herself against the headboard, and did one last sketch of Brie. Pen poised over the paper, she saw it. *That place, just above the belly button, down across the hips, top of the legs. That's it.* She laid the pad of paper by Pete's photo, glanced at the picture, then reached for it. Jenna really did look like her father. She rubbed her thumb on the frame. Their marriage had a rough beginning but they'd managed to become more than sexual partners. They'd become lovers and friends before Pete had died. She missed the friendship. She missed him.

"Maybe it's time for a friend," she said to the photo. In the last five years, after Pete had been killed, she'd let her friends go, one by one, until it was only herself and the kids. Disgusted and disappointed in herself, she hadn't wanted anyone around. Until tonight. Jordan replayed the dinner in her mind. Brie had listened so carefully to everything they'd talked about, as if she was searching for something. At the same time, she'd seemed a little off balance, almost as if she was unused to smiling and laughing. When Jordan asked her to go out and eat again, Brie had looked surprised, almost hopeful.

Jordan rolled to her side, looking out the window at the oak tree and the moon hanging behind it like a lantern. Brie's thick and tousled blond hair had fascinated her, curling back around her ears, long in the front, falling across her forehead. Jenna was right. Brie did look like the woman in the painting that hung on her wall. The woman was wearing a simple little top and skirt, much like Brie had worn today, and her hair was bright like the moon. Brie had unusual pale blue eyes, but something was wrong with them. They looked sad or old. A woman like that had to be married, but she hadn't mentioned a husband. Maybe a recent breakup? Or a divorce? She'd worn a ring.

The scene at the park had been so confusing when they'd crashed. The sister had said Brie lived across the street and she'd immediately turned to the English cottage, the house she'd looked at often when she had the kids out there. The one-story house she'd been looking at when she crashed into Brie. It had a faux-thatched roof with tall windows, and the prettiest yard. When they'd driven into Brie's driveway tonight, she'd caught her breath at the coincidence. She'd always wanted to see the inside of that house, and it was all she could do to keep from asking for a tour right at that moment.

Jordan sank further into the comfortable bed. Something about Brie made her feel like helping her. Just before she fell asleep she knew one thing for certain. She was going to have to feed Brie, a lot. She was too thin.

CHAPTER SIX

The next morning, Brie shoved her chair back from her desk and closed two of the three books she'd been working out of. Three years ago, before she and Niki were shot, she had published an academic position paper that said America was sinking into a highly unstable political climate after 9/11, paralleling the shocked years after the Civil War. Afterward, mired in the trauma of recovery for almost a year, she couldn't have told anyone what the initial reaction had been to her paper. However, last winter, a respected professor from the East Coast had written a direct challenge to her work and, for the first time, her foggy mind stuttered alive as she read his publication. She would defend her position but had more work to do. "A *lot* more work," she said, rubbing her eyes, "and I think I need glasses." She dialed Dr. Mary Kramer, her first lover and her best friend's older sister.

About sixty minutes later, she was waiting for Mary at the Inlet, an upscale restaurant frequented by Milwaukee's business and professional people, known for its good food, good drinks, and casual liaisons. She braced herself for their usual confrontation. Mary, Nora, and Brie had known each other since before grade school, and Mary never let them forget that she was two years older. They had an odd argumentative relationship but, despite their history, Brie wouldn't want anyone else for this. She looked at the menu with a wry thought. If Mary had taught her to kiss—and other things—she could certainly take care of her eyes.

"Hey, blondie, what's up?" a husky voice said behind her. Mary never simply walked into a restaurant, she always *arrived*, and Brie smiled inwardly. Mary eased into a chair across from her. Her white business suit draped her body with a casual elegance over a gray silk shirt that matched her eyes, the eyes that fixed Brie with a piercing stare right now. "My God, you've lost weight. What the hell, Brieanna, put some meat on those bones."

Brie sighed. "That's why I'm here, eating."

Mary picked up the menu and ran her eyes over it quickly. She probably knew it by heart, Brie thought as Mary gestured impatiently at the waiter. "Have you made up your mind?"

"Of course," Brie said. The waiter was beside them in a heartbeat and Brie saw him look anxiously at Mary. Obviously, he had waited on her before.

After he left, Mary leaned over. "He's the slowest waiter here and I hate having to deal with him." She took a drink and cruised the women in the restaurant over the rim of her glass before looking at Brie again. "What's up?"

"Promise you won't laugh?"

"You know me better than that," Mary said with a knowing smile. Brie did know her, better than she was comfortable with.

"I'm fairly certain I need glasses."

Mary's husky laugh carried over the conversations and music in the restaurant. "Christ! I thought this was serious. We'll finish and go back to the office. How old are you?"

"Same as your sister, Nora. Thirty-nine this summer. This isn't about vanity. I just don't want to wear the damned things."

"You're so freaking serious." Mary laughed again, turning heads around them.

"And you're the same arrogant bu—" Mary's large hand quickly covered her mouth before Brie could finish.

"You can't say *that* here. Some of my patients are sitting around us."

The waiter came and they were quiet while he nervously placed food on the table.

"This afternoon? My eyes?" Brie said, daring Mary to take the offer back.

Mary took a bite of her pasta with a suggestive smile. "I can do more than that."

Brie felt her face warm but kept her words even. "Stop it." They stared at each other over their food and Mary was the first to drop her gaze.

"All right. Other than losing way too much weight, how are you?"

"I'm surviving, still volunteering at Omni, and I like it. Classes begin next week and I'm actually looking forward to it. I have to defend my last paper soon and I'm chugging along. In the grand scheme of things, I'm breathing." She took another bite of her BLT, glad to be hungry enough to eat. She glanced at Mary. There was kindness in the normally predatory eyes. "The most exciting thing that's happened was getting hit in the park by a skateboarder."

"What?"

"It was my fault. I stepped into her path."

"A teenager?"

"No, a full-grown woman." Brie almost added *good-looking* and then irrationally remembered her dream last night.

"Sometimes I forget who I'm talking to, Brie."

"I've known you for over thirty-five years."

Mary looked up with mild surprise. "It's been that long?"

Mary ate for a moment, her eyes distant. "I remember you hanging out in the library in high school. You had the best figure."

"Me and about twenty others."

Mary gave Brie a warning look, pushed her empty plate to the side, and stood. "Then you won't mind if I make a trip to the ladies' room." She grinned and Brie wondered what lucky woman she had spotted in the restaurant. Watching Mary leave through the noisy crowd, she was shaken by a gut-wrenching memory. She gripped her glass of iced tea. It was one of Mary's bathroom breaks that had led her to Niki.

Sixteen years ago, Brie had been home for her dad's funeral and had stopped in the restaurant for a quick meal and a moment alone. Mary had simply wandered in, sat with her, and talked. Devastated and wounded by the loss of her father, Brie had fallen into Mary's arms, taking up where they had left off four years earlier. Mary had been gentle and understanding for several nights, taking Brie to her bed, but then she disappeared. Finally, on the day Brie was to go back to college, they had met here, at the Inlet. Brie had been so shaky emotionally that anything Mary did made her giddy. She'd been checking her airline ticket, talking about her master's program and summer plans. Their summer plans.

Mary had not said much and excused herself to go to the restroom. Brie waited, checking out the restaurant. A woman at the bar with beautiful dark curly hair caught her eye and smiled. Immediately fascinated by the lovely hair and smile, Brie stared at her, then looked away, flustered. Was she flirting? A few minutes passed, then more minutes. No Mary. Brie restlessly looked around the restaurant. It was the usual crowd of under-forty-year-olds, drinking hard, laughing loudly. Still, her gaze would always come back to the pretty young woman who continued to look right at her with that intriguing smile. Finally, she had thrown her napkin on the table and walked toward the women's bathroom.

The young woman then did something no one had ever done to her, before or since. She did a slow three-sixty as Brie walked toward her. Her yellow spring dress, flared at the waist, ended just above the knees with yellow heels to match. It was a perfectly symmetrical body. The scalloped V-top ended just above the waist with a glimpse of breasts. Distracted, Brie had almost walked right into her. The slender, toned athletic muscles had her full attention.

"Hi," Niki said in a soft voice, her hands on Brie's hips to balance her. Apologizing, Brie had introduced herself and started to move around her.

"Wait with me? She'll be out in a minute, I'm sure." Niki said, putting a light arm around Brie, moving her toward an empty bar stool. Suddenly Brie had understood that Mary was meeting someone else in the bathroom.

Niki had laid her fingers lightly across her arm while Brie waited on the stool next to her, completely embarrassed.

Finally, Brie spoke. "You must know her?"

"Only too well, I'm afraid," Niki answered. Brie could still remember the look in those brown eyes. Not an inch of pity but a lot of understanding. Those eyes had given her courage.

"I have a while before my plane leaves. Why don't you come with me, drive along the lake?" The interesting eyes with thick eyelashes had lit up with a silent cheer and Brie swore later *that* was the exact moment Niki Willis had stolen her heart. She had paid for the entire meal and walked out the door with Niki. They had driven up Lake

Drive and talked for over an hour before she dropped Niki back at her car. Later, she had flown back to school with a smile on her face and Niki's information in her purse. Now, in the same restaurant, sixteen years later, Brie looked over at the bar and the empty bar stool. Mary had given her Niki and the best years of her life.

She was still smiling as Mary examined her eyes.

"What the hell's wrong with you?" Mary growled and Brie almost laughed out loud but didn't answer.

She did indeed need glasses, and she picked out frames with Mary hovering about her, trying to choose for her.

"You said just for reading. Who cares what they look like?"

"It's important, Brie. You never know who's looking."

"Oh, I think I do," Brie said, looking over the selection. "No one."

That night, sitting at her computer, Brie slipped the letters from Niki's foundation back into the folder. She had set up an appointment with Thomas Teller at Smith & Teller. As general counsel, Thomas handled the distribution of the foundation's multiyear pledges. Niki's father and grandfather had been well-known architects, and they'd begun the Willis Foundation in the forties. When Grant Willis had died, Niki had taken her father's place on the foundation board under Thomas Teller's guidance.

The last five years had been spent on the new athletic center close to Lake Michigan. The dedication was only several weeks away at the annual softball awards banquet. It was the first project of Niki's that Brie had worked on, and Dannie Brown, Niki's best friend, was doing a piece for the ceremony. Brie picked up the phone and left Dannie a message to call her when she could. She left her therapist a message as well. The therapist had asked her to check in when she had dreams like she'd had last night. She tossed her pen onto her desk and picked up the two envelopes lying off to the side. Maybe it *was* time to sell the house and move. Two West Coast universities had invited her to teach next year. She looked around her office, then closed her eyes. Should she leave *their* home? Could she?

Her stomach clenched as the familiar questions ground through her brain. *Niki. Did it hurt when they shot you? Did you see me get shot? Were you ever awake…conscious…in the hospital when I wasn't?*

Brie took a deep breath and rubbed her temples. This was a constant battle she endured. Her mind loved to taunt her and she wiped her wet eyes. She simply could not remember anything beyond a certain point that day. Anything. And she'd give *anything* to remember.

Jordan Carter's business card was propped against the wooden pelican that always sat on her desk, a little thing Niki had bought for her while they were vacationing one summer. She stared at it for a minute, then turned back to the photos of the Willis Athletic Center on her computer. She had helped decorate the main arena and gym, trying to keep Niki's ideas in place. It included a large playroom for children. She and Thomas had enjoyed picking out toys and playground equipment. What would Jordan's children think of the equipment, she wondered. Maybe she should call Jordan and ask if they'd care to give it a test run?

She picked up Jordan's card, rubbing the embossed surface with her thumb. Staring out at the September dusk, she thought of that unexpected flash of sensual heat in Jordan's eyes.

CHAPTER SEVEN

Jordan whistled, cleaning her kitchen. It had been a good morning. It was fun, being off work, even if she had to pay for it with a black eye. She had fixed the kids chocolate chip pancakes this morning and was sure it was the equivalent of fourteen Twinkies. She grinned, remembering her teaching days. She was certain both kids would bounce off the walls in their classrooms. Usually the children caught the bus in front of the house, but this morning she had driven them. Tyler joked with her about her black eye but Jenna had fussed over it. Jordan had held her on her lap before they'd left and let her touch the eye. Once she could see that her mother was fine, Jenna had gone on to other things. Jordan was still pondering their different reactions. Was it their different personalities? Age? Gender?

She changed her clothes and sat at the kitchen table over a fresh cup of coffee and the paper. "Oh, a new gallery, downtown," she said and saw a familiar name, a local woodcarver she knew. "I'll go and see what he's up to." They both belonged to the same Milwaukee artists' group.

She gathered her briefcase and the sketches she'd done of Brie and went to the studio.

Sunlight caught the remaining dew on the grass, throwing shards of light into the air. "It still smells like summer," she said as she walked across her yard and entered the dark silence of the studio. Waiting for her eyes to adjust, she felt the rush this room always gave her.

The row of sketches above her workbench caught her attention. They'd been done in an anatomy class she'd taken. Then she'd searched for the wood that she'd been interested in. She and Pete had brought it in together, then sat there and looked at the drawings together. The next day, she'd begun the carving. Jordan hung the three new sketches of Brie and sank back onto a high stool. *Seven years? Was that possible? Jenna wasn't even born yet.* She turned and looked at the unfinished piece in the middle of the room.

"Let's get some light in here," she said to the quiet. She opened the windows, then the shades on the skylights. Blue light and cool air rushed inside. She walked around the unfinished piece, a carving as tall as herself. *What's happened to me? I understand that everything stopped when Pete was killed, but shouldn't some inspiration be creeping back? At least a little knock on the door?*

Jordan walked back to the sketches again. Most of them were faces or quick impressions of what her vision had been. Brie was the first she'd added in years. She concentrated and searched her mind one more time. At first, nothing. Then she looked back at the new sketches. Suddenly she saw Brie, moving toward her from the hospital doors. The graceful economy of her body. It was just a flash as it passed her mind. She blinked. "Yes," she said.

Jordan reached for her briefcase and left, shutting the door firmly behind her. She'd stop at the construction site on the way downtown.

Jordan slipped between the wood framings on the second floor. Bix, her foreman, was not on-site so she'd come upstairs to check the master bedroom herself. She scanned it, thinking of the blueprints, and reached for her tape measure, then laughed a little. She wasn't wearing her tool belt. Well, it *looked* much better. She'd measure it later. She turned slowly, looking at the room. The tall windows were as graceful as she had hoped when she'd first looked at the designs. A gust of wind blew through the enormous room and she shielded her eyes from the blowing sawdust and dirt. The sounds of hammers, nail guns, and saws echoed around her as she turned to go.

John was looking at a generator when she got down. He looked at her, surprised. "I didn't know you were here," he said. "You look nice." Jordan was wearing dark blue pleated slacks, a light blue tee, and silver earrings. "Goes well with the black eye." He grinned. "Do you have an appointment?"

"No, just felt like something other than jeans. Have you seen Bix?"

"I sent her for those customized parts for the fireplaces. Our client is due in a few minutes. His wife's changed her mind again. Maybe you can get him settled down?"

They walked toward their trailer office. "I'd be happy to go home and change if you need help. I was on my way to see a carving exhibition at a new downtown gallery."

"No. You're off duty. Go to the exhibit," John said, holding the door for her. "Or go shopping, buy some books. Have you found time for your studio?"

She shook her head. It was an ongoing discussion with them. She could still do the small carvings, the whittling, but nothing more. "I swear, John, it all died with Pete," she said and looked away from him. *And then I did the unthinkable. Traded in my carving for the bars.*

The smell of freshly brewed coffee greeted her as they entered the big double-wide trailer. John immediately poured a cup for both of them and she looked at it tentatively. Even as fresh as this coffee was, she couldn't handle it without cream.

She heard John talking to someone in the front. A distinguished older man followed him into their office.

"Jordan, this is our client, Thomas Teller." John pulled a chair to the side of his desk. "Thomas, this is Jordan Carter, our finishing expert and third partner in the firm." He poured him a cup of coffee.

They shook hands and Jordan watched the man take a tentative sip of the coffee. She grinned inwardly at his face as his taste buds got hit with the full force of John's coffee.

"Would you like some cream or sugar?" she asked with a straight face.

He gave her a grateful smile and held out his cup. "My wife keeps changing her mind," Thomas said and laid a handful of brochures on John's desk. "Help." He held up his hands.

Jordan spread them out and studied each one. "Are we still doing a primarily white kitchen?" she asked.

He nodded.

Jordan looked at the wood and color samples before her. "Would you like me to meet with her, Mr. Teller?"

Once again, he looked grateful. "It's Thomas, Jordan. Yes, could you?"

"I'd be happy to take these samples and the designs we gave you in the beginning and go to your house. Or we could meet here."

"That would be excellent," he said and gestured at the brochures. "She's been poring over different samples every day. It would be better if you went to the house."

"I see. Just give me your address…or call her from here, now."

He pulled his phone from his suit pocket. "Let's do that."

John got up and went to the front office. Jordan waited a moment to make sure the wife answered and left as well.

"That was a nice touch." John smiled at her.

"You said no work till Friday. What could it hurt?" Jordan said.

Thomas called for them and they walked back to the office. "Could you go this afternoon?" he asked. Jordan nodded and he smiled, still talking on the phone. He hung up and took a notepad off John's desk. "This is wonderful," he said several times as he scribbled his address and his wife's first name on the paper. "Right now, I'm so busy. I really appreciate this, both of you."

"I have a little space this week, Mr.—" Jordan caught herself. "Thomas." She took the piece of paper. "I'll go now, if that's all right."

"That would be great," he said with a genuine smile and looked at her face. "That's a spectacular shiner. Did you have an accident here?"

Jordan laughed. "Not at all. I have two children and I was showing them a new skateboard in the park, the one by Whitehall. I ran into someone."

"It's a beauty." He grinned. "One more thing." He relaxed back into the chair. "When we called for bids for the Willis Athletic Center, why didn't you place one?"

Jordan raised her eyebrows at John. She had no idea.

"It was the wrong moment," John said and looked out the window.

"Kelly Construction could have managed that project easily."

John nodded. "I know, Thomas. The timing was off."

"How long ago was that?"

"Five years ago, approximately."

She glanced at John but saw that he wasn't going to say more. "John was helping me then. My husband was killed at that time. He was a Milwaukee fireman and one of the victims in the Haben fire. October, five years ago."

Thomas looked up, startled. "The roof collapsed, if I remember correctly. They couldn't find the bodies?"

Jordan nodded. "It took them four days."

There was a small space of quiet as Thomas absorbed the words. "Yes, that would have been around the time we were taking bids." He sighed audibly. "I'm sorry to hear that. Death is never nice, but it has a special, hard feeling to it when the person is young. And you have children?"

Jordan nodded. "A boy and a girl. Tyler is ten and Jenna is six."

"I didn't mean to bring up something sad. Your firm has always been so aggressive that I was just curious," Thomas said. "The foundation has another project coming up soon. It's much bigger than the athletic center we just finished. It'll be up for bid next week, and the window of opportunity to reply will be short." He gave John a youngish grin. "Of course, if you get it, you have to finish my house first."

Jordan packed her briefcase with everything she thought she'd need and left the men talking about the new project. She took the shortcut to the interstate and drove north into Milwaukee. She'd call John about the bid tonight. That sounded really good, and it was more their area of expertise than houses. When she'd come into the firm three years ago, John had told her that he was consistently being underbid on commercial work, and that was true. She'd seen the figures. However, now that residential work was slowing down, it would be nice to catch some commercial work. She tapped the steering wheel, thinking about the bid five years ago. It probably was called for when John was helping her deal with Pete's death and he simply missed it.

Something white was lodged in her car's visor and she reached for it. It was Brie O'Malley's professional card. She must have left it there after the meal the other night. Just as she put it back in the visor, her cell phone rang and her hand automatically went to her front right pocket. Then she remembered her phone was in her briefcase in the backseat. She'd just have to call them back, whoever they were.

❖

The meeting with Thomas's wife had gone well, Jordan thought as she wandered through the new art gallery later. The woman was as nice as Thomas and she had been very precise about what she wanted. Jordan stopped in front of a delicate carving of cattails with a splash of color. Nice, she thought. A woman's voice interrupted her thoughts.

"Do you like that?" a woman asked.

"I do, but is that a sandpiper?" Jordan pointed at the bird nestled in the reeds.

"Yes. I like the California bird and Wisconsin cattails. A unique mix."

Jordan took a second look at the woman. She looked familiar but Jordan didn't think she was a carver. She would have known her. "This is a nice gallery, and Emma Fiona's is a memorable name. I like the pieces I've seen so far."

"Thanks." The woman smiled and held out her hand. "Emma Fiona O'Malley."

"Oh, the owner," Jordan said and shook her hand. "O'Malley?" Her brain shifted. "Any relation to Brieanna?"

"Indeed. She's my older sister. There are three of us. Sisters, that is." Emma laughed easily and Jordan saw her look at her eye. "Do you mind telling me where you got that wonderful black eye?"

"That's how I met Brie."

"Oh no." Emma began to laugh again. "You're the woman on the skateboard."

Jordan's eyebrows shot up, sending a little pain through her eye. "She's all right, isn't she? It really was an accident."

"She said it was. Actually, she said it was her fault."

"No. I should have been more careful. I took her out to eat that night, after we both checked in at Urgent Care."

"Brie could use a friend right now," Emma said. "What brought you to my gallery?"

"I'm a local carver and always try to see anything new. Are these your pieces? I don't see a name."

"Oh no, I just own the gallery. I have more carvings in the back. Would you be interested?"

"Certainly," Jordan said and followed Emma as they went toward the back of the gallery. "Seriously, is Brie all right?"

"We O'Malley women are tough," Emma said and winked at Jordan. "She did talk to me about the accident. Actually, I thought she said you were a finish carpenter for a construction firm. And you had taught school?"

Jordan nodded. "The family business, but I have a studio at my home."

"Have you studied with anyone?"

Jordan shook her head no. "My father was a carver and I keep up with the locals."

Emma opened the door to the back storeroom and Jordan saw an intricate abstract. They began to talk about carving.

It was only later when she got back to her car that she thought about another cosmic bump with Brie O'Malley. *Emma said Brie could use a friend right now.* She took her phone out of her briefcase. Perhaps she could take Brie out for pizza with the kids tonight.

CHAPTER EIGHT

Footsteps echoed on the marble floor as the last graduate student disappeared down the hallway. Brie collapsed into her chair and closed her eyes. Her new glasses would be in tomorrow. "I could have used them today," she said to her empty office. When she had returned to teaching after the shooting, she had dropped a course but taken more graduate students to compensate. It kept the workload balanced and made her department chair happy.

She rubbed her temples and felt her stomach complain. Her appetite had finally found life after that meal with Jordan, and it reminded her that it'd been more than six hours since the cereal she'd eaten that morning. She'd called and left Jordan a message about taking the kids to the new playroom at the sports complex. Brie checked her phone. Jordan hadn't called back.

A light knock sounded on the door and she looked up to see Patrick leaning on the frame.

"Hello," she said, happy to see him. George followed him into the room and they settled into the comfortable chairs across from her desk. "I always think of you as some Celtic queen, up here in your castle," Patrick said and began humming "Camelot," looking around the turret-shaped room. Books lined the walls, and two of the eight tall, narrow windows were stained glass. It was beautiful in the sunlight and comfortable in every season except when the wind blew hard in winter, howling like a true castle. He gestured at the stained glass. "That was the best glass Niki ever did." Two women, one blonde and one with dark curls, wearing medieval dresses, both holding an armful of lilies, graced each window.

Brie got up carefully and walked to the windows. "These were the coldest, leakiest windows in the office until she worked on them. She reframed the casing, caulked them, and put these in. It's been warmer ever since."

They'd thrown a small party in here the night Niki had finished the windows and, after everyone had left, they had locked the door, finished the wine, and made love on the new carpeting. Niki had pulled herself up on an elbow and whispered to her, "Baby, whenever you're mad at me about something, look at these windows and remember this moment." Brie stared at the windows, remembering Niki's sexy voice and exactly what they had been doing at the moment she had spoken those words.

She turned too quickly and pain shot up her side, doubling her over. Both men were beside her in an instant.

"Damn," she gasped. "Remember the party that night?"

They all began to laugh. Patrick had fallen on the last step and been on crutches for several weeks with a bad ankle.

"We brought the wine," George said with a grin and picked up a sack off the floor. Patrick put three wineglasses on Brie's desk. The cork popped and George filled the glasses halfway.

"A toast," he said quietly, lifting his glass.

Brie drank the tears back down her throat and gave them a wobbly smile. George poured more wine and Brie protested.

"This is good for you, Brie," he said. "We need to talk, and both of us feel bad that we have left you alone so long. Niki would have kicked our butts for this."

They laughed, remembering Niki's incredible butt kickings. She was famous for dispersing crowds in a single moment and could have cleared a football stadium if she were angry enough.

"True," Brie said with a shaky breath. She lost count of the drinks as they talked. By the time they were ready to go, George had to lock the door for her, help her down the steps, and drive her home. He talked to her quietly as he drove her Subaru through the narrow streets by the campus. Brie leaned against the window, feeling well and truly drunk, watching the lovely September day fade and streetlights come on. Every piece of her ached for Niki.

George hit the brakes. A sporty silver Camry sat in her driveway, lights on and motor running, and a figure was just leaving her front door. George got out. Brie raised her head, peering through the dusk and headlights, trying to see who he was talking to. Squinting, Brie thought it was Jordan and opened her door, carefully negotiating her way to them.

"This is not a good night," she heard George say and Jordan turned to Brie.

Brie said a few words and caught herself slurring, so began again. "Is too   good night, I mean, we've been drinking   don't listen to him. Have some wine."

"I got your message about the kids. I thought you could go out with us tonight and have some pizza," Jordan said as Brie began to lean sideways and she grabbed her before she toppled. "I agree, not a good night for that, Brie." She began to laugh.

Frustrated with herself, Brie leaned into Jordan. "I smell like a bottle of wine. Or two."

"Or two," Jordan said softly, steadying Brie with an arm around her shoulders.

"But I'm hungry and these mean men haven't fed me," Brie mumbled petulantly. "Pizza sounds good." She snuggled against her, sighing with pleasure at the feeling of the warm and secure arm once again.

"Missed them," she mumbled into Jordan's hair.

"What?" Jordan asked.

"Your arms."

Jordan tucked Brie into her body as Patrick unlocked the front door. They got her to the couch and Brie stretched out. This felt good too. Her mind made a try at staying alert, then settled as someone covered her with a blanket.

❖

Jordan draped the blanket over Brie and felt that strange tug toward her once again. She straightened and looked around. What were the odds that she would be standing inside this house? A home that she'd been interested in for years? The ceilings were low but the rooms were big. Two walls were devoted to books. A stone fireplace dominated the living room in front of the couch where Brie lay. Large easy chairs sat on either side. There was no television, but a large sound system stood in the corner. It was inviting and she liked the bright blues, shimmering greens, and grays in the room. They were the colors of Lake Michigan.

Patrick's cell phone rang and he talked briefly. "Damn," he said, looking at George. "Jordan, can you stay a while?"

Jordan held her finger up. "Wait a minute," she said and dialed her mother.

"Okay, no problem," she said to the men. "What's happened?"

"The restaurant's sprung a leak in the kitchen," Patrick said. "We didn't mean to get her drunk. The moment just got away from us." He paused and looked at George. "Perhaps we should take a minute?"

George nodded, turning for the kitchen. "You'll need to feed her if she wakes up before we get back. She doesn't drink very often, but when she does, she's always ravenous. By the way, she does love pizza, all pizza. She'll eat anything. She also swears like a sailor when she drinks, so brace yourself. Here, let's go to the kitchen." They walked into the next room and Jordan took a deep breath when she saw it.

Three walls were entirely bricked, floor to ceiling. A stainless steel double oven, oversized range, and refrigerator sat against the bricked walls. The remaining wall was white with a grouping of three framed newspaper articles. Dark oak beams ran the length of the ceiling. A large trestle table sat on the largest oval rug she'd ever seen. Wide glass doors led out onto a deck. Blue glass jars with white and blue flowers brightened the room.

"Want a beer?" George asked, opening the refrigerator. "Patrick, come here."

"Niki *would* kick her butt over that," Patrick said, looking inside with a frown. "No wonder she's so thin."

"Beer's great," Jordan said, sitting at the long table. "Wow, this is a working kitchen. Someone likes to cook here. Brie? Her boyfriend? Her husband?"

"No," George said as he popped the cap on a bottle of beer and handed it to her. "Would you like a glass?" She shook her head and took the beer as they sat across from her.

George looked at Patrick. "Damn, it isn't our place to talk about this."

Jordan grinned at them. "I'm thirty-six, almost thirty-seven. What could you tell me that I haven't heard, seen, or even done? And, Patrick, you know about Pete. What I did after he died."

"It was Niki that cooked," Patrick said. "They owned this house and lived together for thirteen years." He continued, explaining the relationship, and then, the shooting. "Brie has lived here alone for a little over two years."

So many things were swirling through Jordan's mind that all she could say was simply, "That's a shame."

Patrick looked at his watch. "We have to go," he said. "Is there anything you need? George, look what we did, and now we're leaving her." They stood, both of them unsmiling, looking at Brie.

Jordan gave them a look. *Men!* "My children are with my mother, so I'm good to go here. Brie's fine with me. I'll stay until she's awake. She'll be okay. What's wrong with the refrigerator?"

"We teased Niki about that refrigerator because she always had it crammed with food. Now it's almost empty."

"Niki cooked with me, part time, when I owned the catering business," George added.

"Go on, you two. I'll be fine."

The minute they left, she went to the refrigerator. "Good Lord, almost bare." The fridge held only beer, juice, bread, and cold cuts. There were cheese and apples in the crisper. And skim milk. *Skim milk?* She pondered that, thinking of how slender Brie was. Shaking her head, she shut the door and looked around the kitchen again, letting her fingers run down the cupboards. Lovingly made, each of them. Not a crack or an open corner in the group, and the wood was solid. There was no veneer in this kitchen. Whoever had done this work was very good. She wondered if the rest of the house was this interesting. She moved down the hallway, turning on the lights. The first room was an office and she flipped the switch, starting to move inside, but then stopped. This wasn't her house. Still, she'd wanted to see it for years, and it was Brie's house. She'd just take a quick look.

First, she saw books and a beautiful desk. The desk looked like real wood. Walnut? She touched it but it felt funny and she looked at her fingers. They were covered with dust. A drawing board with a triangle hanging on the side stood in the corner. *All those books*, she thought. *This must be Brie's office, but the dust?* She took two more steps for a better look at the photo on the desk. It was a younger Brie, wearing a swimsuit, and her hair was longer. Jordan looked at the luscious figure. This was the lover's office. Niki?

The wall directly in front of her had four framed professional photos, all of Brie. She seemed to be modeling clothing. They definitely were posed shots. Jordan frowned. Brie was a model? She had said she was a professor.

She flipped the light off and went on down the hallway. There was a bedroom off to the left and a huge bathroom to the right, complete with spa tub and separate shower with room for two. A double sink took up an entire wall, but only one side of the sink and counter was in use. The delicate light peach color and beige tile with small characters glistened and she looked closer at the tile. Tiny faeries danced over each square, and they looked hand painted. Moving nearer, she discovered that each tiny figure was indeed hand painted and beautifully done.

She thought she heard a noise in the living room and went back down the hallway, but Brie was still sleeping peacefully. Jordan leaned over the couch, absently running her fingers through the thick blond hair, pushing it off Brie's face. It never would have occurred to her that Brie was a lesbian, nor did she care. The murdered lover was the information that had jolted her. No wonder Brie was thin. She should have recognized the expression in the eyes. She'd seen it in her own mirror enough after Pete was killed.

"Dummy," she said, thinking of their conversation. Most of her softball team was gay, and she'd been in their bars with them without thinking twice about it.

Brie moved restlessly. Jordan leaned over again, looking at her face, wondering how old she was. She had laugh lines around her eyes, something Jordan always liked, and long, dark lashes. They were probably around the same age, she decided as she straightened. One thing was certain. Brie was one of the most genuinely beautiful women she'd ever seen. She'd been right about one thing. Men probably *did* fall over looking at her. And drool. And reach. She smiled. "Sorry, boys, this one's not available."

There were photographs on the mantel and she wandered toward them, looking at the people. The first obviously was Brie's family, three little blond girls with a tall man and woman standing behind them. Probably Mom and Dad with kids, she thought, looking for Brie as a child. She spotted the wide quirky grin with dimples on the tallest child. Brie looked like the woman standing behind her. The next was of another family. A dark-haired man stood behind a slender woman with dark curly hair. A young boy and a little girl with the woman's curly hair stood in front of them. The people got older in each picture and, finally, there was a photo of a younger Brie and a cute woman with curly black hair, sitting at a table beside some sort of water with sailboats in the background.

"We were in Italy," a sleepy voice said behind her. A very rumpled Brie sat up on the couch wrapped in the soft blue blanket. Her hair stood straight up and she looked impossibly young.

"Your hair." Jordan broke into laughter.

"Shut up." Brie smiled sweetly. "I'm starving. Did I dream it or were you talking about pizza? The pizza menu is beside the phone on the kitchen counter."

Jordan got the menu and ordered pizza, but Brie was gone when she came back. Finally she reappeared, barefoot, in faded sweats and a short top. She flopped down on the chair next to Jordan. Her cropped T-shirt revealed an interesting tattoo around her navel and Jordan squinted hard to see it better. Was that a naked lady?

Brie pushed the hair out of her eyes. "I'm sorry, Jordan."

"For what?"

"Didn't you say something about your kids when we came home?"

"The kids are taken care of and pizza should be here in about ten minutes," Jordan said. "How do you feel?"

"Still buzzed. Christ, what the hell did I do?"

"Patrick and George—" Jordan began but Brie held up her hand.

"Classes begin next week and I was finishing grad interviews. They brought wine and talked about..." She trailed off, looking at Jordan.

"Niki," Jordan finished for her, looking into the tired eyes that momentarily flashed with misery.

"They told you?"

Jordan nodded with a little shrug.

"I should have told you at the restaurant."

"It doesn't make any difference, but I'm sorry about Niki."

"I didn't tell you because I forgot. For the first time in over two years, I forgot."

"You forgot?"

"I forgot Niki."

The doorbell rang as the pizza arrived. Brie got up fast, too fast, steadying herself on Jordan's shoulder. "The least I can do is pay," she said, starting toward the door and then looked around. "Where the hell are my things?"

Jordan pointed at an end table in the living room. As Brie turned, Jordan saw the big bruise on her side and her heart skipped. *I did that*, she thought.

"Want another beer?" Brie asked after she brought in the pizza.

"No, I'm good," Jordan said. Brie set a cloth napkin in front of Jordan and a gallon of milk with a big glass in front of herself. Both silent, they dug into the pizza hungrily.

Finally Jordan said, "Milk? And pizza?"

"What's wrong with that?"

"Just strange," Jordan deadpanned, trying to make Brie smile. "Maybe it's a lesbian thing?"

"Shit," Brie said. "You're going to make my life miserable over this, aren't you?"

"Wouldn't you? Beautiful woman lures unsuspecting straight woman into her home..."

"Stop it." Brie narrowed her eyes at her.

"I'm going to blackmail you. I'll put up flyers around campus advertising a certain professor's tattoo. Maybe we could do a contest, the best naked lady tattoo." She pointed at Brie's stomach and the woman curled around her navel.

"That's enough. Where are George and Patrick?"

"The restaurant sprung a leak and I said I'd stay."

"Dumb shits," Brie said under her breath.

"The boys told me that you swear a lot when you drink too much."

"*The boys*...who haven't even bothered in almost half a year," Brie said, standing and swaying dangerously. Jordan quickly half stood, righting her and seeing she was far from sober.

"Did you and Niki find this house together?"

"Of course," Brie said, lurching a little. Body tensed, Jordan watched her carefully, afraid Brie was about to fall.

"I love your house. I've looked at it from the outside every time we've been to the park."

"Thank you." Brie navigated into her chair, bracing herself on Jordan's arm. "I forgot where I was going," she said with a crooked grin. "I need to finish my pizza."

Jordan took another slice for herself. "Do you feel okay?"

"No, I feel drunk and picked on." Brie finished the last of the pizza and the milk. "We bought this house from Niki's parents. The kitchen and living room were finished, but we had to do the rest ourselves. C'mon, meanie, I'll show you the rest." She grabbed Jordan's hand. Off balance, she pulled them both hard, knocking her chair over. It felt like slow motion to Jordan as she saw Brie begin to fall. She gave a hard push with her legs, somehow twisting in midair, ending up underneath Brie with a loud thump, knocking the breath out of herself. Brie peered down at her with a confused expression. "We're always knocking each other over."

Jordan struggled for breath and, without thinking, put both hands firmly on Brie's butt just as a knee settled between her legs. Warm breath mixed with a light pizza scent flooded her face. She looked up into unreadable eyes and felt Brie's fingers run through her hair, down her cheek.

"You have beautiful eyes. Did anyone remember to tell you that?" Brie said softly.

Jordan took a quick breath as the knee pushed harder between her legs and her body began to wake up. Brie was staring at her mouth. *Is she going to…* Jordan spoke quickly. "Brie, are you okay, the fall…?"

"I'm okay. I'm always okay," Brie said and rolled carefully off Jordan and onto her back.

Jordan scrambled up and righted the chair. She held out a trembling hand, heart racing and body ready. She helped Brie stand and they moved to the dusty office. Jordan confessed she'd looked in there earlier.

"I don't have the heart to move anything," Brie said quietly. "I dusted about six months ago but couldn't get any further."

"Those photos?" Jordan said and pointed at the posed photos she had looked at earlier.

"I modeled for money, to get through school," Brie said. "Nothing major, just a catalog house. My mom and dad couldn't afford all of us in school." She dismissed it and flipped the lights off. Jordan followed her down the hallway as Brie touched the walls for balance, pointing out where they'd knocked walls out to reconfigure the rooms. Jordan touched the expert workmanship on the door frames and the coving along the floor. "Who did the work, the finishing?" she asked. "This is real plaster, not drywall."

"We did, and the real plaster was because Niki wanted to keep as much of the original materials as possible in the house."

"Just the two of you?"

"Yes, just us. Who did you think…?"

"When we're on a job, we usually have quite a few people doing work like this."

"Oh, I forgot. You're a carpenter, of course you'd wonder," Brie said. "Niki's dad did the walls for us, but all the rest is ours. I've got all of it on her computer. She was an artist, among other things, but her dad was Grant Willis. We bought this house from him. It originally belonged to his foundation."

"The architect?" Jordan stopped. "No wonder that picture on the mantel is familiar. Good Lord, I've been wandering around your house, looking at the craftsmanship. That explains it." Jordan thought of that morning. The Willis Foundation. "Brie, this is crazy. The house my company is building belongs to Thomas Teller."

"You're kidding. You're building Thomas's house?"

Jordan nodded. "This is a strange coincidence." She was thinking, trying to remember what her uncle had said about Grant Willis. "Wasn't that family killed in a plane crash?"

"Yes. Everyone but Niki died. Here, follow me."

They entered Brie's office and she turned on the desk lamps. "We were in the planning stages of this room when all of that happened. Look at the shape of that wall." She pointed behind Jordan. The wall was concave, loaded with books and a flat screen TV in the middle. Speakers were scattered through the books. Closets on either side squared the room.

Jordan turned slowly. Like the kitchen, it was a large room designed for work. The inlaid shelves were beautiful. The desk was enormous. A state-of-the-art computer was to the side with open books and a legal pad. A long table stretched along the back wall with books and papers scattered over it. Brie turned on the track lighting that ran above the table. An office chair was half turned in front of it as if someone had just gotten up.

Brie stood quietly, gripping the desk. "Niki did this for me. She did so much, left so many things everywhere. She was a small woman, about five foot five, but had more energy than anyone I've ever known. It was like living with a high-performance engine. When I'm in here . . ." Brie went quiet and began to move things on the desk.

Jordan walked to the big table in the back and looked at the books. They looked like history books, research books. Several legal pads were scattered about. The one in the front had written across it, in bold, black block letters: "It should have been me. Not her." Jordan froze and read the words again. The paper was almost ripped as if someone had written with a fist. She turned to look at Brie, still gripping the desk and staring at the book to her right.

"Brie," Jordan said, talking before she knew what she was going to say, "would you come over and have dinner with us tomorrow evening?"

Brie turned back to her, smiling. "That would be nice. Thank you."

"I never thought. Maybe we shouldn't go through the house right now."

"I live here. Come with me."

They went to the master bedroom and Brie showed her the other fireplace with the special tile. "That picture, on the mantel? We were in Italy getting the tile for this and the bathroom."

Jordan examined the tile. It was dun colored with large accents of green and blue.

"The colors in the living room are the colors of water. So is this sand and water?" Jordan said.

Brie nodded. "You'll see a lot of that in this house. We both loved water, tried to be close to it whenever possible. That's exactly what we had in mind in the living room. Here." She pointed at the blue quilt on her bed. The green and gray threaded through it looked like waves. Her brows wrinkled. "You're sensitive to colors."

"I'm a wood carver," Jordan said. She didn't want to talk about her carving right now. Or lack of carving. Or Pete.

Brie immediately looked interested. "You carve? Can I see your work sometime?"

"Of course," Jordan said and turned to look at the rest of the room. One entire wall was a closet and Jordan stared at it for a moment. "This house is a work of art. Honestly, I have to tell you, this will probably be famous someday."

"I never think of it that way. I'm so close to it." Brie listed into Jordan's body, hand around her waist with a bit of a sigh. She pulled Jordan toward the patio doors.

They stood on the deck, Brie's arm still around her. Jordan took a breath of the warm September air mixed with a wonderful flowery scent. The lights revealed an enormous backyard, but it was the flower garden that stopped her. "How beautiful," she said. Moths beat against the large deck lights.

"They're weeds, wildflowers. Niki loved to pilfer the woods. She'd sneak out because it's illegal. Did you know that?"

Jordan shook her head. She'd never even thought of it. "They're the same flowers that you have in your house, in the blue glass jars."

"We'd be out in the woods in the middle of the night, digging up something. She loved any adventure." Brie laughed and Jordan turned to her. The laugh was so musical and genuine. "We both loved this time of year, and Niki searched until she found a flower that bloomed only in autumn. She planned it this way but she never got to see the first bloom. You should see this at dusk. The color of the fieldstone they used to build this cottage is odd. It almost melts into the air at dusk. Niki always tried to photograph it but never quite caught it."

Jordan heard her talking through tears. Brie cleared her throat and moved away. A slight breeze brushed across them with a hint of apples and dry leaves followed by a thin, plaintive note. Jordan straightened, looking around. "What is that?"

More mournful cries followed and Brie looked back at the garage. "It's Charlie," she said.

"That's the saddest sound I've ever heard. Who's Charlie?"

"Our screech owl that lives in our garage. Niki built him a little place at the top and he's lived there for quite a while. Did you know they mate for life, and I think he's had his girl up there for a long time. Charlie was our only pet."

Jordan bent, looking past Brie at the garage with a little shiver. The owl's cry was creepy. "You did say dinner tomorrow night, didn't you? Are we talking raspberry torte?" Brie smiled mischievously, dimples showing for the first time. "Or TV dinners?"

"Neither. I'm not a horrible cook, but I'm not Rachael Ray either," Jordan said, grinning at the tease. "Before I go, could we walk in the yard?" She helped Brie down the steps. They walked slowly across the thick grass and Jordan put a steadying arm around Brie, mindful of the bruise. The moon peeked over the trees and Jordan took a breath of the sweet air.

"How old is this property? Those are old trees."

"The house was constructed in 1915." Brie pointed at a large thicket. "That was here when Niki's dad bought the house. All we've added are the flowers on this side and this brick border. Even those flowers are old." She gestured at the other side of the yard. Something darted at them and they both jumped a little. "Bats." Brie giggled, grabbing for balance, the pressure of her fingers across Jordan's back felt like warm electricity. The hair on Jordan's arms rose, her heart squeezing unexpectedly as Brie turned into her. They stood quietly together in the scented air for a moment until Brie's hand slid down her arm into her hand and they walked back to the deck.

When she was satisfied that Brie was fine, Jordan left. She had waited until the lights in the front went off. What a crazy night, she thought, looking at the waning moon over the lake. Her mind skittered over the terrible story of Brie and her lover. And the writing. *It should have been me. Not her.*

Brie was struggling, just as she had. The everyday stuff had made Jordan stumble constantly as she became responsible for everything. Her mind jerked to Pete's funeral. The marching men and women. The Scottish bagpipes. She'd stood with Jenna in her arms, holding Tyler's hand. The man had stood in front of them with the folded flag, but she had been holding the sleeping Jenna so he'd given it to Tyler. Tyler had clasped it to his body like it was his dad. The photo had been in the paper.

"Shit," she said. Tyler had slept with that flag until they moved to her mother's house. She'd thrown the dress away that she'd worn that day, but Tyler and that flag were imprinted on the back of her eyelids. The only thing that would erase it was the bars and alcohol.

The brake lights from the car ahead of her suddenly flashed bright red, and she adjusted her speed. She wondered if Brie had any of those moments.

Brie had felt good, lying on top of her, and what had she said about her eyes? She felt warm, just thinking about Brie's fingers in her hair, on her skin. "Stop it," she whispered to herself and wiped her sweaty palms on her pants. That woman had just flat out turned her on.

She sped up again. It didn't make any difference that Niki was a woman or Pete was a man. It was the same for Brie and for her. They were alone now, no matter what they were before.

CHAPTER NINE

The next morning, sunlight slammed into Brie's face and she instinctively covered her eyes. "Ow," she said as the phone began to ring, slicing through her brain. Careful of her sore side, she reached for the phone but knocked it off the bedside table. "Shut up, dammit," she threatened but it still rang. She slid to the floor in a tangle of covers.

"Brie, are you there?" Emma's energetic voice pounded her ears.

"Shit," Brie whispered, awed at the amount of pain ricocheting behind her eyes.

"Are you all right?"

"Too much wine, too little sex, a side full of knives—" Brie stopped abruptly, shocked that she'd just uttered those words to her baby sister. "Forget I said that."

"Like I've never said the same things to you. Or worse."

"I'm going to die." Brie laid her head on her knees. "What time is it?"

"A little after eight. Get yourself into the shower right now." Emma gave her survival orders. "I'll let myself in."

Later, they sat across from each other in the kitchen. Brie held a cup of something hot and steaming. "Not bad," she said, tasting it tentatively. "Tastes like chicken soup and chestnuts."

"A doctor in California gave me the basic ingredients. The first time I drank it I totally forgot my hangover. I thought he'd poisoned me. It tasted like bitter stone. I've tinkered with it over the years to perfect it," Emma said as she started the coffee. "You'll be pain free and human in about fifteen minutes." She placed a wicker basket on the table. "From Mom."

Brie parted the checkered cloth. There were five gorgeous red tomatoes and a note.

"The last of the tomatoes." Emma grinned. "You get all the garden goodies this year."

Brie fished the note out of the basket. There was only one word, "Eat," printed in big, black block letters on a piece of stationery.

"Mom speaks," Brie said with a sigh. "They're beautiful," she said but quickly pushed the basket away. The thought of eating anything made her stomach lurch.

"What's up with the empty refrigerator?"

"Going to give me the 'time to get your act together' speech?" Brie said grimly.

"No," Emma said. "I actually wanted to tell you that I ran into a friend of yours. Your famous skateboard assassin."

Brie looked up, surprised. "Jordan?"

"One and the same. She wandered into my gallery. Hard to miss with that shiner."

"Looking to buy?"

"No, she's a carver." Emma winked at her. "She's cute."

Brie smiled a little. "You're telling me?"

"Talks well and has a good sense of humor."

"She's married…with kids…but never talks about her husband. Damn, wouldn't you know? The first woman since Niki to *really* make me look, and…married." She took another drink. "I just found out that she was a carver last night."

"*You* looked? That's something." Emma squeezed her shoulder affectionately. "She's married? Kids? She didn't mention that. We only talked about carving and my new gallery." Emma got up for coffee. "We can all use friends, Brie. I liked her smile and her voice. She has a brightness around her. Do you know what I mean?"

"No. I don't know what you mean. Tell me."

"Ha. You're going to suck me into that crazy conversation you love to pull on me, accuse me of being all New Age whoo-woo. I'm not going *there* with you again." She sat back down at the table. "See, you've got that *oh please* look on your face right now."

"Em…" Actually, she *had* been setting Emma up for that

conversation but had lost the energy even before Emma was finished talking.

"Great. You're in one of your funks again."

"Funk? I'd hardly call this a *funk*." Brie's voice rose.

Emma stared at her coffee, then took a deep breath. "Someone has to say this to you, Brie. I know you're seeing a therapist, but you have to at least *try* to help yourself. You can't hide in this house forever."

"I'm not hiding. I go to work. I'm getting ready for school. Classes start soon and I'll be out every day."

"But people, Brie. People. You don't go out with your friends. It looks like you don't even go shopping. When was the last time you were at the grocery store? You haven't even been down to my new gallery in a month."

"Is that what this is about? I haven't been to your gallery?"

"No," Emma said. "This is about you starting to swim upstream again, meeting new people. You wouldn't have met Jordan if you two hadn't crashed in the park."

They stared at each other. "I had lunch with Mary Kramer the other day," Brie said defensively.

"Great. Your archenemy. You always end up fighting." Emma reached for a napkin. "Wait, don't tell me. You haven't been...seeing her?"

Brie groaned and finished her drink. "No, I need glasses."

Emma gave a little snort. "I've been thinking about something. What would *you* want, if you were killed and Niki was still alive?"

"What?" she said in a cracked voice. Had the therapist ever brought this up? Nothing stirred in her memory. "What are you saying? You know it should have been me...she's..." Brie stopped and fought tears. "Emma, you have no idea what you're talking about."

"Maybe, and I don't have the answer. Nor do I want one from you right now." Emma took her coffee cup to the sink. "But I'm right and you know it. Get your life back, Brie." She smiled a little bit. "Honey, I love you, but I can't stand to see you become part of the walls in this house. Please? I'll take you anywhere. How about a movie? Want to go clubbing? You name it and I'll be here. Just call me." She moved toward the door. "Go back to bed. You'll feel like the sun coming up when you wake up."

After Emma left, Brie went back to her bedroom. She opened

the closet door where Niki's clothes still hung and stood there, staring at them. Thank God Emma hadn't nagged her about the clothes. She usually did. She looked at her unmade bed, the covers still on the floor, and picked up a pillow and blanket, tossed them on the closet floor. She dropped carefully to her hands and knees and crawled inside. Brie closed the door and curled up in the darkness. She took a deep breath and closed her eyes. This little spot still carried a thready scent of Niki. This much was still theirs.

❖

Brie thought about what Emma had said all the way to Jordan's later in the afternoon. Her side hurt from sleeping on the closet floor. What would Emma say about sleeping in the closet? Or her therapist? An enormous house was visible in the woods on the right just after the road curved, and she looked at the number on the mailbox. She stopped the car and checked the address scribbled on a piece of paper. There was another mailbox down the road. She drove up the long driveway and wondered about meeting Jordan's husband.

"Holy bat cave," she said, looking at the huge structure in the woods.

A little blond girl ran down the sidewalk, waving, and Brie smiled. What a cutie.

Brie got out of her car. "Hello," she said and bent to eye level with the child.

The little girl was shy but held her hand out. "I'm Jenna Catherine, but you should call me Jen," she said.

"I'm Brieanna Carmel, but you should call me Brie," she said, taking the small hand. They shook solemnly.

"Mommy says to bring you to the kitchen." Jenna tugged on Brie's hand and they began the long, winding walk up to the house.

"Is this big house all yours?" Brie asked, shifting the basket of tomatoes to her other arm.

"No, Grammie lives in the other half. We used to live in another house, over there"—she pointed vaguely to the south—"but now we live here because…" She frowned up at Brie.

"That's okay, I was just wondering." Brie took her hand again as they walked along. Jenna led her into an enormous kitchen and Brie's mouth immediately watered. Was that grilled chicken she smelled?

Jordan straightened up from behind a cooking island.

"Your daughter—this *is* your daughter?—took very good care of me," Brie said and grinned. "My heavens, Jordan, this house is palatial."

"It was Mom and Dad's and when he died and my brothers left, it was just too big for my mother. Uncle John redid this side for us. I could never afford anything like this." Jordan motioned at a pitcher. "There's iced tea. Pour yourself a glass while I check the chicken outside. Roam around if you want. Tyler's in his room, that's my oldest."

"I set the table," Jenna said, shy again.

"You did a wonderful job." Brie smiled, looking at the carefully placed blue cloth napkins and light blue plates. Bright flowers finished the table and Brie placed the basket of tomatoes beside them.

"I've never set a table before," Jenna confessed, eyes down.

"I don't think I've ever seen it done better."

"Really?" Jenna's eyes sparkled.

"Absolutely," Brie said. "Do you want to show me around while your mommy is outside?"

Jenna scampered off the chair, running ahead with little leaps as she went. "Here, Brie, here," she said. The colorful room was obviously hers. Toys were stacked in a large wooden cupboard in the shape of a teddy bear. "Mommy made this for me," she said proudly, pointing.

"Your mommy is quite a carpenter," Brie said looking at the expertly rounded corners and tightly fitted shelves. She certainly was.

"Here's your picture, on my wall." Jenna pointed at a small painting of a blond woman sitting on a half-moon, amid bright stars and a dark night sky.

"We have the same color hair, that's true." Brie had been about to joke but stopped when she saw the sincerity in Jenna's eyes. She smiled instead. A noise made her turn. Jordan leaned against the doorway. The olive green halter dress and gold earrings vibrated against her tan skin. The dress emphasized a figure that made Brie quickly avert her eyes.

"I had to take my mother shopping today," Jordan said. They locked eyes for a moment. "She's about to go to Ireland." She looked around the room. "Jenna, I want you to spend a few minutes before dinner and pick this room up a bit." She turned back to Brie. "Would you like to do the two-bit tour? I've got a few minutes with the chicken. Did you bring those gorgeous tomatoes?"

"The last from my mother's garden," Brie said and followed Jordan down the hallway.

"They look delicious." Jordan began to describe how her uncle had renovated the house.

"He did a beautiful job," Brie said, admiring the rooms and the decor. The house felt spacious but comfortable.

Jordan followed Brie into her bedroom and leaned against the door. "This house is not as unique as yours. I swear, Brie, I've never seen that quality of workmanship. In fact, the entire house is one-of-a-kind. You and Niki did a superb job."

Brie sat on the built-in window seat. "I don't have one of these," she said and smiled. "I like this touch." Brie saw a photo beside the bed. A tall, nice-looking man in a Milwaukee Fire Department uniform smiled at the photographer. She looked up with a question on her face.

"Pete," Jordan said. She checked the hall and shut the door.

Brie nodded, waiting for more. Jordan sat on the bed.

"Brie, I haven't been entirely honest with you," Jordan said. "Pete was my husband, the children's father. He was a fireman, as you can see. He was killed in that fire at Haben, downtown, five years ago. Like you, I have lost a partner."

Brie sank to the other side of the bed, her heart beating hard. "That's terrible." She stopped when she heard her voice shake. "I'm sorry. Are the children all right? Are you all right?"

"It's been five years. I've had a lot more time than you to deal with this." Jordan's face was composed but she gripped her hands. Brie understood exactly what it cost to speak those words.

"Mommy?" Jenna said and knocked on the door.

"Come on, Brie." Jordan got up and opened the door, smiling at Jenna. "Let me show you the office. You'll enjoy that, I guarantee you." They walked down the hall and Brie followed, her heart still beating hard. She had been totally unprepared for that information.

"Look at the books," Brie said, moving to the shelves in Jordan's office, reading titles. "Someone loves history…and this wood is perfect. Is this your work?" Her body still trembled. She concentrated on the titles of the books to calm herself.

"No, Uncle John did this. Everything I've learned has been from him. Unfortunately, he doesn't have time anymore. The company has grown so fast." She looked toward the kitchen. "I think we could probably eat. How about it? Hungry?"

Brie nodded.

"I know you," Tyler said as he slid into his seat at the table. "You're the woman Mom creamed at the park."

Jordan's head slumped. "Ty!"

Brie could not stop herself from grinning at Jordan's body language.

"Face it, Mom, you're just not as good as I am," Ty said and when he taunted her, Brie could see how much he looked like his mother. Even their gestures were similar. Jenna looked like the man in the photo.

"You're an athlete?" Brie asked him. "How about your mother?"

"Best shortstop in the league," Tyler said. "Her team won the city championship this year. She's the MVP." His eyes shone.

Jordan's face was a little flushed. "It's just something I enjoy." Brie narrowed her eyes a bit. Jordan had teased her last night and Brie was now on a fact-finding mission. She smiled sweetly at him.

"What else does your mommy do?" she asked.

"Don't answer that, Ty."

He grinned proudly. "She was a champion soccer player in college, has all sorts of trophies in the den. Want to see them?"

"No, we're eating," Jordan said with a warning look at Brie, who just smiled and ignored her.

"I'd love for you to show me all those trophies after dinner. What do you like to do, Ty?" she asked, giving him some attention.

He immediately began talking about baseball, football, even soccer, and then switched to video games, bragging that his mother couldn't beat him.

"That's not fair. You have more time to practice." Jordan actually whined.

Brie raised an eyebrow at her.

"You're the first person I've had over. The kids are pretty excited," Jordan said just as the phone rang and she escaped to answer it.

Jordan returned a few minutes later, her shoulders tense. "That was Mom. One of the blouses that we bought today doesn't fit right and she's on her way over."

A tall, attractive woman came into the kitchen minutes later. Salt and pepper shone in hair that was the same deep brown and gold as Jordan's.

After the introductions, Charlotte immediately picked up one of the big red tomatoes, turning it in her hand. "How beautiful, Brieanna," she said.

Jordan reached for a plate in the cupboard and took a tomato from the basket. She began to slice it, arranging thin red circles on the plate. Charlotte held up the bag she was carrying.

"It just doesn't fit. Will you take it back on your way home from work?"

Brie compared the two women. Jordan looked a great deal like her mother and Brie would have bet that Charlotte had the same figure when she'd been Jordan's age.

"Richard is coming for dinner tomorrow night," Charlotte said. "I'll plan on your being there?"

"I'll take the blouse back, Mom," Jordan said. "But I might be late."

Brie reached for the basket as Jordan's mother turned to leave. "Here, take some, please. I'm sure Jordan won't mind."

Jordan walked her mother back down the hallway. The children had been quiet, watching the exchange. She laid the bag with the blouse on the counter as she came back and sat, shaking her head.

"So you'll be going back to the mall?" Brie teased, looking pointedly at the bag.

Jordan sighed. "Right. However, we had the most interesting afternoon. It was just the two of us, and that was a first."

"How do you manage that?" Brie started to laugh. "I'm the official to-the-mall person for my mother."

"Lucky you," Jordan said wryly. "Actually, it was nice. My mother is changing, and frankly, she's much nicer, easier."

"My dad's dead and I've been close to Mom these last few years. She's always been a real stay-at-home mother and I don't know how I would have made it without her."

Jordan shook her head. "My mother was never a stay-at-home mom. When Dad was alive, they were very active socially. I hardly ever saw her." She pushed the food on her plate. "When my father died and

Mom was left here, alone with my two older brothers and me, it was too much. Uncle John and Nancy helped." She looked at Brie and then at her children. "This is better discussed at another time." She pointed at Brie's plate. "You ate it all. Would you like more?"

"I love summer pasta, so more, please, and great job on the chicken." Brie speared several slices of tomato for herself and put one on Jenna's plate.

"I want what Brie's having. Noodles." Jenna pointed at her plate and studied the tomato. She took the last tomato out of the basket. "This is so big."

Jordan laughed. *"Attack of the Killer Tomatoes."*

"What?" Brie looked up.

"Just an old movie that I keep around that makes me laugh."

Brie looked down at Jenna. "Jenna, I have a very important question for you. Does your mommy have a tattoo?"

"That's enough," Jordan said as she dished more food onto the plates. "Don't say anything, Jenna, or there won't be any dessert."

"The way you treat your children." Brie shook her head.

They took their iced tea to the patio after the kids were in bed. The warm September dusk glazed the lake to a warm gray and Brie settled into her chair with a rare peace.

"You know, of course, that Mom was just sneaking over here to see who I honored with my first dinner," Jordan said. "I'm certain she was hoping you'd be six foot five and handsome with a deep voice and manly muscles. Oh, and your name would be 'Bob,' not Brie."

"Don't you mean *Richard*?" Brie said. She shot Jordan an impish smile.

"God. I'd already forgotten. Tomorrow night and…*Richard*." They both broke into laugher.

"I don't care. You can practice on me. Just call me *Richard* now," Brie quipped and they laughed again. Brie stretched her legs out, propping them on another nearby chair. "Actually, your mother seemed nice. Has your family lived here long?"

"I'm third generation in Milwaukee. This city has quite a history.

Well, you teach it. I expect that you know it much better than I do. Pete loved this city's history. He'd pick up every book he could find on it."

"Those are his history books in your office?"

Jordan nodded. "Actually, we both read a lot, but I prefer fiction."

"Would you mind if I went through them? I'm working on a project right now, an election in the late eighteen hundreds, and I'm always on the prowl for something new." Brie relaxed farther into her chair. "On a different note, my youngest sister, Emma, was at my house this morning and kind of rescued me." She kicked off her shoes and sighed.

"Emma? I met her at her gallery yesterday. I would have told you last night but, in the confusion, I forgot."

"Confusion? That's kind. I thought I was going blind when I woke up this morning."

Jordan gave a snort. "I've been there. I kept the entire beer industry solvent after Pete was killed."

"Why didn't you tell me about Pete?"

"I'm sorry. I don't talk about it." Jordan took her earrings off and stretched her legs. "We dated in high school and found each other again the last year of college. He died doing something he loved, and I suppose that's as good as it gets."

"As good as it gets?" Brie echoed, thinking about Niki, how happy they were that day.

"It's been about five years," Jordan said. "It wasn't on purpose that I didn't tell you. I'm simply trying to get on with my life."

"I didn't talk about Niki. We're even," Brie said. "That wallet? It was Pete's?"

Jordan nodded. "It had all of his identification and information. The things I needed for the funeral and everything. I carried it right after he died and never got out of the habit. I still wear the ring to keep the guys away."

"Must be a straight woman thing."

Jordan held up her hands. "I deserve that after last night. All the things I said to you. But you still wear your ring."

"Here," Brie said, handing Jordan the ring. "Niki designed this."

"Faeries. I've never seen anything like this. Beautiful silver and gold. These are the same as in your bathroom?"

"Niki painted those too," Brie said and slid the ring back on her finger. She looked at Jordan with a small smile. "You love to tease, don't you? You'd be dangerous in my world."

"Dangerous?"

"Sure. Cute and cocky with that hint of bad," she said with a hint of come-on.

"It's not a hint. Unfortunately." Jordan exhaled. "I've been a good mother, Brie, but not a very nice woman." She swiveled in her chair to look at Brie. "Were you just flirting?"

"Dream on, Carter." Brie laughed, absolutely flirting and enjoying it.

They stared at each other for a moment, and Brie felt a nice glow slip inside. She hadn't flirted with anyone since Niki and it felt good, but she ended the conversation before it took a turn she didn't want to deal with. "Isn't it odd? Both Pete and Niki dead?"

"And Niki's family gone."

Brie looked out at the lake. "Niki's case is still open."

"Open? George and Patrick said it was a random shooting."

"As far as I'm concerned, it is." Brie bent to pick up her glass. "However, the police don't want to let it go. They still call me occasionally because I survived."

"Survived? Were you there?"

"I was shot too," Brie said after a deep breath. "That part's a blank. I remember waking up in the hospital…that's it. It's part of the reason I volunteer at Omni. It helps, somehow."

"You were shot?" Jordan looked shocked.

"I'm healed, physically. At least to the point where I was just beginning to do a little running." She frowned down at her hands. "I'm actually thinking of selling the house and moving to the West Coast. I've had two offers to teach out there next year."

"Oh no, you don't. You're not allowed to move. I've just met you. There has to be a rule about new friendships." Jordan concentrated. "Let's see, how many seconds when you drop something on the floor? Or the thirty-second time-out in basketball."

"It would be hard to leave my house. Still, I need to get on with my life."

"How do you stay there, alone?"

Brie's therapist had asked her that too but, Brie wondered, where else would she be, other than their house? "I don't know how to answer that. Sometimes, in this mess, I forget Niki's not coming home, but I like the comfort of knowing the little things. For example, where the silverware is, the soap in the bathroom. Do you know what I mean? We put ourselves into every piece of that house. It's almost like another person."

"Are you seeing a therapist?"

"Yes, and she's been an enormous help. A lot of people have helped. Actually, you're helping. I'm really enjoying tonight." Brie tracked some kind of bird across the sky. The evening still felt good to her and something lifted inside her. Hope?

Jordan stood. "Come with me and I'll show you my studio, but I have to warn you, I haven't cleaned in there for quite a while. In fact, I hadn't been in there for weeks until yesterday morning."

"I don't care," Brie said, rising. "I'd like to see what you're working on."

Jordan held out her hand. "Is your side better? You stood easily."

"I wasn't standing *easily* last night," Brie said ruefully and took the offered hand. Jordan's skin felt warm and safe, just as her arms had before. It was the first time anyone had held her hand like this since Niki, and she liked the little tingle that ran up her arm.

"That wasn't the bruised side. That was the wine," Jordan said mischievously.

"I meant to tell you that your eye looks better. That yellow and purple...very attractive with the green dress." Brie scanned Jordan's body, enjoying the bare skin and how the fabric held what must be fabulous breasts. They certainly looked fabulous.

Jordan scoffed a little laugh and, still barefoot, led the way to the studio. The moonlight was so bright that they didn't even need the small lights that lined the sidewalk.

"Careful of your white slacks," Jordan said as Brie moved around the back of the studio. "And watch out for the tools. I always keep them very sharp." Cutting tools were neatly laid out on the workbench.

Brie picked up blocks of half carvings, little animals and birds. "What are these?"

"Every year the local carvers have a booth at the downtown renaissance fair. I offer carvings of birds, little animals, whatever. The kids and I dress up. It's fun."

"I haven't been there in years," Brie said, turning a piece of wood in her hands. "Is this going to be a wren?"

"Yes. They sell quickly. Actually, they aren't carvings. That's called whittling."

"Do you carve owls? Like Charlie?"

"Charlie?"

"You know, my only pet?"

"Oh, Last night, I'd forgotten. What did you say he was? A screech owl?"

Brie nodded and looked hopeful.

"Never tried, but I would for you," Jordan said and turned, seeing Brie look at the sketches she had done of her. "Like those?"

"Is that me?"

"I do quick sketches of things that catch my eye."

Brie turned to her, a quirky expression across her face. "I caught your eye?"

"Uh, your body...the way..." Jordan's voice trailed off. Brie merely smiled and Jordan could feel herself blush. She had no idea how to explain what she had sketched, but Brie had turned to the big piece in the center of the studio. "That's the piece I've been working on for a long time. Take a look, tell me what you see."

Brie was quiet as she walked around the carving in the center, a piece about as tall as herself. "What kind of wood is this?"

"It's Indian rosewood, heavy and hard. It's also used for fine inlays and musical instruments. I was lucky to find it. Another carver had it and we paid a bundle for it."

Brie nodded absently, bending in to see it better. "The purplish and green hues in the wood are unusual. It's lovely, Jordan." She moved to the front of the carving, squinting a bit.

"It's a woman, wrapped in a blanket. A robe? Standing in the wind? She's been around some trouble perhaps? Her face has so much character." She turned and looked at Jordan, leaning against a shelf. "It's very delicate. A little anger, or is that fear?"

"Both. Her wrap is blowing in the wind. See how one hand is just rising, as if to ward off a blow while the other clutches the cloth to her, close and tight for warmth and protection?" Jordan moved to the carving. The bottom was still untouched.

"It's as if the figure is stepping out of the wood. Maybe you should have a single foot showing. Or did you think of that already?"

"No. I hadn't." Jordan concentrated and padded away, making an arc in front of the statue.

"Just an idea and…" Brie began but saw that Jordan was engrossed in the carving. Jordan straightened her body, and Brie saw it, the coil of energy hidden beneath a well-monitored calm. "Jordan, this is very good. You know that, don't you? The face has so much emotion in it. Why aren't you carving every chance you have? It's so alive. Like you."

"Alive?" she repeated and they stared at one another.

Brie blinked, looking at Jordan's beautiful shoulders as something unspoken passed between them. The silence stretched until she said, "What were we talking about?" She felt a little dizzy.

"I don't know," Jordan said, equally bemused.

"Oh, the carving." Brie was confused by what had just happened.

"I have a problem with carving," Jordan said. "I haven't been able to work on this since Pete died. It's weird."

"How did Pete feel about your carving?" Brie turned her back to Jordan, looking at the statue again. She couldn't look at Jordan without staring.

"One hundred percent behind me. We both were so busy, and then, the kids. About the only thing we did away from the house was camp now and then."

"We camped too," Brie said. "Want to take the kids sometime?"

"They're a lot of work, but that sounds good. We'd have to go soon, while the weather's nice."

"I know a perfect place for kids, safe and fun," Brie said.

"Jenna would be easy, but Ty's a handful."

"Like you?" Brie teased, finally turning.

❖

After Brie left, Jordan Googled "screech owl" and printed a photo from her computer. It looked like a quick piece of work. *Her only pet. Charlie?* If it took that sometimes-lost look off Brie's face and made her smile, it was worth it. Lost? No, *hurt*, and it was still thrumming just below Brie's surface, something Jordan was only too familiar with. She wondered if Brie was as angry as she had been.

Jordan cleaned the table and caught the moon framed in the window. It had tarnished Brie's hair to silver tonight as they walked back from the studio. Those long legs in white slacks with the wine-colored blouse completed the image. If Niki had been the artist Brie had said she was, she would have watched Brie all the time. Every movement was unconsciously graceful...and sexy. Jordan unloaded the dishwasher, seeing Brie move in her mind. It had always intrigued her, those unplanned gestures and moves that some women had.

She hung the damp cloth on the sink to dry and remembered Brie's body on hers last night. She had automatically pulled her close, but it had felt good. *Face it, she just plain fascinates you. You haven't felt this alive in years. When she said "alive" you knew it was true.*

CHAPTER TEN

B rie pumped her fist in triumph as she left Mary's office with her new glasses in hand. She'd managed to avoid seeing Mary. Still smiling over that, she arrived early for her appointment with Dr. Wolfe at Urgent Care.

"I can really see," she exclaimed, looking over the paperwork he handed her.

"Just need more red blood cells, girl." He smiled across the desk at her. "You've let yourself get run down."

Brie scanned the test results, adjusting her glasses. "What do I do now? I finally have my appetite back."

"I'm going to start you on some special multivitamins, for openers."

"Is that all?"

"Set up an appointment with me for the first week of October to check the blood work. If it's better, you're off the hook. Your side looks better but I'm keeping you away from Omni for another week. I've already called them so you don't have to." He set the papers aside. "How's it going with the therapist?"

"I have an appointment with her tomorrow. I see her every week."

"Are you having any anger issues?"

"That's a therapist question."

"I know it is, but I want to know. It's important, Brie."

"Maybe." Brie stared into space. "My sister said something to me."

"Which sister?"

"Emma."

"She would," he said and shook his head a little. "What did she say?"

"She asked me what I would have wanted, if Niki had lived and I had died. What I would have wanted Niki to do."

"Whew," Dr. Wolfe said.

"Usually I just go into a kind of white noise or cry myself to sleep," Brie said and felt tears threaten but held them back. "Why can't I remember? It's crazy. I can remember the senator from Virginia in 1875, but everything after the dirt bike and the gunshots is a blank. All I remember is waking up in the hospital."

"The hospital," he repeated and Brie shivered, the memory still making her faintly nauseous. "I'm sure the therapist has said this to you. It's trauma, the mind, protecting you. It may just suddenly hit you and all that memory will flood your mind. Then again, it may never come back."

"She's talked a lot about trauma and remembering," Brie said. "But something's better. You know I've only been pretending to be alive the last few years but, the other night, I took someone through our house for the first time since Niki died. It wasn't as bad as I thought it would be. Something's shifting. I found a new friend and she helps."

"Friends are good. I'm simply saying, be on guard, Brie. A number of things can trigger a recall."

She sighed. "I'd rather remember."

"I would assume you wouldn't try anything silly, like running?"

"Running? Not a chance until I can move easier. Ibuprofen is my closest friend."

"All right, but take it easy. I don't want to hear that you're swimming across Lake Michigan, trying to set one of those crazy records."

"Thank God for helpful people. My department chair has been wonderful, but I think this is the last year I'll be able to get away with this light schedule, and I don't even have to tell you about my publisher. They've been very understanding, but I have to get things going again so I don't use up all that goodwill. My friends, *our* friends..." She frowned and went quiet.

"Your friends?"

"Absent." She looked at him. "I'm finally missing them, so I guess I'll just have to go find them. I'm going out in a couple of weeks."

"Will you still volunteer at Omni after classes begin?"

"It makes me feel like I'm doing something worthwhile and it's helping me deal with this mess." What Brie didn't say was that it also was a great insight into how others dealt with horrific events. "I've been thinking of moving out of state, teaching somewhere else, maybe sell the house or rent it out."

"Move?" he said. He gave her a sharp look. "Where?"

"Two universities on the West Coast have made offers," she said. "I've talked to the family. Also, we're going to be taking bids for Niki's foundation's next project. The sports complex is done. I enjoyed the parts I was able to do. I think we did what Niki would have wanted." Brie picked up her purse. "I have to be at school in a little while. Evening classes begin tonight." She put her hand on his shoulder. "Thanks. I'll make an appointment and see you next month. Have a good September."

❖

After a quick shower, Jordan hurried over to her mother's side of the house, tucking a yellow blouse into her tan slacks as she walked down the hallway. She could smell something on the grill and her stomach grumbled. "Show time," she said, rounding the corner into her mother's kitchen. She fully expected to find a new man, ready for action—but totally uninteresting.

"Mommy," Jenna said, jumping up. "We saw you come home."

Jordan gave her a hug and a kiss. "Thanks for watching out for me." Tyler grinned at her around a big hamburger and she tousled his hair. A gray-haired man walked in from the patio with a platter of hamburgers and grilled vegetables. His face was ruddy from the barbeque, and warm September air followed him inside. Her mother was positively glowing as she did the introductions. Speechless, Jordan simply stood and almost forgot to return his handshake. This wasn't about her. It was her mother's date.

"I thought you should meet the man I'm going to Ireland with," her mother said with a twinkle in her eye.

"Mom, this is great," Jordan said. She'd been wrong. *This* was interesting.

Jordan cleaned up after the meal, listening to everyone else laugh outside. It made her smile as she turned the dishwasher on. "Wait till I tell Brie about Richard." She chuckled.

Her mother stepped back into the kitchen. "When the kids are asleep, will you come back for a while? We'd like to give you the trip's itinerary, where we can be reached."

Jordan came back for coffee and took the opportunity to get to know Richard a bit better. He was a retired businessman, active in her mother's church, and had adult children and grandchildren. She liked him and liked watching them together, enjoying their conversation and comfort together.

"How did your dinner go last night?" her mother asked.

"Good," Jordan said and set her coffee cup in the sink. "Brie's a professor at Sparta University."

"I liked her, Jordan. Did she mention anything about writing books?"

Jordan nodded. "I picked up one of her textbooks, the day we collided in the park"

"Perhaps," her mother said, "but I believe she also writes fiction." She got up and left the room, returning with two books. "Isn't this her photo?"

Jordan took the books and looked at the photograph on the flyleaf. It was Brie. "I didn't know," she said, surprised. "Did you read these?"

"They're excellent. Great historical mysteries. Here, take them. I guarantee you'll enjoy them."

The minute Jordan got back to her side of the house she stopped at her office and turned on her computer. She looked at the Sparta University site and found Brie's faculty information. It was long, but at the very end there was a paragraph about her fiction. Jordan checked the titles. The second one had been a best seller. Jordan frowned at her computer. Brie had also published quite a bit of academic work and there was a column of awards. Why hadn't Brie mentioned this?

She rapped the desktop with her knuckles, thinking. That answer was easy. Brie was just beginning to fumble her way back. She'd probably simply forgotten. Books had to be the last thing on her mind. She'd bet the most Brie could manage were everyday things. Her house was orderly, which meant she was paying attention on some level. Some things Jordan could help her with. The basic things like eating, getting out now and then, or just laughing.

She closed the house up and got ready for bed. It was after nine thirty. Good. She wanted to tell Brie about Richard. She picked up the phone.

"Is this *Richard*?" she said in a low voice, sliding over the words when Brie answered. Brie laughed and Jordan smiled. Brie's laugh was special.

"Just walked in the door, but I'll be anything you want," Brie said.

"Well, guess what? Richard was my *mother's* date. He's the man who's going to Ireland with her."

Brie laughed again. "So, it's *not* all about you?"

"Guess not, and I wanted to share that with you." Jordan laughed too. "How was your class?"

"I always enjoy this one. All the new ideas and new people. It was a good night."

"I wanted to tell you about Richard, but I also wanted to remind you about our dinner at Patrick's tomorrow night."

"I hadn't forgotten. Do you want to meet there?"

"That would be a good idea, if you don't mind. I have to stop at school, talk to Tyler's teacher, and then give the kids a ride home. Uncle John's wife, Nancy, is having them over for dinner before Mom leaves."

"You're not going to dinner with your mother and children?"

"No, I have to go back to work and meet my foreman. We're going into the next phase on the house and I want to make sure we're on the same page. I'll make it to Patrick's in plenty of time."

"Okay, I'll see you out there about six. I have an appointment with my therapist at four thirty, so if I'm a little late, be patient." She gave a little giggle. "*Richard* is probably never late, but *Brie* sometimes is."

❖

When Jordan walked into Patrick's the next night, something happened. Her eyes connected with Brie's and she felt something she hadn't felt in a long time, like an old song you hadn't heard in years that reminded you of a very good feeling. A warmth collected inside her as they smiled at each other and Jordan almost stumbled. George was standing by the booth and reached out to steady her.

"Would you like to try my special tonight?" he asked. "It's chicken and has a special drizzle that I put over it."

Jordan nodded but looked at Brie. "Do you mind eating chicken so soon, after dinner at my place?" Her words sounded a little breathless to herself.

Brie shook her head. "This is an old recipe of George's that I really like. I've eaten it as he's experimented with it over the years. It's always delicious but also always slightly different." She made a face at George. "He's kind of an experimental cook."

"If you recommend it, I'll give it a shot," Jordan said, sitting across from Brie and noticed she was drinking coffee. "Coffee?" she asked.

"I probably should have made it whiskey. Rough night at the therapist's." Jordan took a closer look at Brie's eyes. Had she been crying?

"I'm sorry," Jordan said. "Let me see what you're wearing. Nifty blazer." It was blue with gold buttons with a white shell underneath. Jordan peeked under the table top. Blue jeans and half boots. "You look nice." *She'd look nice in a cardboard box*, Jordan thought and smiled across the table.

"Thanks," Brie said but her smile was weak. "Look at these." She put on gold-rimmed glasses.

"Glasses? Since when?" Jordan tilted her head at Brie. The glasses made Brie look serious, focused, a little brainy. *What am I saying? She is*.

"Since yesterday. I wanted you to see them, get used to seeing me wear them. I can hardly believe how much better I can see." She smiled and Jordan was happy to see that it was a stronger smile. "How'd your day go? Why were you seeing Tyler's teacher?"

"It's been rough for him since Pete was killed. Jenna was too young, but Tyler adored Pete. We have good times, and then we have bad times. It's day by day. He's been bullying several boys at school and the teacher called me."

Brie frowned a little. "This has to be rough. I was thinking about Jenna and Tyler today. In fact, I talked about all of you to my therapist."

"Did you tell her that you have a new name? *Richard*?" Jordan teased.

"No, of course not." Brie laughed for the first time.

There was a glow on Brie's face. Jordan couldn't remember anyone with that same bloom when they laughed. "Before I forget, were you serious about camping?"

Brie nodded. "You bet. My family has a cabin on a nice little lake not too far from here."

"Why don't you follow me home and we'll look at what equipment I've got? Do you have time tonight?"

"Of course. I have more time than anyone I know." Brie lost the smile.

"Was the session that bad?"

"Just about," Brie said as George brought their food. They continued talking about Tyler over the meal. "He has months when he's easygoing, just normal boy stuff. Then he sinks into anger and takes it out on his classmates." She pushed her empty plate away. "It's still… grieving, the five steps. You probably know those by heart. I certainly do."

Brie nodded and propped her head in her hands. "My anger seems to be turned inward."

Jordan wanted to be very careful here and remembered the paper in Brie's office. *It should have been me, not her!* "What went on with your therapist?"

"Oh, the usual suspects. I think I see Niki in a crowd or hear her voice. I dream of her and, of course, I talk to her."

"And," Jordan said, trying to coax it out of Brie but gently.

"Emma kind of jumped on top of me the other day, the day she saved my life." Brie's smile was sad. "She said I was becoming part of the walls in my house, that I should get out. Then she—" Brie stopped.

"She…what?"

"Asked me what I would want for Niki. If I had died and she had lived." Brie's voice trembled slightly and Jordan reached for Brie's hand. Brie lifted her eyes to Jordan. "I don't know. That's the hard part." She cleared her throat. "How did you do, after Pete was killed?"

"Terrible." Jordan took a drink of water. "I'll tell you about it sometime." She folded her napkin into little squares as they both were quiet. "I'm going to change the subject. Why didn't you tell me you wrote fiction?"

Brie gave a small laugh. "Do you realize that it's going to take us months to catch up with each other at this rate?" she said. "I didn't tell you because I didn't think of it. In fact, I hadn't looked at my third book in over two years until recently." She told her about Niki finding the old letters and the stories that had come from them. "I really enjoyed writing those books. After all the academic work I've done, it was just pure fun. And Niki had fun with it as well. She was always my first reader, then Mom."

"You have a third book that you're writing?"

"*Trying* is more accurate. I'm way behind. I have to see my editor soon and hopefully, I can find my story again before then."

"Niki helped?"

Brie broke out in a laugh. "Well, help? Niki loved to debate. However, she was always honest and when you're writing, that's worth its weight in gold."

"What else did Niki do? Besides art, I mean."

"A lot of work with her family's foundation. She also managed her father's business." Brie gave a little shrug. "A fabulous athlete."

"Any sports in particular?"

"You name it, she did it. We ran together and skied whenever possible, but I could whip her rear in tennis. I truly suck at softball, but she didn't. Like you, Miss Shortstop MVP."

Jordan shook her head. "Stop. What leagues did Niki play in?"

"The South Shore."

"What position?"

Brie grinned. "Shortstop, for the Ravens."

"You're kidding."

"Remember, I said she was only about five foot five, small for an athlete, and that just made her try harder."

"I might have played against her at some time, but I don't remember."

"Didn't you ever go to any of the banquets? She won the MVP three times."

"No, we were just so busy. I was only there when we played. No socializing." She concentrated, remembering something. "Wait, seven years ago, the city championship. The Ravens beat my team in the semis and went on to win. Lord, I remember that game and I remember Niki. Eleven innings without a score. One of the best defensive games I've ever played in. How about that? I actually played against her."

"I was at a university conference in Boston that week and missed that game. Otherwise, we probably would have seen each other," Brie said. "When I got home, it was the first thing Niki talked about."

❖

Brie followed Jordan home from Patrick's and parked her car to the side of the garage as Jordan turned the lights on. Brie took a good look at the T-shirt, khaki shorts, and construction boots ahead of her. *Those legs.* She pulled in a steadying breath.

Jordan moved boxes away from the wall in the garage. Everything looked good, surprising Jordan. "This hasn't been used since the last time we camped. Tyler was four and I didn't know I was pregnant with Jenna." Hands on hips, she looked at the blue tent. "Sleeps six," she said.

"We have a cabin, so I thought we'd sleep inside. Unless the tent experience would be more fun for all of you," Brie said. It was warm and she took her blazer off, hanging it on the lawnmower handle. She bent to look in a box. "Let's take my car, more room. You guys and your sporty cars." She pointed at Jordan's tricked-out two-door Camry. "Is that one of those street cars?"

Jordan laughed. "No. I bought it off one of the guys at work. He was getting married and his wife wanted a minivan. But I have to warn you, I love speed."

"Why does that not surprise me?" Brie said, grinning, checking out a hatchet. "Wait, I'll make a list." She reached into her back pocket and brought out a pen.

"A pen?"

"Always, just in case an actual thought crosses my mind. I have my cards too." She pulled out a few note cards and laid them on the counter, beginning to write.

Jordan looked at the tools hanging on the wall and reached for an adjustable wrench. She put a hand on Brie's shoulder and leaned fully against Brie's back, stretching for the tools. "For the propane," she explained, stepping away and holding up the wrench.

Brie froze, feeling firm breasts pressed into her back, and closed her eyes. It had been so long.

Jordan held up a note card. "Always prepared, huh?" she joked.

Brie shook her head, still looking at her list. "Not recently."

CHAPTER ELEVEN

The O'Malley family cabin on Half Moon Lake was only a couple of hours north and west of Milwaukee. Brie coasted to a stop beside the wooden building and pointed out the large beach. Both kids behind her yelled at the top of their lungs. Startled, she put her hand on her chest and laughed. "You can't go into the water until your mom says it's time."

"Unpack first," Jordan said.

"Mom," Ty complained.

"I'll need your help, Ty. Then we can all go in."

Brie rummaged around in the car's glove compartment, finding the keys. This was a childhood memory she looked forward to sharing. "They only said 'are we there yet' ten times," she said with a grin at Jordan.

"You got lucky," Jordan tossed over her shoulder as she got out. The cabin hadn't been used since June and a hot, stale, musty scent assailed Brie's nose when she unlocked the door. "Whew," she muttered. Everything was just as it was when she was a child: Bunk beds and big fireplace on one wall. Sink, refrigerator, and stove across the room. A full-sized bed nestled in the southwest corner and an ample table in the middle. Her sister Val and brother-in-law usually brought the kids up here, but their oldest boy had broken a leg so it had been months since anyone had been here, and the cabin felt neglected. Brie began to open windows to let the place air out.

"Where do you want the food?" Jordan called.

"Come inside and help me open this." Brie pointed at a stubborn window.

"You're such a girl, O'Malley." Jordan grunted, opening the window.

"Just because your black eye is gone doesn't mean my side is ready. I'm just cleared for duty."

"Whiner," Jordan said, opening the final window. "Besides, your side looks great." She snagged Brie's T-shirt and traced a finger across her soft skin. "See? Just a faint mark left." Goose bumps rose immediately on Brie's skin and she stepped back, blushing.

"Who built this place?" Jordan looked at her finger and then at Brie.

"My grandfather. I'll check the electricity before we use it," Brie said, thinking that the electricity between *them* was just fine. "My brother-in-law rewired it two years ago when he added the shower, toilet, and new stove." She engaged the switch for the water. "Let's put things on the porch until it cools off in here." She came back into the main room to find Jordan standing in the middle.

"Look at this. The kids are going to love those bunk beds."

"I always did," Brie said.

"Okay, kids in the bunks and we're in the double bed," Jordan continued.

"Sleeping with you?" Brie made her eyes wide. "Nice," she teased.

"Let's ask the kids," Jordan said.

"That's a new one," Brie said as they stepped out on the porch. "I've never had to ask the kids for permission to sleep with their mother."

"Shut up," Jordan said but grinned.

Jenna and Tyler came inside and immediately began to argue over the top bunk. Jordan put a hand on each of their shoulders. "You know how we settle this?" She dug in her shorts pocket for a coin and flipped it. Jenna called heads but it was tails, and she began to sulk. Jordan tossed her swimsuit at her, saying, "In that case, go get your suit on," and Jenna was gone in a flash.

Brie showed them where it was safe to swim, to the end of the dock. After that, it dropped steeply. They lathered the kids up with sunscreen and watched them race down the beach. Jordan laughed at them as she stepped out of her shorts and then took her T-shirt off. Brie froze at the sight. Long, well-defined muscles were highlighted by a sheen of sweat. She had to look away.

"Should be nice and warm," Brie said and shed her own T-shirt and shorts. They both had worn their suits under their clothes for the trip. "It was such a hot summer and the lake is shallow." She took a few steps toward the water. "How much supervision do the kids need out there?"

"Not much. I've had them swimming since they were little." Jordan squinted up at Brie. "Wait a minute, O'Malley. Come back here." She rummaged in the little first aid kit. "Here." She held out a Band-Aid.

"What's this for?" Brie took the Band-Aid and tried to keep her eyes away from Jordan's sleek body.

"Your tattoo, dummy. You think I want my impressionable sweet young boy, my son, looking at a naked woman?" Jordan's eyes sparkled and the corners of her mouth tilted up.

Brie covered part of the tattoo with the Band-Aid. "You know how silly this is? Look at us." They both looked down at their skimpy suits.

Brie finally gave in and just stared. She'd been right, those breasts were scrumptious. "Hussy," Brie taunted, moving toward the lake.

"Tramp," Jordan said.

"Race you in."

"Cheater," Jordan yelled, running, but Brie was underwater by the time she got her feet wet.

❖

They took a break in the shade on the porch. Brie shook her hair, water flying everywhere, just as she had as a kid. She got the kids to do the same, all of them laughing, and she caught Jordan staring at her. Brie raised her eyebrows in a question. *Was Jordan just checking me out?*

"Why don't we use the stove inside?" Jordan said, clearing her throat.

"Fine with me. It's cooled down and I'll do the steaks on the grill anyway." Brie pointed at the barbecue on the porch.

"What else did you bring? The coolers are jammed."

"Mom tossed in the last of her sweet corn and butternut squash. I love fresh vegetables."

"Did you mention a canoe?" Jordan said.

"Yup." Brie pointed at a fieldstone structure at the side of the property.

It didn't take them long to get the boat in the water. Brie put Jordan in the front and she took the helm, the kids safely between them. Jordan wiggled the long craft, making both kids squeal with fake fear and Brie smiled. Jenna and Tyler were like their mother, confident and unafraid of just about anything.

"This lake's bigger than I thought," Jordan said, taking another deep cut with her paddle.

"What?" Brie said, her mind absorbed in the play of Jordan's muscles in front of her. She snapped her attention back to the canoe just as they came out beyond the land that jutted out into the water. This was Brie's favorite moment, where you could see the other, bigger side of the lake. She had grown up boating from one end of this lake to the other and knew it like her own hand. She and Niki had used the Willises' enormous cabin up north instead of coming here and she'd missed this little lake.

They weren't quite far enough north for loons but Brie did spot a crane. She called Jordan's name softly so she could show Tyler and Jen. The boat slowed in the water as they watched the tall bird until it caught sight of them and lifted off, its strong wings carrying it away.

Jordan hung the kids' suits out to dry and got the bunk beds ready while Brie cooked. Jenna and Tyler were still so wound up that they talked through the entire meal.

"I can't believe it," Brie said later. They had eaten everything. "Okay, now this is special," she said. "It's an O'Malley tradition to sing a song or tell a joke after dinner."

"Oh, no." Jordan shook her head. "I don't tell jokes and I *don't* sing."

"Mom," Jenna said, eyes wide and very blue against a sweep of sun on her fair skin. "That's a fib. You tell me jokes."

Tyler gave a snort. "Those are my jokes, Jen. I tell them to Mom and she just repeats them to you."

Jordan tried to keep a straight face. "I'm serious, Brie. All I know are kid jokes. Like why did the chicken cross the road kind of stuff."

"I'll settle for that. It's a joke?" Brie snickered, unrelenting. "However, if you prefer to sing…"

"No," both kids shouted and Brie burst out laughing.

"Are you serious?" She looked at Jordan, who had her hands over her face. "Your own kids don't want you to sing?"

"Couldn't carry a tune if my life depended on it."

"Okay, you're off the hook but, as punishment, you have to build the campfire so the kids and I can roast marshmallows for dessert while you do the dishes."

They laughed at Jordan's pretend-sulk and Brie began to clean plates. Suddenly, she was aware of Jordan standing at the end of the table.

"What?" Brie said with a sweet smile.

"Your swimming suit," Jordan said. "I like it." She turned quickly and went toward the beach.

"Ha," Brie said softly. *Jordan* was *checking me out.*

The family had always used a deep pit for their fires, surrounded by big stones placed there by four generations. There were five huge rocks at a comfortable distance from the fire and Brie settled against one. She sipped her coffee, listening to Jordan. She might not be able to tell jokes, but she could tell a story. Jenna's eyes grew wide and Tyler grinned at Jordan. *This is nice*, she thought and then, without warning, she heard Niki say "Baby," very clearly. Brie scanned the beach, her stomach muscles clenched. Jordan had stopped talking and was looking at her across the fire. "You okay?" she asked. "You look as if you saw a ghost."

Brie studied her, pondering Jordan's smile and Niki's voice, but pointed at the sky. "Look at the stars. Everything's in place."

Tyler began to name the stars and Brie relaxed, listening to his youthful recounting of the constellations hanging above them. Her gaze slid back to Jordan's animated face.

With a physical jolt Brie sat straighter. For the first time in over two years she understood that she was going to survive. But as *what,* she thought. She knew *what* she'd been with Niki, but what would she be *without* her? Staring into the coffee cup, she went over the things that had been floating in her mind. Rationally, she understood that Niki was dead, but she had taken so much of Brie with her that she didn't know what was left to work with. She heard her name and looked up to see Ty and Jordan looking at her.

"What?"

Jordan pointed at her lap and a sleeping Jenna. Brie put her cup in the sand and rose to help. They tucked Jenna into the bottom bunk and Tyler scrambled up to the top with a monster grin, but he looked as if he'd be following Jenna at any moment.

"We wore them out," Jordan said as they went to the closet for warmer clothing.

"The kids are so well behaved," Brie said, choosing a long-sleeved shirt. Jordan took it from her and stepped behind, helping her into it as if it was something they'd always done.

"Ha," Jordan said, pulling a sweatshirt over her head. "You just haven't been around them enough. Ty's such a smart-ass and Jen's a real bully at times."

"Jen, a bully? I can't believe that."

"Believe it. They're a handful. There's something about you, Brie, but they'll revert to their normal grumpy selves soon."

"They're kids. It'd be normal," Brie said as they walked back to the campfire. "I like them and your mother as well."

Jordan stared out across the water. "What's happening between Mom and me is weird. I was so young when Dad died and Uncle John and Nancy took me in. I never really got to know her and now here we are, finding each other after all these years." She scooped sand into her hand, letting it trickle through her fingers.

"Moms are important," Brie said, part of her mind still thinking of Niki. She took a deep breath and looked at Jordan. "When we were at Patrick's you promised to tell me what happened to you. How you handled everything after Pete was killed." Jordan nodded but didn't say anything, just looked thoughtful and played with the sand. Finally she spoke. "In the beginning, the children and the funeral kept me so busy that it didn't hit me for a while, but later I was…not good."

"I understand," Brie said.

"No." Jordan said the word softly, drew it out. "You don't. Our experiences have been very different." Jordan expelled a long breath. "Pete and I dated in high school but went to different colleges. Somehow we met again in the summer before our last year of college and picked up where we left off. I had a job and had to work spring break before we both graduated. A group of us got together for just a night. Pete and I ended up in Chicago, drunk and then…pregnant."

"Oh." Brie looked at her quickly. "That changes things, doesn't it?"

"A lot."

"Would you have married him if you hadn't been pregnant?"

"I'm not sure, but *probably*. We had a lot in common and were always good friends. I don't regret marrying him." Jordan let sand trickle between her fingers again. "True, I married him because I was pregnant. It was rough at first, but we learned together. I don't know. Maybe we were just growing up?" Jordan looked at Brie with a kind of half-question on her face.

Brie was the first to look away. She didn't have an answer.

"Then I hit the bars after Pete was killed. You said I had just *a hint of bad*? It was more than a hint, Brie. I didn't even wear underwear." Jordan stood and poked the logs in the fire. "I've only told my psychiatrist this. I'm not sure why I'm telling you."

"Underwear?" Brie repeated, not sure she'd heard correctly.

"I'd drop the kids at Nancy's and run for the bars."

"You'd go out without…?"

"Underwear." Jordan nodded. "It was faster."

"So, it was just for sex and…"

Jordan settled back down beside her. "No excuses. I was angry… and disgusting. I don't know how else to describe it." Jordan took a nervous breath and hurried on. "Of course I quit. I mean, I haven't done anything like that since."

"Wait," Brie said, laying her fingers on Jordan's arm. "How long ago was this?"

"Three years or so."

"Then it's over. You're not doing that anymore."

"I can't let it go." Her face was bleak in the shifting firelight and darkness.

"Tyler?" Brie suddenly understood. "When we were talking about him at Patrick's. You feel some of Tyler's behavior is because you were in the bars and not home with him?"

Jordan nodded and looked down at the sand. "Yes, it's partly that. It's also a lot of other moments. For example, I was mad as hell when I learned some idiot had set the fire. It was arson. I even went to his trial one day. Then the memories of the funeral just wouldn't leave me alone. I was even mad at myself because I'd gotten pregnant and the first two years were really rough. Finally, we called a truce and worked at it. Brie, we worked at it every day until we finally regained at least the friendship by the time he was killed, even a little love. And then what? He's dead." She threw up her hands. "The only thing that calmed me down was the bars and alcohol. Sex."

"And you're still seeing a therapist?"

"I have my last appointment soon. That was as much about the alcohol as it was Tyler."

"Does it bother you to discuss it? Could we talk about this again?"

"You're the first person I've talked to, other than the psychiatrist. Actually, it feels good." Jordan straightened, surprised. "There's one more part to this. I can't carve anymore. It's just gone. Remember what you said about your writing? That's how I feel about carving. I'm a blank."

Brie didn't know whether to laugh or cry. She pulled her legs up to her chin and wrapped her arms around her legs. Jordan's words had hit her like a freight train. Here was someone who got it, who understood.

"Did you ever go to a survivor's group?" Brie said.

"I went to one meeting." Jordan shook her head slightly. "They were like the emotional Nazis." Jordan looked at her. "I'm sorry. That was mean. It works for some people."

Brie rested her forehead on her knees with an almost profound sense of relief. "I've wondered why I haven't done something like what you described. The bars and a lot of women. Maybe it was the trauma of being shot, the long healing process." She shrugged. "Maybe they shot my hormones too?"

"Shot your hormones?" Jordan said with a quick short laugh and got to her knees. "Show me. Where you were shot."

"Below my left shoulder blade." Brie twisted and lifted her shirt.

"Oh, I saw those two marks."Jordan rubbed the raised edges of the scars with her fingers. She let the shirt fall back, but left her hand protectively over the rough skin as they both settled back into the big rock. "How long did it take to heal?"

"Over a year and lots of physical therapy. The muscle damage and left lung were the most serious." Brie pushed against Jordan's fingers, enjoying the feeling and thinking about what Jordan had told her. Something rustled in the tall grass next to the beach and they both turned. An enormous raccoon waddled toward the water.

Jordan put her hand over her heart with a little half-laugh. "Startled me. By the way, why did you look so spooked earlier?" She scooted closer to Brie.

"I thought I heard Niki say something to me."

"Does that happen often?"

"Not so much anymore, but enough. That and very occasionally, the damned dirt bikes."

Jordan shifted closer. "Dirt bikes? The day we had the accident in the park, you mentioned a dirt bike."

"When we were shot, I heard a dirt bike. I could even smell the exhaust. My therapist says I'm hyperaware of them now. The bikes aren't real. It's just something I imagine." She exhaled. "Remember, the other night, at Patrick's? I told you that it was a rough session with the therapist." She hesitated, debating how to tell Jordan more of this.

"Look what I just told you," Jordan said and urged her on.

"I know. One of the issues is Niki's clothes. I can't seem to let them go, and worse, I get into this strange place in my mind where the only safe place is in the closet. If I close the door… Niki's scent's in there."

"And?"

"The worst. I can't remember the shooting. I remember the dirt bike and then…waking up in the hospital. It's dumb. I mean, my mind *wants* to know if it hurt. Did she see me get shot? Did she say anything? Something else. What if I did see something that might be important to the police that would help them find the murderer? Stupid mind."

"Did she die, there at the scene?"

"No, they kept her alive for almost two days on life support so I was with her when she died, officially. Dr. Wolfe somehow managed to put us in the same room and I tried to stay conscious but couldn't.

The few times I'd come around she wasn't…there. There was never a response, according to the hospital."

Jordan put her arm around Brie. "I think this is something we share. They didn't find Pete for four days. At first they wouldn't tell me if he was alive. Later, I understood that they didn't know. Then they got the fire out and found Pete and three other men. I used to lie awake at night and wonder about those things too."

Brie turned in Jordan's arm to see her face. "Do you still think about that?"

"No, and you won't either, eventually."

"It just wears me out."

"Stick with me," Jordan said and cradled Brie back into her shoulder with an arm around her waist. "We'll figure this out."

The smell of lake water and sun on skin drifted into Brie's senses as she relaxed her head against Jordan's shoulder with a sigh.

"How did you meet her? Niki?" Jordan asked, her breath warm against Brie's ear. "You've said little bits and pieces, but what about the special things?"

Brie began telling the story of the restaurant and Mary Kramer. Before she knew it, she was sitting up on her knees, laughing over the details of that afternoon. Her own humiliation, followed by the surprise and delight of Niki. She giggled. "I just remembered how I used to tease Niki about that moment. "That I was *frock fucked* that afternoon, done in by a yellow dress!" Brie moved back against Jordan as they laughed a little.

"Wait a minute. Are you telling me that woman went into the restroom at the Inlet and…at lunch?"

Brie grinned. "Yep."

"Good Lord, where have I been? I mean, I know it's easy to pick up a guy there. I've done it, but I didn't know about the women." She tipped her head back, looking at the stars. "And I've been to the Crow's Nest, seen women together…"

"The Crow's Nest? For a beer after the game?"

Jordan nodded and sat up. "Did you ever do guys?"

"Hey." Brie's head snapped up. "What kind of question is that?"

"You don't have to answer. A lot of women do both."

The question had been asked kindly and Brie tilted her head to see Jordan's eyes. "No, I don't do both. It would confuse me, and that's not too hard to do these days. However," she grinned, looking away, "there were a few."

"Ha." Jordan laughed. "I knew it. I can't believe men just don't mob you."

Brie grimaced. "The men happened because my first woman totally befuddled me. When I went to college, I tried guys the first year and I have a lot of good guy friends, but I..." She shrugged. "I prefer women."

Jordan shifted against the big stone. "Most of my ball team are fairly butch." She looked at Brie with a question. "It would be hard to be more feminine than you are."

"Niki too, but we have good friends that are butch. As a matter of fact, I'm going out with one of them and her partner next weekend."

"Where do you go?"

"Wherever there's good food, like anyone else. Probably the Milwaukee Brewery, but they're still treating me with kid gloves and—" She stopped. "Did that happen to you? Did people treat you like you're going to break?"

"Sure, for a while, but I complicated it with the bar scene," Jordan said with a derisive little snort. "Like you, I also saw a therapist. He helped, a lot. And then there's Mom. Every time I turned around there was another guy at the table."

Brie chuckled. "Richard." She leaned against the rock, quiet for a bit. "My friends have suddenly left me alone. I don't think they know how to handle me. They tend to try to think for me when we're together."

"What are these women like, the ones you're going out with next weekend?"

"Nice. Peg's an OR nurse with my sister, the one you saw, and Vet is a paramedic for Omni. She's the one who got me to volunteer there."

"Vet? What kind of name is that?"

"She was in the military and that's why the name. She's tough and totally butch. Her real name is—" Brie clamped her mouth shut. "I can't tell you. She'd kill me."

"What?" Jordan said mischievously. "Do you think we'll run into each other and I'll give it away?"

"You'd do it on purpose. You love to stir things up."

"Sure…but look who's talking. I think we're about even. Besides, if you worked where I work, you do it to survive. My foreman, Bix, and most of my crew are butch and I can handle them."

"Handle?"

"They tease me constantly but I give it right back. So does my ball team."

Brie laughed. "Oh. I see. You understand butch rules?"

Jordan raised her eyebrows. "Rules?"

"Okay, not exactly *rules*, but let's say, accepted behavior."

"How hard could it be?" Jordan said with a cocky grin. "I mean, we're all women…the same equipment."

"You think?" Brie laughed even harder. "Oh brother, Carter, you have no idea. Competitive, are we?"

Jordan gave her a sassy smile. "You're right, I am. Did you and Niki argue?"

"Of course. Who doesn't?"

"How'd you settle it?"

Brie shrugged. "Like everyone. Yelling, talking or…in bed."

"Sex?"

"Well, it's been a while, but if you insist."

Jordan threw her hands up, laughing. "See what I mean?"

Brie turned to watch the moonlight on the lake, quiet again. "All my life with Niki wouldn't have been enough. How about you? Anyone ever make you…catch your breath when you looked at them?"

Jordan shook her head. "No, not even Pete. Worse, after those miserable two years, I've lost interest. I've let my friends slide and don't go out. It's just the kids and me. Nothing seems to catch my eye or…" She shifted so she could look at Brie. "Whatever it is that gets caught in those moments."

Held by Jordan's eyes, warm in the firelight, Brie lost her place but had a sudden idea. She should take Jordan with her this weekend. Her friend wouldn't nag her to get back out into the dating world, for one thing. "How about going out with us next weekend? Run interference for me? I need to see my friends and you need to get out."

Jordan accepted without hesitation. "Not a bad idea. Maybe it's time to stop being such a hermit."

Brie smiled. *Perfect.* Then she frowned. Jordan was so cute, what if someone came on to her, tried to pick her up? "Do you think you could handle someone making a pass at you?" She stood, brushing sand off herself. "Think about it while I use the bathroom. Do you want anything from inside?"

Jordan shook her head and watched Brie move away. "Women are just women," she said to herself and shrugged. "How hard could it be?" Then she groaned. "Why in the hell did I tell her all of that?"

Brie returned and held out a beer. "Let's split this. After tonight, I think we've earned it," she said and rearranged the logs before settling down next to Jordan. "So, you'd be comfortable, out with me? You'd have to wear underwear, however." Brie bit her lip against a grin, testing Jordan's comfort level. She didn't want Jordan to regret their conversation.

"You'd never know if I didn't, and I never should have told you that," Jordan said. "I love a challenge. Let's be the odd couple. I'll be your token straight woman and you'll be my lesbian."

"And if someone tries to pick you up? I'd bet money on it."

"Easy. I'm not interested. Twenty dollars says you're wrong."

"Twenty dollars? You're on, Carter." Brie put her hand out to shake.

Jordan had a smug look on her face as she shook hands and Brie collapsed on the sand, laughing. "Sucker."

❖

Late the next afternoon, Jordan tossed the last bag in the back in of Brie's car and slammed the door shut. Brie and the kids were on the pier, still in their swimsuits. More time would have been nice. Brie had curled up on her side of the bed last night, falling asleep almost immediately, but Jordan had lain there quite a while, hands under her head, thinking about their conversation on the beach. Those scars on her back were real. She'd never felt a gunshot wound before and couldn't imagine what that was like. Brie hearing Niki speak was odd, but with all that had happened, it made sense. Sleeping in a closet to be next to Niki's clothes? That was strange as well. The other thing, the not remembering, had to be horrible. She was going to have to treat Brie cautiously.

She had rolled onto her side and watched Brie sleep. Simply talking to Brie and telling her the worst thing she could tell her about herself had made her feel like an idiot, but Brie had seemed to just accept it. Now she was glad that she'd shared it with Brie. It was a lot worse than sleeping in a closet.

She remembered what she'd seen scribbled on the paper in Brie's office at her house. *It should have been me. Not her.* She'd meant to ask her about that but had forgotten.

Finally her mind got around to what she'd been avoiding. Something else was happening too. Standing on the porch, looking at Brie in that swimming suit, had literally made her heart skip. She'd been checking her out, the same way she checked out a man. *Exactly* like she checked out a man. *That* had made her sit up in bed, get up, use the bathroom, and take a drink of water. She'd fallen asleep then, but it was the first thought she'd had this morning. It was another reason she was going to have to be careful of Brie.

That was something she was going to have to sort out later. It had been a great weekend. The kids laughed at something Brie said, pointing out to the water. Jenna and Tyler definitely liked Brie and she certainly had something special going on with them. She looked closer. Brie seemed to be gaining a little weight and the sun had colored her skin nicely.

Jordan walked around the car and bent inside, looking for her camera. Brie's swimming suit hid absolutely nothing. Leaning on the hood, she took several photos. She'd do sketches off these shots. If Brie ate properly, she could get back that luscious figure she had in the photo on Niki's desk. It was more than luscious. Sexy.

Jordan began to walk toward them, smiling over the bet they'd made last night. Someone make a pass at her? Not likely, but someone certainly *would* make a pass at Brie. If she were a lesbian, she certainly would.

CHAPTER TWELVE

B rie took a step back from her bathroom mirror and checked herself out, adjusting the waist of the pants a little. This was the last outfit Niki had bought for her for that wonderful night in Chicago. She drifted a moment, remembering. Not too long ago, this outfit would have made her sad. The hollowness inside her was beginning to fill even though it was a slow trickle.

Tonight was the Annual Women's City Softball Awards Banquet. They would announce Niki's new two-and-a-half-acre sports center plus—*ta da*, she said softly—she was going to give Jordan the MVP Trophy. Brie mentally went over her speech again, repeating parts of it out loud.

Dannie Brown, Niki's best friend and a well-known local sportscaster, had created a filmed preview of the Willis Family Center that would open that weekend. Brie had worked to keep tonight a secret, even when Jordan had cancelled their dinner at Patrick's, explaining that she had a softball "thingy" to go to.

The two days at the cabin had been a miracle. The sunlight and water had cleared her mind. Pieces of herself that she had thought lost had floated to the surface. She laughed a little at the memory of Jenna and Tyler roasting marshmallows. The kids had been fun. *So had their mother.* The secrets she and Jordan had shared that night on the beach had been more than a relief. It was a beginning of something new for both of them.

She frowned at herself in the mirror as she adjusted her silver earrings. The regret and embarrassment on Jordan's face as they sat on the sand stayed with her. *Her days in the bars are over*, Brie stubbornly said to herself. She was certain she could help Jordan believe that as well. Brie gripped the counter. The interest and questions she had seen in Jordan's eyes that weekend at the lake stayed with her as well.

The doorbell rang and she set her brush down. Dannie was giving her a ride to the banquet.

❖

Jordan flew into her house, headed for the shower. The kids were staying all night with Uncle John and she had a fleeting impression of how quiet the rooms were without them. Forty-five minutes and she'd be at that damned banquet. Not that she wasn't grateful, but she'd rather be at Patrick's with Brie.

After the shower, she stood in front of her closet in a lacy black bra and panties, hands on her hips. "What?" she yelled at her clothes. She'd planned on her standard black business suit, but then remembered she'd have to say a few words when she received the trophy. Pushing each hanger aside slowly, she saw the rich, dark burgundy Oscar de la Renta suit that her mother had bought for her. She gave a little laugh. An Oscar de la Renta for a softball banquet? Adding a soft pink silk tee and gold accessories, she thought of Brie. She'd still rather be with her tonight.

It took Jordan twenty minutes to drive into the city and Montgomery Hall. Jordan hurried across the parking lot with Kay Kendall, her first baseman, both of them complaining about traffic and praying the food would be good. They were starving.

Jordan finger-combed her still-damp hair and nudged Kay. "Is my hair standing up or…"

Kay snickered. "Would I tell you if it was?"

"You clean up nicely, Carter," Shelly, her catcher, said, "for a straight woman."

"Go to hell," Jordan said in a low voice and caught sight of Dannie "Downtown" Brown, the WLAK-TV sportscaster. Jordan pulled in a breath. Dannie was holding Brie's hand, firmly tugging her along as Brie lingered, speaking to people. There were those gorgeous feminine moves again. Brie was not only the most beautiful woman she'd actually known but she was accessible, stopping and talking with a genuine smile. Women's faces lit up as Brie went down the line, speaking to them. Dannie didn't let go when they stepped up onto the platform, her hand casually on the small of her back. *Damn, she just pressed Brie's hand to her cheek. Is this a date?*

Jordan followed Brie's every move. She was dressed in white flowing pants and a top. No, not white. Was it barely blue or was it silver? Every way Brie turned, the clothing changed color. She was bright and shinning. Jordan shifted her gaze to Dannie Brown. Tall and lean, she wore a black suit with a dark purple vest and a white shirt open at the neck. If this had been a bar with guys, Dannie Brown would be the female equivalent of a stud, Jordan decided. Brie leaned past Dannie and shook hands with the Softball Association president. Jordan's eyes widened. Brie's low cut top gaped open and some of the audience got a stunning view of gorgeous breasts. Jordan heard her entire team take a collective breath.

"What's wrong with you?" Kay nudged her with her elbow.

"Huh?" Jordan mumbled.

"You're practically touching that woman with your eyes, the blonde with Dannie. You know who she is, right?"

Jordan came back to earth, realizing her entire team was staring at her.

"Carter, have you been struck by lightning? We've played ball together over nine years, and I've never seen you look at anyone, man or woman, with that expression," Kay said and began to laugh.

"Ha, Jordan, I knew it'd catch up with you sometime." Bev snickered. "You're finally batting for our team."

"Stop it," Jordan said.

"Here. Let me wipe your chin. You're drooling."

"Shut the fuck up," Jordan said and the team hooted at her.

Brie looked out at the crowd and Jordan caught her eyes. Brie smiled and wiggled her fingers at her. Jordan knew Brie had caught the surprise on her face.

The food was good. Jordan ate steadily, watching Brie at the head table. For the first time since she'd known her, Brie was literally sparkling and truly alive. *This must be what she was like...before?* The talk at the table ran around her and it occurred to her that no one knew that she was Brie's friend. She smiled inwardly. She was going to have some fun with this...particularly with Brie, *flashing* the audience like that.

Finally, the meal done and cleared, Dannie Brown stood and picked up a microphone. "Good evening." Dannie grinned at the crowd and was met with huge applause. Everyone knew Dannie and that smooth television delivery. "LAKE-TV is here tonight," she began, pointing at the cameras in-house, "because we are honoring a very special lady." She turned to the three large screens slightly above and behind her that showed a gangly young girl with curly hair. "This is Niki Willis, the first week that I met her. She was just thirteen years old and already a phenom."

The room broke up with an enormous ovation.

"Niki and I..." Dannie's voice broke a little and Jordan saw Brie look up anxiously. "We finished high school, attended college together, played in these leagues until I broke my arm and had to quit, something she never let me forget. I never knew she was two years younger than me until our second year in college. She actually went through high school in three years and was only sixteen when we entered college." Dannie stopped again and took a drink of water. "We were out drinking one night and they carded us. They should have. She was only eighteen and I didn't even know it." The crowd laughed as someone yelled "jailbait." Dannie just grinned. "I wasn't legal either, so you know what that meant." Whistles and laughter interrupted her again.

"I got off the subject, didn't I?" she said with a crooked smile at the crowd. "I get to be the first to show you what Niki has left us." The screens behind Dannie came alive with film of the new sports pavilion. "In conjunction with her foundation, I'd like to present the Willis Family Center." She pointed at the film as it did a tour of the facility. "There is a gym, an Olympic-sized swimming pool, and ten softball, baseball, and Little League diamonds, all free of charge to everyone in this city."

The applause began again as the film ran on, showing Niki playing at various moments on the ball diamonds throughout the years. Finally, the film stopped on a breathtaking few seconds in slow motion of Niki at shortstop, catching the ball mid-air and throwing across her body to first base, the famous eleven-inning championship game that her team had won seven years ago, one to zero. It was the game that Jordan had remembered.

Dannie gestured at the film and began speaking again. "I present to you my best friend, Niki Willis," and the center panel showed Niki accepting her final MVP award, the only player to win it three times and the night she announced her retirement.

Like everyone else, Jordan's eyes were riveted to the screen, but she looked at Brie in the semidarkness. Brie's head was down, her eyes away from the film. Dannie took her glasses off and reached for Brie's hand again. The piece ended with Niki handing the trophy to her team and blowing a kiss to the crowd.

The quiet that followed was intense and Jordan saw many of the women wiping their eyes, but finally, the applause thundered again around the hall. Dannie straightened as the lights came back up and she put her glasses back on. "There's a lot less warmth and goodness in the world without Niki Willis." She cleared her throat. "It is now my true pleasure to present the woman that Niki constantly talked about, driving us all crazy." She stepped back. "Brieanna O'Malley. We just call her *Niki's girl*."

"Thank you," Brie said as the noise quieted. "We were all the better for knowing Niki, and she loved this game." Another ovation stopped her and she waited, smiling and poised. "As some of you know, from now on the MVP trophy will be named the Niki Willis Trophy. The other trophy has been retired in the new gym that Niki designed, and I sincerely hope all of you are able to use that facility. It's free and the entire area belongs to all of you. Tonight, I have the honor of presenting the new trophy to this year's MVP. I used to keep stats for Niki, so I understand and appreciate the figures I've just seen. This woman earned the award with some impressive batting, outstanding defense, and a love of this game. She was fourth in the city in home runs, but led all of you in RBIs. Her team elected her captain and she is a true leader. It is my honor to present to you your new MVP, Jordan Carter."

Applause and the noise of chairs being pushed back as women stood assaulted Jordan's ears. She walked numbly to the podium where Brie stood, waiting with the big trophy. Brie's eyes shone and her warm hands covered Jordan's cold ones as she handed it to her. Brie leaned in, kissing her on the cheek, and the crowd whistled and cheered. Jordan stood absolutely still, feeling the warm mouth on her skin, stunned at the gesture. Dannie jammed the mike in her face.

"Uh," Jordan began and heard her team laugh.

Dannie grinned. "I know you can talk, Carter. I've heard you yell out there on the field. Okay, the name of your team, the team that won the championship?"

"Whitney's," Jordan managed.

"And your league?"

"Greenlake," Jordan said as the spell on her tongue broke. "The best team in the city this year." She took the mike and turned to the room. "I'm sorry, I was just a bit overwhelmed for a moment." She touched her cheek. "This is a tremendous honor and I want to thank my team because without them, I am nothing. Also, our sponsors, the league, the association, Dannie and..." She turned to Brie with a smile. "Niki's girl." She held the mike away and leaned in, whispering, "Are you aware you flashed the crowd? Have you no modesty?" Brie's hand flew to her chest and she blushed as Jordan walked back to her table, handing the trophy to the first woman sitting there so everyone could have a moment with it.

"Congratulations, Carter," Bev said. "The rest of us would have committed murder for that."

"It's a beautiful trophy," Jordan said.

"No, that kiss, dummy." The whole team clapped and Jordan could feel her cheeks warm. She looked up, right into Brie's eyes, and got the most intriguing smile she'd ever seen.

"Damn," she said, eyes locked with Brie.

Kay nudged her. "You're staring again."

"And at a woman," Bev pointed out. "Are you going to ask her out, Miss *Straight* MVP?"

"I could," Jordan said.

"Maybe you *should*, because you're drooling again."

"She's just a woman," she said, feeling cocky, remembering that her team didn't know that she knew Brie.

Kay pulled a fifty dollar bill out of her wallet and tossed it in the middle of the table. It was followed by a flurry of tens, fives, and other bills from the rest of the team. "We dare you," Kay said and the women at the table began tossing money at Jordan.

"I repeat, it's just another woman," Jordan said, shaking her head .at the money accumulating on the table.

"Not *that* woman," Bev said, laughing.

Slowly, with a very cool smile, she stood and made her way to the front once again. Brie had been watching the table and raised her eyebrows at Jordan.

"Brie?"

"Yes?"

"Can you do something for me without being terribly obvious?"

"Maybe." Brie raised an eyebrow.

"Look over my left shoulder," Jordan asked.

"Do you mean that pile of money that's scattered in the middle of your table?"

Jordan nodded and checked out Dannie, who was talking to the association president. She still wasn't sure this wasn't a date.

"They bet I wouldn't walk up here and ask you out."

Brie's face opened up in a surprised grin. "Are you?"

"I am. Will you go out with me?" Jordan's gray eyes were warm and happy. Brie realized how tired she was of sad eyes, something everyone but Jordan seemed to have when they looked at her.

She took a card out of her purse and wrote on the back of it, handing it to Jordan. "The answer is yes, because you're going to run interference for me with Vet and Peg this Saturday night." She handed the card to Jordan. "Do you remember our bet?"

"Of course."

"This is kind of *after the fact,* isn't it? Since we've already slept together." Brie smiled innocently.

"Brie!" Jordan exclaimed. She could feel her face warm.

"What?" Dannie said, paying close attention to Brie and Jordan. "Did you really?" Dannie looked at Brie, surprised.

Brie held up both hands. "We took her kids and went camping at the cabin, last weekend." She gave Jordan an extra-warm smile. "I'm sorry. I was just joking. Let's have some fun with your team, a little razzamatazz. Put that cocky grin back on your face and toss this card on the money. Tell them that I'm worth a lot more than that."

Sauntering back to the table, Jordan held the card up to her team, tossed it on the money, and flashed a big grin. "Girls, she says she's worth a lot more than this."

They all grabbed for the card and threw more money out, holding it up to Brie, laughing.

Kay picked up the card and read out loud: "Sounds like fun. See you at seven thirty. Brie." She looked at Jordan with wide eyes. "For Christ's sake, Carter, how'd you do that?"

"She's just a woman, like you and me," Jordan said calmly but looked back at the head table. "Use the money on the table for the team dinner next year."

CHAPTER THIRTEEN

D one," Jordan said, and slid the hammer into her tool belt. She headed outdoors into the late Saturday morning, air so fresh that all she could do was take a big breath as she surveyed the construction yard. "Where are you, Bix?" she said, looking for her foreman. Finally, she spotted the gray-haired woman sitting on a stack of lumber.

"We're finished," Bix said as Jordan scooted up next to her. Bix was one of the first women her dad had hired, and Jordan had grown up around her.

"I need a favor."

"Sure," Bix said a little warily. "Something wrong?"

"No, not at all. I'm taking a woman out tonight and I need—"

Bix choked on her coffee and looked hard at Jordan. "A woman. You?"

Jordan ignored the choking and continued. "Here's the story. A good friend of mine is a lesbian. A very pretty lesbian. She's going out to eat with some friends of hers tonight and they're pressuring her to get back out into the dating scene. I want to go along and kind of…" Jordan stopped. How did she want to say this? She frowned. "Hell, Bix, I'm just going, all right? Anyway, I've never done this before, been out on a date with a woman, and I need your advice."

"Are you sure this is a date and that she's a lesbian?"

"A date? Okay, a meal out. I know she's a lesbian because we've talked about it."

"Why would her friends pressure her?"

"Her lover was murdered. She needs help."

"Murder?" Bix gave a low whistle. "Maybe her friends are just trying too hard."

"You should meet my mom," Jordan said in a low voice. "She made my life a living hell after Pete was killed. She pushed one guy after another at me."

Bix grinned and screwed the cap back on the top of her thermos. "How can I help you with this 'date'?"

"I'd like to do this right, so for openers, should I wear any special clothing? I want to blend in."

❖

Brie navigated the screaming ambulance up the hill, cars scattering in front of her. Sean checked his seat belt and held on, molded to the seat.

"We're almost there, Brie."

"Check the address again. I haven't seen a fire truck or a cop, and we had the farthest to go."

"They probably used the freeway," he said.

Brie grinned when she saw that his eyes were closed. It was her first time driving the ambulance on a real call and she careened around a corner. They were lifted out of their seats as they topped a sharp hill and Brie hiccupped as they hit bottom. She'd get them there safely.

"There it is," Brie said, hitting the brakes and angling the ambulance to block the road.

Two cars were in shambles in the middle of a busy surface road and they saw a third, off to the side in a ditch. An ambulance, two fire trucks, and the police were already there and everyone was out on the road. Brie and Sean grabbed equipment, going toward the mess on the pavement.

"Brie." She turned to see Vet running from the first ambulance toward her. "You and Sean take the car in the ditch. Stay away from here." Brie changed direction and adjusted the backboard in her hand. The car engine was steaming. She leaned in and turned the ignition off. An elderly lady lay quietly across the seat of the older model car, eyes closed. Her seat belt held her in an awkward position and Brie bent quickly to her face and chest, catching a whiff of an old-fashioned sachet. A narrow line of blood laced across the woman's face and she had a good-sized bruise on her forehead. A cut intersected the skin. Brie checked the victim's neck alignment and spoke clearly. "Are you all right? Can you hear me?" Two firemen finished stabilizing the car with wood blocks and one leaned in with a questioning look at Brie. She nodded an okay at him.

"What happened?" The woman's words were faint and reedy.

"I think you were run off the road," Brie said reassuringly as Sean began to take vitals.

"Brie, Sean," Vet yelled across the road, "how many?"

Sean held up one finger, indicating the single victim as Brie continued talking to the woman, gathering information. The woman was alert but they checked her again before they eased the board underneath her body. They prepared to transport and Brie noticed that Vet was still there. She looked at the crashed cars and knew it was serious. Brie pulled the rig carefully away from the scene.

The accident had made Brie late, and she began taking clothes off as soon as she was inside the house. Jordan would be here soon. She stepped into the shower, thinking of Vet at the scene of the accident. Vet had kept her away from what appeared to be a serious crash, trying to protect her. She ducked her head under the water, scrubbing her hair. Somehow she'd have to convince Vet that she wouldn't shatter. She took a deep breath and rinsed her hair. "Maybe tonight, when we're out," she said, toweling her hair as she went into her bedroom and stood in front of her closet, naked.

Nothing leapt out at her as she trailed her fingers along the hangers. Dress or pants? Pants, she decided, more casual. Something caught her eye and she pulled a light yellow outfit out of the closet. She liked the slight flare at the bottom of the pants. The top was a white camisole with a sweater that matched the pants. She could wear both if they just ate, but if they went out later, it would be too warm. Was this camisole too daring? She put it back and then pulled it out again, remembering the swimming suit. She'd certainly worn less around Jordan. She slipped into the camisole and looked for jewelry.

The long gold earrings would do and she took them from the jewelry box. No. Niki had bought these for her. She searched further and found the new ones she had bought for herself last spring. Quarter-sized gold hoops with a tiny crystal teardrop. New earrings for a new friend.

She grabbed a brush and headed to the bathroom. Just as she applied light, faintly pink lip gloss, the doorbell rang. "Crap. My clothes are all over the living room," she said, and raced down the hallway. She gathered everything and tossed it into the closet.

Jordan was jingling the car keys nervously in her fingers when Brie opened the door and they stood, assessing each other.

"You don't like it," Jordan said, frowning.

"Yes," Brie said a little breathlessly, pulling Jordan inside. "Oh, yes I do."

Dark brown leather pants caressed Jordan's hips like a whisper, and they hit her matching half boots perfectly. Brie murmured, "Oh my." The white collarless blouse fit Jordan superbly, finished off by a gold pendant hanging between the open top three buttons. *Perfect breasts.* Brie swallowed hard.

"Your turn," Jordan said. "Wow…Brie."

"Thank you," Brie said absently, enchanted by what she was looking at.

Neither moved for a moment until Jordan finally asked, "Do we have time for a beer?"

Brie blinked. "Of course. Vet's going to be late. She and I were on a call for Omni this afternoon." She gathered herself. "I've got to call Peg and tell her that Vet's going to be late." She turned quickly, going to the phone in the kitchen. She leaned against the wall, unbelievably nervous.

"Why am I so jittery?" Jordan said under her breath as Brie disappeared into the kitchen. "We haven't even left yet."

❖

Dinner went well and they lingered over the last of their wine, deciding if they were done for the night. They had talked about everything from books to sports, and the food had been wonderful. Peg and Vet obviously liked Jordan, talking easily and laughing.

"How are you, after this afternoon?" Vet leaned toward Brie, talking softly.

Brie knit her eyebrows. "Fine."

"We had a bad afternoon. Did she tell you?" Vet said to Jordan.

Jordan looked at Brie with a question on her face. Brie gave the barest of shrugs but Vet interrupted before she could say a word.

"We had an accident call out on State Street, one fatality."

"Vet—" Peg began but Vet lectured on

"Brie, you have to talk about this."

"You never even let me get close to the primary scene. I'm sure the woman we transported to the hospital will survive. I stayed until her husband got there." She set her glass down deliberately. "I'm okay. Otherwise, I shouldn't be doing the job." She left a little warning in her voice and held Vet's gaze.

Vet nodded slightly and shifted her focus to Jordan. "Did you grow up in Milwaukee?"

"On the north side."

Vet finished her wine and looked at Peg. "After today, I need some dancing and my girl in my arms. Could we go to the bar for a drink?" She looked at each of them for confirmation.

❖

Loud music blasted them as they opened the door to the club. They stood for a moment, letting their ears and eyes adjust. A yell turned them all to the bar. Most of Niki's softball team was suddenly upon them, grabbing Brie and rolling her physically into the group. Jordan walked to the edge of the mob scene.

"Better grab your girl," Vet said into her ear.

"I've probably played against most of them," Jordan said, standing straighter.

"Jordan," Brie yelled from somewhere in the middle. Brie saw Jordan looking at the group, deciding her next move. Their eyes found each other and Brie wanted to gather her close, hold her. *Show her off?*

"Jordan Carter," a tall woman said and the whole group looked in Jordan's direction. "Come on, Miss MVP. We only beat you, we don't bite." Jordan waded through the women and the moment broke with laughter. Brie put her arm around Jordan, smiling. She wanted them to see her with someone else and imprint it on their minds. Especially *this* someone.

The Ravens' first baseman handed them each a beer. Brie felt a bit giddy as she explained they were with Vet and Peg, and guided them back to the booth.

"That was a moment," Vet said.

"It had to happen, sooner or later," Peg added.

Brie glanced at Jordan from under her eyelashes. "Sooner is nice."

"Been in here before?" Vet asked.

"No, this just opened," Jordan said, taking a drink of beer.

Brie looked at her, surprised. How had she known? *She* didn't even know about this place, and she raised an eyebrow as Vet and Peg left to dance.

Jordan inched closer to Brie. "You okay?"

Brie nodded.

"How am I doing?"

Brie studied her before she spoke. "You're good. Confident, interested, just the right amount of attention. Almost too good," she said, narrowing her eyes with a tease.

"Maybe I'm just good." Jordan grinned. "You know what's coming next, don't you?"

Brie shook her head.

"She'll want to know why she hasn't seen me before if I grew up here."

"Tell the truth, that you were married. Talk about the kids."

"This is too much fun. Can't I just wing it?" Jordan said with a sassy grin.

"Okay, I'll play along, but you could just tell them. They would accept it," Brie said, looking at Vet and Peg on the dance floor.

"If they ask, I'll tell the truth," Jordan said. "I'm having such a good time, Brie."

Jordan got up to find the bathroom and Vet stayed on the dance floor, talking to some women. Peg sat with Brie and they both watched Jordan walk away. "Look at that cute little butt. Where in God's name did you find that luscious woman?"

"That's the woman I crashed into in the park," Brie said, her eyes still on Jordan. She covered her face with her hands. "You won't believe this. Can you keep a secret?"

Peg grinned at her, fanning her face.

"She's straight."

"What?" Peg sat up, eyes wide. "No way."

"She's a widow with two great little kids. If she's gay, she doesn't know it." They both laughed. "I'm trying to get her to tell you, but she hasn't been out like this in years. She's having a good time, and you know what, I am too. Thanks for tonight, Peg."

Jordan threaded her way through the crowd of women, looking around at the club. This certainly wasn't a dinky little bar like the Crow's Nest. This was a true club with a what's-happening ambience, lots of mirrors, leather, and plenty of room. She didn't recognize the music, but she liked it. The women were dressed to kill but she hadn't expected all that sexual energy and good looks.

Some of Niki's ball team had given her knowing smiles. They had thought Brie was hers. She walked a little straighter, feeling good about the moment, and grinned to herself as she stepped aside, allowing several women to exit the bathroom. It was empty, or so she thought until she heard breathy words and some heavy-duty moaning. She listened for a moment and tried to wait them out but finally just said to hell with it and flushed the toilet.

As she walked out to wash her hands, a stall door at the far end opened. Jordan kept her head down but peeked at them in the mirror. Still embracing, the two women moved to the sink. The blonde straightened her dress and kissed the dark-haired woman passionately, letting her fingers linger over her face, then left, the door closing softly behind her.

The remaining woman smiled at Jordan and peeled a condom off something in her pants, tossing it in the trash. Jordan froze, processing what she was seeing, and then she understood. The woman zipped her pants, washed her hands, and started toward the door but stopped.

"Interested?" she asked.

"No," Jordan said, trying to shut up, but she was having too much fun. "It's a little small."

"Small?"she said, all flirting gone.

Jordan turned the water off and reached for a towel. The woman leaned against the wall, bracing herself with a leg.

"Small? You show me yours, I'll show you mine."

"I'd hate to embarrass you." Jordan leaned against the sink, daring the woman. She crossed her arms, enjoying the adrenaline rush and recklessness.

The door opened and Brie walked into the bathroom, looking at both of them.

"Mary," she said to the tall woman at the wall. "I see you've met my Jordan."

Mary's head snapped up. *"Your* Jordan?" She looked from Jordan to Brie and suddenly was sociable. She held her hand out to Jordan. "Mary Kramer. Hey, girls, two for one. I'll buy you both a drink."

"No, this one's promised me a dance," Brie said smoothly, a firm arm around Jordan's waist, moving them to the door. Mary staggered a little against the wall.

"I insist, Brieanna."

"You really ought to go home, Mary," Brie said, moving quickly, almost pulling Jordan to the other side of the dance floor.

Still riding high on adrenaline, Jordan grabbed Brie's hips and brought her close. *"My Jordan?"* she teased, mouth close to Brie's ear. Hands and arms snaked around her neck.

"Umm" was all Jordan heard as the feeling of Brie's body against hers registered. Jordan backed away. "Who was that woman?" she said.

"Remember the woman I told you about, the day I met Niki?"

"The woman in the bathroom at the Inlet? That's her? She wears something in her pants."

"Oh yes, she packs," Brie said with one of those cool, raised-eyebrow looks.

"She and some woman were going at it in one of the stalls."

"And you said we all had *the same equipment.* I suppose she offered you the opportunity?"

"As a matter of fact, yes."

"I told you someone would make a pass at you. You owe me twenty bucks, Carter," Brie said but Jordan caught the twinkle in her eyes.

"As you said, you're worth a lot more than that." Jordan pulled

Brie close again. She caught her breath at the unexpected pleasure as their bodies connected, but this time she held her tight and didn't step away. "You were right about Vet," Jordan said. "She's overprotective."

"The last time I was out with them, Vet even ordered my meal." Brief misery slid across Brie's face and Jordan immediately began to tease, trying for a smile.

"That was a beautiful outfit you wore to the banquet. The top was a little revealing, but this one . . ." She leaned in, pretending to peek down Brie's white camisole.

"Hey, eyes here, Carter," Brie said, pointing at her face.

Jordan smiled when she saw the grin back on Brie's face. "I can almost see your tattoo."

"What?" Brie burst out laughing. "You wish," she said with a little snort. "Do you even have underwear on?"

Jordan blushed but held Brie's hand firmly as they sat down. She watched women look at Brie, then slide their eyes to her. Brie had what made men stand straighter. Women too. Whatever *that* was, Brie had it.

"What went on over there, at the bathroom?" Vet asked.

"Just the infamous Dr. Kramer, out in full force tonight," Brie said, shaking her head.

Peg looked at Brie and began to laugh. "She nailed Jordan, didn't she?"

Jordan lifted her chin. "I kind of provoked her."

"There's something wrong with that woman," Vet said, frowning. "One more dance, Peg? I'm ready to call it a night. How about you?"

"Wouldn't you know? I finally get back to a bar and Mary Kramer's here too," Brie said. She looked at Jordan. "First time with Niki and now you. Mary's got some mojo."

"Mojo, like hell. She's just a jerk. Let's dance and forget it." They had just begun when a strong hand grabbed Jordan's right shoulder.

"Cutting in," Mary said, lurching into both of them.

"No, you're not," Jordan said, turning Brie, talking over her shoulder. "The lady doesn't want to dance with you."

"C'mon, Brie." Mary stumbled, trying to push between them.

Brie took a step away.

"*You* know how good I am, and I taught Niki everything she ever knew. You should be thanking me," Mary slurred, falling into them.

Brie took another step backward and Mary fell to her knees, then tried to crawl up Brie's leg.

"Mary, stop. Go home," Brie said, but Mary's hand crawled higher.

Brie was losing the battle. Jordan reached for Mary and stood her up. She gripped Mary's wrist, hard. "Fuck," she said hoarsely and increased her grip. Several women stopped dancing and tried to help, but suddenly Vet was there, hauling Mary backward.

"She just pisses me off," Jordan said, her hands on Brie's shoulder, feeling her tremble. "Are you all right?"

"No," Brie mumbled, sinking into her. "Just embarrassed. I'm sorry."

She held Brie protectively, watching Vet escort Mary out the door. Jordan ran her fingers through Brie's soft, thick hair and found herself aiming for the slightly open pink lips. At the last second, she kissed the forehead instead and wrapped her arms tightly around Brie. "Stick with me, we'll make it," she said softly, her lips resting against the soft ear. "Would you like to sit down?"

"Don't move. You have no idea how good this feels," Brie whispered against her cheek. Jordan shivered as the warm breath slid down her face. "Do we have to go when Peg and Vet go?"

"No," Brie said, tightening her arms.

Every single part of Jordan's body moved toward Brie. Christ! She was more than just attracted or turned on. It thrilled her but it also frightened her, and she felt her hard-won control slipping away rapidly.

Peg walked up with their beer and Brie's purse. "That woman is despicable," Peg said as Vet found them. She grinned and slapped Jordan on the back. "That was a hellava move, Jordan. Minimum effort, maximum damage. I'm not sure that you didn't break her wrist. She whined all the way out the door and it's for darned sure it'll be sore. Let's do this again," she said, taking Brie out of Jordan's arms for a hug. Jordan almost reached for Brie, trying to keep her arms around her.

There was an empty booth right behind them and Jordan placed their drinks on the table. "Don't tell anyone, but I almost *slapped* that woman. That would have been a real statement," she said, trying to ease the moment. "Brie. That's not acceptable anytime, anywhere."

Brie sank into the booth. "It was disgusting and Niki will…"

"Niki...? What?"

"Kill her," Brie said and took a long drink of her beer.

Jordan looked down at the table, quiet.

"Did I say that?" Brie said, shaking her head slightly. "Sometimes my brain just goes on default. God, I am sorry." She cleared her throat. "All right, do you want to tell me where you got the information about this bar?"

"A woman at work that I've known forever."

Brie finally smiled. "I knew it."

"Can't I just be good?" Jordan said, turning her bottle slowly. "I could have been better. That damned doctor."

"You *are* good," Brie said softly.

Jordan stared at Brie's mouth. *I almost kissed her* kept running through her mind. "Would you like to go?"

"I'm ready. Damn, what a night!"

Brie was quiet the entire trip home and Jordan walked her to the door. "Could we do this again?"

The light September wind lifted Brie's hair a bit with a brief scent of apples and fall leaves that seemed to linger around this house. "You'd go through...that? Again?"

"It's been years since I've danced. I don't even recognize the music anymore and the food was good. I liked Peg and Vet. Anyway, we agreed, two dates."

"Okay. I love to dance." She looked overwhelmed. Sad.

Jordan reached for her. "Brie, it'll be all right."

"Thanks. Most of the night was wonderful," Brie said and leaned into her for a light hug before she went inside the house.

❖

After Jordan had driven away, Brie collected her clothes from the hall closet and walked to the bedroom. She tossed the clothing in the bathroom hamper and braced herself against the wall, finally sliding to the floor, worn out with alcohol, dancing, and the evening. She took a deep breath, trying to calm herself. Emma's question unexpectedly slid across her tired mind. *If I had died and Niki had survived*—Brie rubbed her forehead, thinking—*what would I have wanted for Niki?*

Her gaze trailed down the hand-painted tiles in the bathroom.

When Niki's family had been killed, she and Niki had discussed death... sudden death, but not their own, for God's sake.

It had been unthinkable.

Brie stood and looked at herself in the mirror. She stripped down to her underwear and went into the bedroom. The jewelry box was still open on her dresser and she carefully replaced her earrings. Jordan had noticed them.

She turned and looked at the closet. She walked across the room and slid the big door sideways. A blanket was still on the floor where she had slept. She picked it up and folded it. She began to look at the clothes in front of her, idly moving garments apart to look at each item. Who on earth could use these, she wondered. The only person she knew that was approximately the same size as Niki was her sister Val. Or girls at the university? These were really nice clothes and they might use them. She saw a deep burgundy dress that was familiar and thought of Jordan at the banquet. Jordan's burgundy suit had fit perfectly, showcasing that riveting body. It had been about the same color as this. She held it up to see it better in the light. Brie remembered how the color had glowed against Jordan's tan skin. Brie smiled. Tonight had been fun, despite Mary Kramer. Jordan, trying to act like she had been in that club a million times.

"Wing it?" Brie said out loud, repeating Jordan's words, laughing quietly. Maybe that's what Jordan had been like, before. Before life had caught her and wrecked her, knocking her into the bars. "Bet you were something else," she said. If tonight had been any hint, Jordan probably *had* been something else. Jordan was always saying that men were falling over in front of her. Brie was certain they looked at Jordan the same way.

She missed Niki, but every part of her body had hardened against Jordan tonight. For the first time since the shooting, she'd felt a sliding touch of need for someone other than Niki. *Did Jordan almost kiss me?*

CHAPTER FOURTEEN

N o," Jordan mumbled into her pillow as the phone rang. She pushed farther into the bed, searching for the phone.

Uncle John's deep voice rumbled in her ear. "Do you want to have breakfast with us when you pick up the kids?"

"Yes," she said, not even trying to open her eyes.

"Don't hurry," he said.

"Couldn't if I wanted to," she said, yawning through the words. "I need a shower. How are my little ones?"

"We kept them up so late that they're still asleep," he said, chuckling.

"Give me an hour, at least," Jordan said, burrowing back into the warm bed, still on the edge of the dream, the fragile shift of Brie's bone and warm muscle as she leaned in to kiss her and... Jordan's eyes flew open and she sat up. Brie's hips and breasts, pressed against her, that feeling of surrender and... "Damn," she said, amazed at how wet and ready she was.

Fully awake, she pulled off her T-shirt. Yes, she sure as hell *had* meant to kiss her.

❖

Brie dragged the garbage through the empty space where Niki's car should have been. Something bright and shiny caught her eyes and she recognized it immediately. It was one of the heavy-duty washers that Niki used for the new pipes in the bathroom. She slipped the washer into her jeans pocket. Why she hadn't noticed it before?

The big workbench made an L around two walls and Brie wandered down its length and hit the switch to open the garage door. The smell of possible rain blended into the fresh air that rushed at her and she took a deep breath. Niki's car had been impounded by the police, but outside of that glaring space, the garage still looked just as it always had. The three big toolboxes on wheels gleamed in front of her. She should give them to someone who would use them. Maybe Dannie or Vet? She'd gotten up that morning with a peaceful, light feeling. Was it finally a good day to do Niki's office? The closet? She took a cup of coffee and swiveled her office chair to look out at the garden. Despite Mary Kramer, they'd all had fun. Jordan could really dance and Brie had never seen her laugh that much. They'd do it again.

"You owe me twenty dollars, Carter," she said. She could have stayed in Jordan's arms forever. Jordan was about the same height as herself, and her breasts…

"Crap," Brie said, standing quickly. "What am I doing?"

She flipped on the bathroom lights and saw Jordan's wallet propped between the soap dispenser and hand lotion. She turned the soft leather billfold in her hand. *How weird. I find one of Niki's special washers that I haven't seen in years, and now Jordan's wallet. It even smells like her.* She grabbed her car keys, tapping the wallet against her fingers.

❖

"Where did I leave my wallet?" Jordan said as they walked up the sidewalk to the house, then laughed. How would the kids know? The last time she'd seen it was last night at Brie's. She dumped the contents of her purse onto the kitchen table and began to sort through it.

Someone rang the doorbell and Tyler ran for the door. "Uncle Mac," he yelled.

Mac Flynn tousled Tyler's hair and grabbed Jordan into a huge hug, finishing with a kiss, a real kiss. "Hey gorgeous," he said. The kids giggled, watching him kiss her.

"Hey." Jordan pushed him away.

Grinning, he closed the screen door and left the inside door open. "Let some air in, Jordan. It's going to rain. You always loved that smell."

She looked at him for a moment. How on earth had he remembered that? Mac had been Pete's partner and, after Pete's death, much more to her. To begin with, Mac had been the only one, but as alcohol and the newly found space in her life widened, Jordan had gone on to others. He had followed for a while until it ended in a fairly violent argument one night in his bed. She had gotten up, dressed, and never gone back. After that, on the rare occasions when they ran into each other, they'd only nodded.

He sat at the kitchen table, looking around. "I haven't seen this place," he said. "It took me a while to find you. I went to the old house, yours and Pete's." He took the coffee that she handed him.

"How'd you find me?"

"The bar. They told me that you'd moved in with your mother. I've been by a couple of times but you weren't home." He gestured at her purse. "What are you doing?"

"I managed to lose Pete's wallet last night."

"You're still carrying that?"

Jordan sat across from him and ignored the question. It was none of his business. "What's up?"

"Nothing. It's been over three years." He appraised her frankly. "You look good. Tasted like old times. Cute outfit. I always liked you in skirts. Shows off your legs."

"Mac, the kids."

He ruffled Tyler's hair again. "You've really grown, Ty, and, Jenna, you're the picture of your daddy."

"Uncle Mac, you should see my games. Come on, I'll show you," Tyler said.

"I need to talk to your mom a bit, but I warn you, I'd whip your rear, kid," Mac said with a laugh and watched the kids leave for Tyler's room. "They've really grown."

"So," Jordan persisted, "what's up?"

"I've missed you, that's all."

She said nothing, mildly irritated.

"Still making the rounds?"

She shook her head. "No. It was just a strange time."

"I'm sorry," he said. "That was out of line." He smiled apologetically. Jordan remembered one of the things that had made her give him a try in the beginning. That little-tease smile and warm green eyes. His curly brown hair looked a little shaggy, but he was wearing a clean dark blue Milwaukee FD T-shirt. "I've finally got a girl." He paused and looked at her. "Jordan, you knew how I felt."

"Never going to happen, Mac. You were about the last thing I needed. I finally quit that kind of drinking and the bars."

"Are you still working for your uncle?"

"Full partner, and I love it."

"Pete would have hated that."

"Pete isn't here."

"Right. Job's not the same either. My girl's from Chicago. I may just move down there. They always need paramedics." He stood. "I've got to go. Tell the kids I said good-bye. Maybe I'll see you again."

"I'll walk you down," she said, holding the door for him, and walked outside just as it began to rain lightly. They stopped at his car and said the usual things. She turned to go but he grabbed her for one last unexpected kiss. Jordan jerked away and Mac laughed just as another car stopped behind his. Jordan turned and saw Brie's surprised face. Brie backed her car away from Mac's so he could get by and then pulled her car up to Jordan. Brie powered the window down and held out the wallet.

"Here," she said. "You left it at the house."

"I was going to call you," Jordan said, reaching for the wallet. "Had breakfast at John and Nancy's, picked up the kids, and discovered it was gone." She felt strangely embarrassed.

Brie stared straight ahead. "I didn't mean to interrupt."

"Interrupt? No, that was Pete's ex-partner. I haven't seen him in years. He just stopped by to—" She stopped and looked at Brie's strange expression.

"You were good friends?" Brie searched her face.

"At one time. Yes." She answered honestly, looking for the usual hint of tease or laughter in those eyes, but she saw only serious blue.

"Okay, have to go."

"Wait. I just made coffee. Why don't you come in?"

"No. I'm going home to try to clean Niki's office." Brie tapped the steering wheel and backed down the driveway.

Jordan stood very still until Brie left, feeling a little queasy.

❖

Brie watched the garage door rumble down in her rearview mirror. "Well, so much for that. Wake up, Brieanna," she said to her quiet car. A big clap of thunder shook the house. "You can say that again." She looked up.

She hauled the vacuum cleaner into Niki's office and relentlessly tackled every corner. Finally, she collapsed in the big chair and tossed the dust rag on the desk. The image of the man kissing Jordan seemed to be stamped on her brain, and she scrubbed her eyes with the heels of her hands. She could have sworn Jordan was going to kiss her last night, but she must have misread it.

She looked at Niki's desk."What am I going to do with all of this?" she said. There were four deep drawers and she really had no idea what was in there. "Boxes," she said and got up to go to the storeroom at the back of the garage. One side of the room held her file cabinets containing the information for her classes and the academic papers she wrote. Across the small room there was a stack of file boxes and she took four, two in each hand. She stacked them beside Niki's desk and had a sudden flashback to that morning. Jordan had jerked away from the man, not kissed him. She tossed two files into a box just as the doorbell rang.

Jordan and the kids stood underneath the porch while it poured rain behind them.

"Hey," Brie said, going to one knee in front of the children. "Are you visiting me?" Jenna and Tyler had a handful of flowers and held them out, grinning. "Ah." Brie gave them each a hug. She looked at Jordan.

"Let's start this day over," Jordan said and looked so hopeful that all Brie could do was stand and smile. "I thought maybe pizza? I brought a movie for the kids."

"I'm cleaning Niki's office. Could the kids have a root beer?" Both Jenna and Tyler turned to look at Jordan, but Brie turned them toward the kitchen. "Come on. If you're going to hang out here, you have to know where the root beer lives." They followed her and Brie gave them each a soda. "Jordan, put the movie in while I find a vase." She saw the puddle in front of the sink. "Oh, shit," she said. Jordan and the kids swiveled.

"I'm sorry, kids. I didn't mean to swear."

Jenna giggled. "We have to stand in the corner if we say those kind of words."

"I'll stand in the corner. I was wrong." Brie looked at Jordan and raised her eyebrows.

"We forgive you. How about it, kids?" They nodded. "Did we do that?" Jordan pointed at the puddle.

"No, it's just the same loose coupling under the sink that we've battled forever. Drove us nuts." She moved past them toward the tools in the garage. "Why don't you get the movie going and I'll fix it."

Jordan sat at the table, watching Brie scrunch under the sink. "You know how to do…plumbing?" she said.

"Dad owned a hardware store and I worked there every summer. Not much I haven't done in the way of plumbing." She locked the pipe wrench around the fitting and glanced up as Jordan pulled a chair nearby. Her legs were crossed and a sandal dangled off a foot. Her dark purple skirt had hitched, exposing those lovely legs. Brie's gaze ran up the casual mauve tee. *My God, look at her.* She swallowed hard and focused back on the pipe above her. No wonder men wanted to kiss her. She did.

"That man, this morning?"

"Pete's partner at the firehouse. After Pete was killed, we were more than friends for a while."

"I saw you jerk away," Brie said, trying to be clear. She concentrated on the wrench.

"He was just being a creep this morning," Jordan said. "Need some help?" she asked and then laughed. "Honestly, Brie, I've never done that in my life."

"Never?"

"Pete or Uncle John usually took care of it."

"Umm," Brie grunted, giving the wrench once last firm tug. She noticed a neon red paper tag hanging from the top of the pipe. She reached and turned it slowly. *Thanks, hon, I love you*, it said in Niki's writing. She laid the wrench on the floor and undid the string. "I'll be darned." She scooted out from under the sink and ran water in the drain, checking the pipes. "Perfect," she said, pointing at the dry pipes and dusting her jeans off. Jordan bent to look under the sink and picked up the red tag.

"What's this?"

Brie shook her head. "A note from Niki. I didn't know she knew I was working on this sink all the time." She mopped the puddle dry and picked up the wrench. "We had our hands full with this place. Would you like some iced tea?" Jordan nodded. "Take it into Niki's office and I'll put the tools away."

❖

Brie carried the vase of flowers into Niki's office.

"Looks better in here," Jordan said.

"Did you have to do this, with Pete? Go through a desk?"

"Some, but not to this extent. We shared an office and used the same desk."

Brie opened file after file, going over the information carefully, and made three stacks of papers, brochures, magazines: information for the house, business, and personal. Jordan got up, looking at the sound system, and took a dust cloth to it. She hit the On button. A woman's voice filled the room and Brie froze. Jordan quickly turned it off.

"What was that?"

"Niki," Brie said faintly and put her head in her hands. "Oh God. This never occurred to me. She always carried a little recorder, called it her 'notes to self' and ran it off to disc. Open that cupboard above the CD player."

There were three rows of discs, and Jordan tilted her head to read the dates. It began over fifteen years ago. "Wow," Jordan said, sitting back down beside Brie. "Can you stand to listen to that?"

"I don't know," Brie said. "This is crazy. I haven't thought of these discs since before the shooting. I've never opened that cupboard."

"Do you want to take a day?" Jordan gestured at the wall. "I'll sit with you, if it would help."

Brie looked unsure. "I have a feeling that's 'us' up there." She took a deep breath. "She talked everything and I wrote all my stuff."

"Yes. You did write. I meant to tell you last night that I finished your first book. It was excellent."

"Thanks. Niki found a family's letters and documents in an old house she and her father were working on. The odd thing about the family's letters and information was that it is exactly the time period I teach, after the Civil War and up through the eighteen nineties. I had a question about the family and that's what started everything. It was fun, relaxed my mind."

"Your second book was a bestseller?"

Brie finally smiled. "Luck and good marketing. I started the third one in the series and have a contract, but it's going to expire if I don't get going. It's all based on that family."

"Are you really an *authority* on an election in the late eighteen hundreds?"

"Where on earth did you hear that?" Brie laughed.

"The university Web site."

Brie shook her head. "Same thing as the book. Just marketing. They'll say anything on that Web site, I swear. Maybe, by the time I'm one hundred, I'll know something."

"Why aren't you writing?"

Brie looked out the window. "Why aren't you carving?"

They sat for a moment, listening to the sounds of the kids' movie floating down the hallway. Jordan cleared her throat. "Carving? I sat at the kitchen table when I got home last night and thought about carving and...dancing."

"I really enjoyed myself, despite Mary." Brie's mind raced. She hoped she understood what they were really talking about. "You know I'm not home free yet," she said. "I'm only finding pieces of life, here and there." Brie took the washer out of her pocket and threaded it through the string from the red tag, all the time thinking about the almost kiss last night. The phone rang and they both jumped.

Brie recognized Detective Jim Carnes's voice immediately and sank back into Niki's chair, listening.

"We have someone that you need to see, here at the station. This may be the break we've been looking for. Can you come down now?"

Brie swiveled the chair and stared at Jordan. "Of course," she said automatically.

Jordan was already moving. "He talks so loud I could hear every word. I'll go with you."

"The kids?" Brie said.

"Let me check with Nancy. Maybe she'll watch them. Let's take my car," Jordan said and began talking into the phone. Brie got up to gather the kids but didn't move.

"What's the matter?" Jordan asked.

"This isn't right. They're grabbing at anything that comes along." She finally started to walk out of the office. "I just don't want to go."

CHAPTER FIFTEEN

B rie had never been in this part of the police station before. The smell of disinfectant and sweat agitated her. Her stomach churned. She wiped her hands on her jeans with a quick glance at Detective Jim Carnes. Every time he opened his mouth she felt as if he was shouting. Did he have a hearing problem? Jordan shifted in the chair next to her.

Carnes looked down at some papers. "We've picked up a man that we've proved was in the vicinity at that time, and we believe he's involved with Ms. Willis's murder, your shooting. Would you be willing to look at a line-up?"

"You know I believe this was a random killing," Brie said, clenching her jaw. Her arms felt heavy. "However, I'll do—"

The detective interrupted with a crisp comment. "We don't have that luxury."

"Luxury?" Brie said with a deep breath and her heart began to pound. "I'm here, aren't I?"

"It's our job." He stared at her. "We've done quite a bit of work on this case and this suspect. The last time we spoke, last month? You said you were still unable to remember anything. What if seeing this man makes you remember?"

Brie began to sweat. The longer she sat there, the worse she felt. "Do you understand I *can't* remember?" Her entire body shook as she stood, leaning on the table. Brie grappled with tears and a quick wash of anger.

"I'm sorry," he said. He reached for a box of tissues.

She held up her hand to stop him but he repeated it. "Ms. O'Malley, please. I'm sorry."

"You're *sorry?*" The slap of her hand on the table was like a gunshot in the tense room. "I try to *remember* every single day of my life. Or what's left of my life." She wiped her eyes. "Jesus Christ!"

Someone knocked and Carnes went to the door. He traded words with a man and turned to Brie and Jordan. "We're ready. Would you follow me, please?"

They were led into a dark room behind two-way glass. Six men came in, all approximately in their mid-thirties. Brie, Jordan, and Carnes stood there, looking at them. Brie wondered who they were or if any of them but one were actually criminals. Suspected criminals, she corrected herself.

The detective was looking at her intently, but she shook her head. "I'm sorry. They look like what I see every day at the university." She shut her eyes and willed her mind back to the shooting, one more time. The sequence began to play once again, that moment. She closed her eyes. "All I remember is what Niki said to me. She told me to put the glasses down. I heard a noise and asked her if it was the waves. The dirt bike was suddenly there. I could smell the exhaust and then, gunshots. There was a flash of red in that direction."

"A flash of red?" Carnes was alert. "You've never said that before."

"I haven't?" She couldn't remember. "There were birds, seagulls I think, after the noise." She opened her eyes and turned back to the glass. "Could it have been blood?"

The detective cleared his throat. "No. I don't think so, Ms. O'Malley. I remember the scene clearly and...no. The shots came from behind." In the darkness of the room, Jordan put a hand on Brie's shoulder.

"I don't recognize any of them."

The detective visibly sagged. "All right, that's enough. Thank you, Ms. O'Malley." He opened the door. "Let me take you ladies out."

They hurried across the parking lot in the rain to the car. Wisps of ground fog sprang up as the day began to end and the temperature dropped.

Jordan started the car. "Let's get the kids and go for pizza, how about it?"

Brie stared out of the window, still shaking.

Jordan reached into the backseat. "You're shivering. Here, put this on." She helped her into the fleece jacket.

Brie turned the collar up on the jacket. It smelled like Jordan. "Do you realize they're never going to solve this? And even if they do, it won't bring Niki back...or un-shoot me. I hate this." She gritted her teeth. "But still...he's only doing his job. I was too rude."

Jordan stared out the windshield. "Have you been at this precinct before?" she asked as she pulled away from the police station.

"Thomas Teller and I were here, after I was released from the hospital. I gave a statement before Niki died, but they wanted more."

"More?"

"I was not in any shape in the hospital to give much of a statement."

"That's right," Jordan said. "You said you and Niki were in the same room."

Brie nodded. "I made the decision to stop the machines based on what the doctors told us. They didn't give me a shred of hope, but even as out of it as I was, I knew she wasn't alive. Thomas could have made the decision but I didn't want him to carry that the rest of his life. He and Niki were close."

Jordan made a left turn onto a quiet street. "That took courage."

"No," Brie said as they pulled into John Kelly's driveway. "It took love."

❖

After dinner, they drove home through the rain. The kids were unusually quiet.

Jordan grinned across the car at Brie. "Food coma."

The pizza and laughter with the kids had brightened Brie's mood and she dashed through the rain toward her front door. Jordan ran after her.

"I forgot the movie the kids were watching. Also, I saw a book about wood finishing in Niki's office. Is there a chance I could borrow it?"

"Sure, as long as you'll let me troll through Pete's books," Brie answered as they walked to Niki's office.

"Thanks for coming over with my wallet," Jordan said. "Are you all right? Would you like us to stay for a while?"

"No, but thanks." Brie said. She turned to give Jordan a light hug but Jordan moved first, holding her hard. The arms felt warm and strong, too good to move. Brie pushed her face into Jordan's hair and inhaled the scent of rain, spicy shampoo, and fresh air.

"I'll call you tomorrow night."

"I have class. Call me after nine thirty." Brie waited at the door as Jordan ran to her car. "Thanks for the flowers," she called after her and Jordan waved.

As Jordan drove away, Brie realized she was still wearing her jacket. "Wait," she called but it was too late. She closed the door and locked it. Coffee sounded good. She started a pot and then hung Jordan's jacket in her bedroom closet, between her clothes and Niki's.

There was a light on in Niki's office and she stepped in to turn it off. The cabinet door under the sound system was ajar and Brie saw something inside. Three letter-sized corrugated boxes were side by side. Brie immediately went to her knees. She had asked Niki to get them from storage that day, their anniversary. They were the letters, the family's correspondence that provided the basis for her fiction.

"I have no mind left," she said. She touched the fragile papers lovingly. She knew exactly what was there because she had packed them. *Why can I remember that I asked Niki to get these boxes that day but not the shooting?* She gathered the boxes and carried them into her office.

Brie turned her computer on and immediately went to her book file. She typed some notes to herself, based on the afternoon at the police station. All the computers and technology in the world hadn't changed a thing. Crime still won.

The smell of coffee drifted into her office and she got up to go to the kitchen. She hated this underlying anger she carried right now. And the hopelessness that hung in its shadow.

The wind practically took the door out of Jordan's hand as they entered Patrick's the following Tuesday night. They were early, and George came out and sat with them before the dinner rush began.

"You look better. You've gained some weight," he said, smiling at Brie. "Nice outfit."

Brie was all business in a charcoal suit with a faint lavender pinstripe and lavender blouse to match. "You look pretty good yourself," she said, bumping him with her shoulder.

"Why the serious clothes?" Jordan asked and leaned in, examining the small gold necklace that glimmered in the hollow of Brie's throat.

"I had a meeting today," Brie said and held the necklace closer.

"What is it? It looks like a flower."

Brie watched Jordan examine the necklace. She rubbed her tired eyes. The last two days had been busy, and she had written on her book as late as possible every night. Her mind was still in bits and pieces after the police station, but her emotions were in worse shape. After a shower, she had fallen asleep almost immediately but both nights had shimmered with strange dreams and interrupted rest. Nightmares of Niki at the police station, anguished, pressed against the glass while Brie could only stand, mute and helpless on the other side. Last night's dream was the most unsettling. She and Jordan had waited in an unfamiliar room. Jordan had faced her and slowly undressed. Brie had woken, got out of bed, and taken her first sleeping pill in months. Now, searching Jordan's eyes across the table, she was glad to be here, but the dream lingered.

George spoke up. "The flower on the necklace is a calyss."

"What's that?" Jordan asked.

"A mythical flower that some French woman drew about a million years ago," he said, with a little laugh. "Brie tried to tell us that they grew wild, all over France."

"I was teasing," Brie said defensively. "You guys are always so cutting edge. It was my turn."

"Niki backed you up," George said and turned to Jordan. "Here's the deal. Niki was always putting us on with that incredibly quick mind, but Brie was usually quiet. Patrick didn't buy it, but I did."

"What?" Jordan scoffed at Brie. "You tease me all the time."

Brie made a face at both of them.

Jordan frowned at George. "Brie was actually quiet?"

George nodded. "Niki would be out front, quick and talking." He looked at Brie. "You were the detail person, the one that tied up all the loose ends."

Brie nodded with a little shrug. "It's true. I don't care. It worked for Niki and me."

"Ah," Jordan said and raised an eyebrow at her. "You were the closer."

"Talk on," Brie said. "I have to wash my hands."

In the bathroom, Brie dribbled soap on her hands, remembering the day they had tried to convince George and Patrick that the flower existed. She soaped her hands. Niki had picked her up on campus in her work pickup, an old relic that Niki and her father both loved. Brie had immediately laughed at the streaks of red and brown that covered Niki's face and clothes.

"If that's lipstick, you're dead, but…" She had licked her fingers and ran them over Niki's cheek. "But since it's brick dust, you may live a little longer."

Niki had taken her eyes off the road with a sexy smile. "You want to put those fingers somewhere else?"

George was right. Niki had been more out front. Brie scrubbed her hands. Jordan was more subtle. Her slow, sensual invitation in the dream last night had been without a word, but her eyes had burned with desire. Brie had stared at the angles of Jordan's tanned arms as clothing fell to the floor. The taut stomach below round, tight breasts with dark nipples. She had shuddered against her raging body, then finally able to move, she had reached for Jordan but woken instead with a sharp breath.

Brie automatically shoved her hands under the water but jerked them back. It was steaming hot.

"Damn," she said and adjusted the water temperature, trying to calm herself. "What now?" She ran a damp towel across her face. She gripped the sink to steady herself, fully wet and ready. Just as she'd been after the dream.

Brie came back to the booth, still warm and aching. She fixed her gaze on Jordan's wide, expressive mouth. What would it taste like?

"Are you all right? Your face is flushed," Jordan asked.

Brie shifted in the seat. "Do you know what I did after you called last night?"

"Called some cute woman? Phone sex?"

Brie adjusted her body, trying to ease the pressure. "Watch your mouth."

"I'm just a tramp. What can I say?"

"Say you're sorry. And you're not a tramp."

"I'm sorry. What did you do last night?" Jordan said with a sassy grin. "Your face is still rosy."

"Stop it," Brie said but wouldn't look at her. "I wrote a few thousand words on my fiction."

"That's great."

"You know what that means?"

"Yes, you're writing again. Great news."

"That means you have to go to your studio and work."

Jordan held her hands up. "Well then, guess what I did last night?"

"Called some cute guy and…" Brie countered and finally looked at her.

"No, I did some carving." Jordan's smile curved into a tease. She had begun work on Brie's owl.

They finished their meal and walked across the parking lot to their cars.

"You had a meeting today? You don't teach on Tuesdays," Jordan said, putting an arm around her as they walked.

"I had a meeting, downtown, with a committee. A paper of mine is being challenged. No biggie. I'm on solid ground and maybe it'll help me stay focused on my book. God, I hope so. I have a meeting next month with my fiction editor in Santa Fe."

"Editor?" Jordan said, her expression interested again.

"For that third book," Brie said. They cut across between cars just as the wind gusted and blew leaves back at them. Laughing, they turned their backs to the commotion for a moment.

Jordan put her arm around her and pulled her close again. Brie leaned her face briefly into Jordan's cheek, the faint scent of wood mixing with cool air. The dream shaded her mind for a moment and she looked at Jordan. Jordan was looking at her.

"Let's get together at my house tomorrow after my therapist's appointment. Some of Pete's books might help," Jordan said.

They reached the cars and Jordan put her hands on the car on either side of her. Brie blinked. A kiss right now would be perfect. Instead, she said, "I have tomorrow off from both jobs and I'll take you up on that offer for Pete's books, and explain what I'm going to have to do in January."

"Thanks for tonight." She took Brie's hand and studied it. Finally, she brushed her lips across Brie's knuckles. "I'll call you after my doctor's appointment."

When Brie got home she didn't even bother to turn the lights on and walked through the dark house to her bedroom. There was a constant tick-tick-tick of yearning in her body even though she was worn out. Had she taken her vitamin? Maybe it was just PMS. She mentally calculated. No.

After her shower, she went immediately to bed. The only light in the room was a small light beside the bed. She took the framed photo off the bedside table and laid it over her heart, the glass cold against her skin. Jordan's lips had felt warm on her hand.

She held the photo up. "How am I doing, girl? Maybe I should say, *what* am I doing? I'm still a little foggy, but my hormones have certainly found daylight." She put the photo down carefully and then punched her pillows. Now she'd have to tell her therapist about that dream, the one of Jordan. And the therapist would just tell her it was because her mind was working again, the writing, creative side of her mind. Or would she? Who knew?

"I probably should just move to California," she grumbled. "Night, sweetie. Wherever you are, I love you."

Desperately tired, she turned the light off and let her eyes close. Suddenly she came up to her elbows. *It's the first time I've ever had a sex dream about anyone other than Niki.* "Crap!" she said out loud and collapsed back on the bed.

CHAPTER SIXTEEN

D r. Joel Bauer slid into his chair the next morning and Jordan immediately thought of hobbits. She was starting the Tolkien series with Tyler, and Dr. Bauer had morphed into one of the characters. Short and round. All he needed were some of those odd little slippers and a cloak, and he'd be a perfect hobbit. The psychiatrist ran his hands through his thinning, rusty-colored hair. "It's crazy out there. I'm thinking of checking myself in." He made a face at her over his half-glasses. "You look great. I like your new hairstyle."

"Someone canceled at my hairdresser's. I got in early this morning."

Leaning back, he surveyed her. "You're smiling and the tan looks healthy." He grinned. "What's this? Sparkling eyes?"

Jordan unbuttoned the cuffs on her navy blue shirt and pushed them up a little. "We all had our checkups. Everyone's in great shape."

"How's Tyler doing?"

"He had an episode several weeks ago, but he's been fine since then. I spoke to his teacher yesterday afternoon."

He shuffled papers. "Let's see, we set this appointment up over a year ago. Time flies when you're having fun, huh? How's the drinking?"

"Occasional."

"What kind of drinking?" he asked.

"Just beer or wine."

"When?"

"Usually when I get home from work. Very occasionally, Joel, and then just a beer. One." She thought about that and added, "Well, last weekend I did a little more than just one."

"Jordan, that's drinking. Period. You've got to be careful." He bent, scribbling on the paper. "Charlotte still lobbing guys at you?"

"Wait until you hear this." Jordan started to chuckle and told him about her mother, Richard, and the trip to Ireland. "Oh, and Mac Flynn stopped by. He gave me an opening, but I'm still not interested. It's like I used it all up in that two-year binge."

"Used all *what* up? Does that mean you haven't had sex in three years?"

"I never said that."

He looked at her and let the papers fall back on the desk. "I apologize. I'm only trying to find out what put the smile on your face."

"As if it's any of your business," she said. "Actually, it is your business. That's why I'm here." She checked out the colorful barberry bushes against his windows. "No."

"What?"

"I said no. I haven't had sex in almost three years."

He absently cracked his knuckles. "You said you've had a physical recently?"

"You should have the paperwork. I had Dr. Kittel send it over."

They were quiet as he found the information and looked across it. Jordan noticed the plants in his office needed attention and got up to get a pitcher from one of the cupboards. She filled it with water and began to water each plant. At one time she'd been in here so often that she knew exactly how many plants there were and how to tend them.

"My plants have missed you," he said drolly and tossed his glasses on the desktop. "Okay, I give up. Something's changed in your life. You're shining…or something."

"I made a friend."

"That's always good," Dr. Bauer said.

"I was showing Tyler a new skateboard in the park. There's a house, a cottage, out there that really fascinates me, and I wasn't paying attention. I hit Brie and knocked us both down. I gave myself a huge black eye and she had a big bruise. We ended up at Urgent Care and I took her out to eat. Since then, we've gotten to know each other. We even took the kids camping at her family's cabin. That was a great weekend." She filled him in on the last weeks.

"So, you went to a lesbian club with your new friend, Brie?" he said and cleared his throat. "You confront the woman in the bathroom and then, the same woman makes a scene later?"

"That woman reminds me of bar women I used to hang out with. Not people I want to know anymore. She crawled right up Brie's leg."

He stacked the papers on his desk and shoved them off to the side. "Jordan, I'm just testing the water because you seem to be alive again. Does this mean you're changing your lifestyle?"

"I was helping a friend." They stared at each other until Jordan held her hands up in surrender. "All right, more than a friend. I've personally never known anyone as beautiful as Brie, but she's interesting. She's warm, smart, and articulate. Uncommon. I don't know what it is, and you know what, Joel? I don't care."

"Does the fact that she's a lesbian have anything to do with... anything?"

"Of course not."

"It's not a sexual attraction?"

"No," Jordan said. "Well, maybe. I almost kissed her."

"Kissing? Isn't that a little sexual?"

"I suppose. It's confusing." She studied her hands thoughtfully. "There's something else, Dr. Bauer. She lost her partner of thirteen years to a murder, so you could say we have that in common. It just occurred to me that I've told her things that I've only told you. And every time I do that, it's a good feeling. *Freeing*."

"Murder?" he said. "Whew."

Jordan nodded. "A little over two years ago."

"How's she doing?"

"She's trying. It's funny, it's the first time I've been able to see my own progress. I've never known anyone to compare it to, and it's an odd feeling."

"Jordan, think about where you were a few years ago with the alcohol and the bars, and then you dropped into, what did you call it?" He stared at the ceiling, thinking. "The dead zone? You sound as if you're enjoying life." He checked his notes. "Do you remember how we ended our last session? You said nothing interested you but your job, carving, and the kids. And you're not carving."

"No, but I'm doing more than whittling. More importantly, I'm getting that little feeling right here." She patted her heart.

"That's good. Jordan, I'm not advising you to fall in love. That's not the issue here. What I'm talking about is the way you locked up your feelings. Hid them away." He smiled kindly. "If you're attracted and you've found someone *uncommon*…and perhaps it's a little sexual? Plus, you're carving? Maybe this is it? You're moving out of that dead zone." He opened a desk drawer and pulled out some papers. "Have you had any questions about Brie's lifestyle?"

She gave him an are-you-kidding look. "Sure I have."

He handed her the papers. "This is something you should read, then. It's interesting information on your relationship with Brie. We have a new term that we're using in our profession. Sexual fluidity. It's based on current studies, specifically directed at women. I'd like you to read it."

Jordan reached for the stapled papers and read the date. "This was done last year?"

He nodded. "Basically, it confirms something I've been seeing for quite a while. Women connect with the person, not the gender. It's something you probably already know, as a woman. The emotional connection is much more important than the physical to most women. I'm not saying women don't like men sexually. I'm simply saying the *important* connection is the person. Women are more open to a *variety* of relationships."

Jordan scanned the first paragraph. "This looks interesting."

He stood. "Would you make another appointment in a month? I'd like to see where this goes. When I see you again, let me know where you weigh in on this information." He stacked the papers on his desk. "What about Pete?"

Jordan stood as well. "What about Pete?" She pulled her shirt cuffs down and began to button them but looked at him. "Pete. I forgot. It was five years ago, yesterday, and I forgot."

"Why should you remember?"

"I'm not sure. I've never forgotten before."

"I think it means you're getting on with your life." He walked to the door. "Make that appointment. One last session and I think we're done."

Jordan closed the door quietly, her mind racing. Was that what this was with Brie? *Attraction?* No. *Attraction* was the bars. *This is different. More of…something. Christ, but what?* She'd never been so aware of anyone. She pulled her phone from her pocket but let her arm hang at her side. She didn't know what this was between herself and Brie except that wherever *Brie* was, she wanted to be there too.

❖

Brie leaned against the doorbell of the service entrance to Emma's gallery. Her hands were full, holding two large lattes. It was a peace offering for not getting down here nearly enough. It would be a good time to talk with Emma, before the gallery opened.

Emma opened the door, obviously surprised. "Oh, the latte that I love. You are a sweetie." She held the door open and Brie followed her to her office.

"Ah," Emma crooned, taking a sip of the hot liquid. "My taste buds bow to you." She scanned Brie's button-down white shirt, washed-out jeans, black leather boots, belt, and jacket. "Going to a biker convention?"

"How'd you know?" Brie deadpanned. "This is how I'm going to handle all of this crap. I'm heading west on a hog."

"Going alone?"

"If I took anyone, it would be Jordan."

"Jordan? Mom said you took her out last weekend?"

"Yep." Brie took a drink and looked around the office.

"Did you forget she's straight?"

"Maybe. Lay off, Em. I'll handle this."

"As I said, did you forget she's straight? Also, I think you should know that her reputation isn't all that great. Some of my friends remember her from the clubs, several years ago."

"I know about that. What's more important is that she hasn't done that in over three years and there's a woman that's finally caught my attention."

"Think of how Niki would view this."

The temperature in the room plunged as Brie swiveled to her. "Tell me. *How would Niki view this?*"

Emma took a deep breath. "Sorry. That was incredibly stupid." She took another drink of the coffee. "George and Patrick were in here the other day. They picked up some paintings, one for their restaurant and one for Patrick's office downtown. They said you've been meeting Jordan for dinner? You may as well know that I talked to Mom about you two."

"You what?" Brie's eyes widened.

"Mom asked how you were and told me what you'd said about last weekend. And I told her about the dinners at Patrick's, you and Jordan."

"Why on earth did you do that?"

"I did it because I felt you'd need someone to talk to, just in case. Things happen."

"She's seeing her therapist this morning and is going to call me when she's done. Her husband was a history nut and I get to look at his books today. She wanted to know what started all of my books, so I'm going to show her some of my dissertation." Brie set her coffee on the desk and gave Emma a disconcerted look. "Emma, for God's sakes, I didn't come by for a lecture. I just wanted to see your gallery and visit a little." Just as Emma began to answer, Brie's phone rang.

"Hey," Jordan said when Brie answered, "what are you up to?"

"I'm at Emma's gallery, downtown."

"How about some lunch? It's after eleven, and I'm only about ten minutes away. Why don't you leave your car and I'll pick you up?"

Brie turned to Emma. "Could I leave my car here in your private lot?" Emma nodded. "Pick me up out front of the gallery," she told Jordan.

They drove to the restaurant, a small place out by an inland lake. It was busy but they found a table by the windows and were able to order quickly. Jordan took a quick breath as she watched Brie take her coat off, framed in the October sunshine. "That's a nice look."

"Emma asked me if I was going to a Harley convention," Brie snickered. "Nice haircut, by the way. When did you find time for that?"

"Someone canceled this morning and I went in early."

"It's trendy and fits you," Brie said, appraising the new, somewhat-shaggy hairstyle.

"How'd it go with the therapist?" Brie asked, watching Jordan adjust the shakers, move a napkin, set the silverware somewhere else. Jordan was shifting around in her chair. Something had gone on with the therapist.

"I have to see him again in a month. I hadn't seen him in over a year, so we had a lot to catch up on. My health, the kids, my new mother, sex—"

"Sex?" Brie interrupted, starting to laugh.

Flustered, Jordan made a face. "I didn't mean to say that." She frowned and shifted the shakers once again.

"Too much? Too little?" Brie leaned across the table playfully. "All right, no sex talk, but you should eat," she said, pointing at the food that was being placed on the table.

Jordan looked at Brie's food. It was salmon, drizzled with a spicy-smelling sauce. There was a variety of cheese, fruit, and bread on another plate. "What is that?"

"Their special. I'm not a huge seafood fan, but their salmon is out of this world. Here." She forked a piece of the fish and held it across the table to Jordan. "Open up."

"Omigod," Jordan said, closing her eyes, tasting lemon but also something a little sweet. "You find the best food." She looked at her hamburger.

"I've got to get you off the burger binge," Brie said with a big grin.

Jordan stabbed a slice of peach off Brie's plate. "The therapist and I also talked about Pete, and it reminded me of something. Would you mind if I talked about it? It's the day of the fire."

"Sure," Brie said, beginning to smile, but she stopped when she saw Jordan's serious expression. "Did you and Dr. Bauer talk about this?"

"I told him about our date."

"Date?"

"He said that I'm shining." She made a wry face at Brie. "No one, except you, has said anything close to that for years." She rushed on nervously. "The day that Pete died, we had overslept. I always got Jen ready for the daycare at my school and was in the bedroom, trying to get both of us dressed. Pete was doing the same thing with Tyler, getting him ready for kindergarten. Somehow, we got in each other's way and began arguing. I don't think either of us ever said such mean things to each other."

The waitress came with more coffee, quieting them for a moment.

"Anyway, we took the fighting out of the bedroom and down the hall to the kitchen. Jenna was screaming in her crib and Tyler was standing between us, trying to tell us that she was crying. Pete picked him up, grabbed his bag, and started out the door. He looked at me and said, 'Don't forget to get the damned kids on the way home.' That was the last time I saw him."

"When was this?"

"Five years ago yesterday. It's the first year I've forgotten." She took a drink of coffee. "I'm still mad at him. I never, ever, forgot the kids. I know it was said in anger, but it was such a dumb thing to say."

All Brie could do was reach across the table and take Jordan's hand.

"I've never told that to anyone except the doctor. You're the first real friend I've had since Pete was killed."

Brie looked out at the thinning lunch hour crowd, her heart rate kicking up. "Thank you," she said, her voice breaking slightly. Brie stood and tossed some money on the table. "Come on," she said. "Give me your keys. There's a place we need to be."

Ten minutes later Brie pulled off the paved highway onto a short dirt road, kicking dust up behind the silver Camry. Foliage flew past the windows. Brie never took her eyes off the road until she stopped in a clearing. She tossed the keys at Jordan and walked ahead. Jordan pushed aside a low branch and saw Brie sitting on the ground, head on knees.

"What is this?" she asked.

Brie shook the hair out of her eyes. "I just need some quiet."

Jordan walked over to the edge of a rock to see a small creek. They were surrounded by trees and wildflowers, then Lake Michigan to the east. It smelled like Brie's backyard.

"This is our woods, where we'd dig up the flowers that we planted at our house."

"Your novel? The place where they met in *Midnight Woods*. Is this it?"

"You remembered?"

"Of course, it was an important place. Is it in the second book?"

Brie nodded and took a deep breath, winding grass around her fingers. "Jordan," she said carefully. "I'm not sure I can be the friend you think I am or that you deserve."

Jordan blinked. "No," she said softly, sitting beside Brie.

"What if I want more than *just friends?*" Brie rubbed her face hard."I keep wanting to…" She looked into Jordan's face helplessly. "I keep wanting."

Jordan pulled Brie close and rubbed her shoulder. "We can do this."

Brie shook her head. "I don't know if I can."

"We can be anything we choose."

"I know what I'd choose," Brie said, her voice shaking as she started to cry a little, "and Niki…"

"All right, it's complicated." Jordan exhaled and leaned back on her elbows. "I care, Brie."

"My feelings, my life will confuse you. I can see it coming. You have two kids that I care about and I know you're a talented carver, something you need to be doing."

Jordan stretched out on the ground with her arms over her face. Brie went to all fours above her and pulled Jordan's arms above her head, bending slowly until their mouths almost touched. "Just so you understand me perfectly…I will do this anytime I have the opportunity." She closed the space, kissing Jordan lightly, first on the forehead, then on a cheek and finally, her mouth trailed very slowly down to the lips. Brie thought Jordan was pulling away and then realized she was pushing upward for more. She kissed her again, tasting her thoroughly. She tasted of coffee, surprise, desire.

Brie tried to steady herself against a rush of dizziness. They stared at each other, breathing the same air. The only sound was the light wind in the flowers around them.

"Do that again," Jordan said in a low voice. When Brie hesitated, Jordan cupped her face in her hands and pulled her mouth back to her own. "You taste good," Jordan said, her mouth still against Brie's.

Brie lay fully on Jordan's body, intoxicated and dazzled. If she didn't stop now, there would be no stopping. She pushed up to her hands and knees.

Brie stood. "Come on. It's time to get the kids."

"Wait. Don't stop." Jordan tried to tug Brie back down.

Brie shook her head and pulled Jordan up, holding her hand all the way to the car.

Turned away, Brie felt both embarrassed and pleased. "I didn't expect to do that, but I'm not sorry," she said.

"I'm not confused, Brie, just high. Nothing about you is confusing. That was perfect." Jordan said, her face glowing. "I want to do that again."

❖

They made tacos together with the kids. Brie dared Tyler to cook with her, showing him how to melt cheese over nachos, cleverly getting him to do almost the entire dish. She had Jenna help her with the salad, patient as they tore the lettuce. As Jordan watched Brie play around the kitchen with her children, her heart gave a strong tug. It looked right to see her here. She finished setting the table and realized she couldn't remember driving to the school. It was as if they had gone from the woods to here. When had they picked up Brie's car? There it sat, in her driveway.

After the kids were in bed, they curled up on the couch together as if nothing had happened and read through parts of Brie's paper. Politics or history had never interested Jordan, but Brie's ideas immediately intrigued her, and suddenly it was late.

"You need to get up early," Brie said, slipping into her boots. "Let me check Pete's books and I'll go." Jordan followed her into the office and helped her look through the books from the Civil War. Brie took two books. Jordan didn't move. They were a breath away from each other. Her eyes began to close, heart racing, leaning to the lips in front of her when two little arms wrapped themselves around her legs. They jumped apart.

"Mommy, I had a bad dream," Jenna said. Jordan gathered Jenna and carried her to her bedroom, soothing her. She tucked her in and made sure she had fallen asleep before she left.

Brie was ready to go when Jordan came back into the living room. She gave Jordan an inviting smile, held her face in her hand for a moment, then gave her a light hug and brushed her lips with a light kiss. Her leather jacket creaked against Jordan.

Later, Jordan lay in bed, feeling as if her world was upside down. Or maybe it had just rotated into the right position? Dr. Bauer had said she was *alive*. Alive would be Brie kissing her. Or leaning into her on the couch, reading, as if they did that every night of their lives. Jordan turned over restlessly and watched the breeze move the curtains on her open window. All she could hear in the dark night were the oak leaves touching one another. *Touching.* Brie had touched her every possible moment all night and stayed close. Then the moment in her office tonight, and Brie's eyes, warm and wanting.

Brie had whispered something as she left, but Jordan wasn't sure what she had heard. "Thanks." Had that simply been it? She thought again about the kisses. One thing was certain. Of all the times she'd been kissed, she had never imagined anything like Brie's mouth.

CHAPTER SEVENTEEN

After a night of deep and dreamless sleep, Brie woke early, full of energy. She tugged on a pair of heavy sweatpants and a hoodie, humming an old TV orange juice ad from her childhood. First cup of coffee in hand, she stepped out to the deck and looked over the glistening backyard. It had rained last night. The flowers were still perky even though there'd been frost warnings around Milwaukee. Something caught her eye. A spider's web floated across the yard, sparkling in the early sunlight. Sparkling, like Jordan's face yesterday. She felt a punch of exhilaration and walked along the deck, almost dancing.

She had left as early as possible last night. Jordan needed time to think about yesterday. Never mind wanting to rip her clothes off as they sat on the couch, Brie laughed to herself. How had she gotten through that paper she had read to Jordan?

The steps creaked as she walked off the deck to the grass, and she tested several boards. Perhaps Jordan would help her with those? The foundation of the cottage had to be visually checked every fall. They had reinforced the structure inside, in the basement, but the outside, almost one hundred years old, was untouched. Niki had wanted to keep the ambience of the cottage and refused to put anything over the old fieldstone.

The ivy that ran up the back of the house was still green. She touched the leaves, sending a shower of droplets to the ground. Her mother had contributed this ivy and Niki had loved it.

The long windows were next. They had redone the casings five years ago, one of the hardest jobs they'd undertaken. The old windows were uneven and odd-sized. She ran her finger along the bottom and the side. Everything felt tight, but she leaned in closer, testing the caulking with her nails. What had Niki said? Check for long cracks. She did, but there weren't even any short ones.

Almost an hour later, she had gone entirely around the cottage and went back inside for a bowl of cereal and some fruit. Afterward, with another cup of coffee, she stepped into Niki's office, opened the cupboard, and stared at the discs. "Chicken," she said. "Come on, Brie, suck it up." She started to walk away and then turned back. Did she have to listen to the discs?

She had a departmental meeting today at eleven thirty that was combined with a lunch. It certainly wouldn't be anything like yesterday's lunch with Jordan. Was there time to see Jordan this morning? She went to her bedroom to dress.

Jordan checked a window sill on the second floor and pushed against it. She'd check it again. In fact, she knew she'd check all of them again before they moved forward on this house. The yard was busy below her. It had rained earlier and the construction site shimmered with puddles. She watched Bix carry a small saw toward the house, navigating the wooden planks they'd thrown down against the mud. She tapped her fingers on the window casing and considered talking to Bix about last weekend and maybe yesterday. In less than twenty-four hours, her life had somehow turned around and faced the other way. Someone had jerked a filter off everything and the world was bright again, for the first time in years. "Happy," she said out loud. "Revved up," she added and started down the steps with her thermos.

Bix was sitting against the wall in the framed-in porch when Jordan reached the bottom of the stairs. She was just pouring herself coffee. Jordan settled down against the wall beside her and opened her own thermos.

"How'd it go last weekend?" Bix asked, stretching her legs out in front of herself.

"Good," Jordan said as she screwed the lid back on her thermos. "Do you ever get out like that?"

"Sure. We had just had our thirtieth anniversary and I took Carol out. Did you go to the new club?"

"Thirtieth? Congratulations," Jordan said, grinning. "Yes, we went to the new place. I'd only been to the Crow's Nest, so it was kind of a surprise."

Bix grinned back. "I like that club. Carol likes the music but I like the wood, the way the place is designed. Lots of room to dance but also private places where you can hear yourself talk. Did you notice the wood?"

"The wood? No." Jordan thought about that. She hadn't noticed wood? How had that happened? "We're exciting dates," she said drily. "Looking at wood?" They both laughed.

"It was from an old bar, downtown. It's real wood, not the new stuff. One of my friends co-owns that place and we got to see it before it opened." Bix sipped her coffee. "Everything else went fine?"

Jordan nodded. "I loved it all. The food was good and the clothing you recommended was fine. The music was great, but the women were different than I expected."

Bix nodded. "Times are changing. It used to be that everything was like the Crow's Nest, but today's woman is a different person than what I grew up with. Now we just look like everyone else, some better, some worse, a sort of anything goes atmosphere. The new clubs are fun and classy." She took a drink of coffee. "How'd it go with your friend?"

"Wonderful," Jordan said enthusiastically. "I haven't danced that much in forever. We had a little scuffle with someone but, other than that, it was a great night out."

"Scuffle?" Bix frowned.

Jordan started to answer but saw that Bix was looking over her shoulder, her attention riveted on something behind her. She turned and her heart bumped hard. "Oh, it's her," she said and scrambled up. Brie was moving carefully on the temporary walk, her trench coat open to a form-fitting light gray dress and high heels.

"That's the woman you took out?" Bix said, her eyes widening. "It's Niki's girl, Brie O'Malley."

Jordan went out to meet her and led Brie back to the porch where Bix stood.

"That was a trip." Brie laughed and flashed her dimples as Jordan did the introductions. "I hear you helped Jordan," she said to Bix and then took a second look. "I think we've met before."

"Jordan and I talked, and yes, we've met. Carol and I used to volunteer for Niki now and then. Good to see you again, Brie." Bix smiled as she picked up her thermos and left.

Brie stepped back a bit and looked up at the house. "This is Thomas's new house? Wow, it's huge."

"Do you have time? I'll take you through it." Jordan pointed to the second story. "Look at those lovely long windows."

She turned and caught Brie staring at her.

"Busted," Brie said, with a little half-embarrassed smile. "I admit that I just wanted to see you this morning. And, yes, I could have called." Brie's eyes twinkled. "I told you, anytime, anywhere..." She ran her fingers down Jordan's bare arm. "I have a meeting, so I have to go. Talk to you tonight?" Jordan escorted her back to her car and stared at the empty street after Brie drove away. She'd dreamed about the kisses last night and woke up ready. Still ready. "No wonder men like to kiss us," she said as she walked back to the site.

Bix was waiting for her. "Jordan, I'm not sure what you're doing," she said.

"I'm not either," Jordan replied, staring out into space. Then she grinned. "But I sure love it. Something else, Bix, I'm beginning to think of carving again. I'm about done with a small piece."

❖

That night Jordan read to her kids for an extra half hour before bedtime, thankful down to her bones for both of them. How did Brie stand it, living alone? She opened Brie's second book, noticing the acknowledgments and dedication. Of course, it was dedicated to Niki. What wasn't dedicated to Niki? She stared at the writing. "Grow up, Carter."

History was fun when Brie wrote it, the way she included the small things and understood feelings, the humor, making her feel as if she were part of the story. She checked the clock. It was about time to call Brie. Then she had a sudden thought about the weekend. She called her mother and asked if she would watch the kids. Next, she dialed Brie.

"Caught me, just getting in the house." Brie sounded a little breathless.

"Want me to call you back?"

"No, just hang in here with me. I'll be done in a minute."

Jordan could hear Brie moving through her house. "The briefcase is in the office and I'm going to put the phone on speaker, okay?"

Jordan grinned. "Are you getting into something comfortable?"

"If I don't get these stupid panty hose off, my toes are going to turn blue."

"What are you wearing? The light gray suit you had on this morning?"

"Yep." Brie exhaled. "It's hard to get out of. Hang on."

Jordan concentrated, visualizing Brie's every move. *Top is on the bed. Does that mean she's down to her bra?* Brie sighed audibly. *There went the bra.* She heard a zipper release. *And the skirt. Now the panty hose.*

"That's better," Brie said. "I hate panty hose. If I had my way, I'd wear something like a sarong or whatever it is those lucky women just get to wrap around themselves." She laughed a little.

Jordan was riveted. *Brie, standing in her bedroom...naked?* Her mind lept to Brie in that swimming suit and had that off in a heartbeat. She'd love to touch her body, run her hands over that...tattoo. Her hands were sweaty and other parts were getting wet as well.

"What the hell?" she mumbled.

"What?" Brie asked.

"Nothing," Jordan said, more curtly than she meant to.

"You said 'What the hell' out of the blue." Brie took a big breath. "I love my bed," she said and turned the speaker phone off. "...it was something else."

Jordan hit herself in the forehead with her fist. What had Brie just said? She looked around her bedroom for something, anything, to take her mind off Brie, naked on the bed. She found herself staring at Pete's photo and turned it around.

"How are my favorite two children in the world?" Brie asked, her voice relaxed and even.

Jordan told her about the hobbits and Tolkien.

"Are you going to do Harry Potter for Ty?"

"No, I thought I'd do the hobbits first. By the time we finish, he can read the Potter series on his own."

"What else are you reading to Jenna, other than the book I read last night?"

"I have this down to a science. Tyler gets his hour of games while I read to Jen in her room. Right now she's into horses, as I'm sure you heard last night. She always falls asleep and then Ty and I tackle the hobbits. Truthfully, I'm enjoying them as much as he is."

"Next time we get together, I'd like to read to her again."

"What are you doing Saturday night?" Jordan asked casually, rubbing her hands, which were sweaty again. "How about another meal?"

"Are you asking me out?" Brie said softly.

"I am. Maybe some dancing...?"

Brie responded with a sexy laugh. "I certainly want to dance with you again. And—"

"Stop it." Jordan grinned but hoped she wouldn't. God, she was going to have to take another shower.

❖

Brie lay on her back and stared at the ceiling. She pulled the sheets up, thinking about the construction site that morning. She was glad she'd remembered Bix. She would be helpful to Jordan. She could still see the look on Jordan's face when she left, watching her in the rearview mirror. Those astonishing eyes, silvered by sunlight, narrowed slightly as Jordan had stood, perfectly quiet, watching her drive away. It was Jordan's *I am thinking of what to do next* expression. They would either be just friends or, lovers. "I vote for lovers," Brie whispered into the silence of her room.

Turning onto her side, she stared at the photo of Niki. "Well, baby, here I go. For better or worse, I'm going to try. I might get my heart hurt, but what could hurt more than you? You always used to say that we should take a trip around the moon, just once. Wouldn't that have been fun? I hope you do that. Night, darlin', wherever you are, I love you."

CHAPTER EIGHTEEN

"Calm down," Jordan said to herself in Brie's driveway. She had been sitting there for what seemed like hours, but she knew it was just minutes, trying to decide how to handle this evening. "It's just dinner and dancing." She laughed a little. "And touching and looking and kissing."

The door flew open before she could even ring the bell, and she looked into Brie's happy eyes.

"Hey, gorgeous, get in here," Brie said and pulled her inside. "Let me see you."

Jordan wore a dark green silk shirt with a chained belt and black pleated pants. Her heart beat so hard that she was certain Brie could hear it.

"You're going to kill me, Carter," Brie finally said breathlessly.

"Your turn—" Jordan began but immediately went quiet. The light blue dress stopped right at the knees and matched the color of Brie's eyes. Matching strappy heels made her legs go on and on, but it was the front that knocked Jordan into silence. Or lack of front.

"Sweet mother," Jordan said, staring at the vee of the halter dress that barely covered her beautiful breasts, screeching to a stop at the navel, mid-tattoo. "Are you even wearing a bra?"

"Ah, my little secret," Brie teased, watching Jordan's eyes. "You're the one who didn't wear underwear."

"You're going to freeze."

"Not if you hold me."

Jordan pulled in another deep breath, thinking of all that skin against her. "Where's your coat? You have to wear a coat with that."

"I wasn't planning on it."

"Oh, yes, you are planning on it. You're wearing a coat," Jordan said, leading her to the closet. "In fact, can you dance in a coat?" She went through several garments hanging in front of her. "Brie, damn, you're...exposed."

Laughing, Brie held out a coat that matched the dress and let Jordan help her into it.

As Jordan drove, Brie talked about the Ice House, located in the Riverwalk section of Milwaukee. It was surrounded by a number of small bars, good restaurants, and trendy shops. Emma's gallery was only a block away.

"I don't know if the public should see you in that dress," Jordan grumbled as they got out.

"You're going to like this place," Brie said, tugging Jordan toward the neon signs that lit up the entrance.

Jordan hardly heard her, looking at Brie's sensuous mouth, remembering the taste. She tried to swallow but her mouth was too dry. "If you're there, I'll like it."

"Wow," Jordan said as they walked inside. The entire room was patterned after a professional hockey arena. The dance floor was shaped like a hockey rink and the surface was constructed out of a material that resembled ice. Jordan followed Brie up to the fourth level that looked down on the entire club. The music was loud and the crowd was noisy, but the high-backed booth was quiet. The couple in the next booth broke apart as they sat down, and Jordan watched one of the women close a button on the front of her shirt. She turned to Brie, who had seen it also.

"What can I say? We're a lusty lot," Brie said but added a mischievous grin.

Jordan helped Brie off with her coat, sighing over the beautiful shoulders and well-defined arms. Brie sat close. They ordered margaritas and watched the crowd for a bit in comfortable silence. Jordan thought of Brie's talent for making people feel completely at ease. There were two Bries, in fact: the one that mourned and flailed at herself over Niki and the murder, then the laughing, easygoing woman that most people came in contact with every day. Over the weeks she had seen less and less of that first woman.

The music changed to something hot and fast and couples flooded the dance floor.

"Come on." Jordan held her hand out. "And by the way, it's official. I can see your tattoo."

Dancing loose and free, Jordan concentrated on Brie and the music. Women were laughing, singing along, moving against her. Even her bones felt like liquid. Brie simmered in front of her and she moved closer, trailing her fingers down the bare shoulders and arms. She tipped her head back and just let herself move, then danced behind Brie, wrapped her arms around her, fingers mapping the skin on her stomach. She saw goose bumps rise on Brie's skin as her fingers inched up muscles that moved in time with the music. Four songs later, the DJ took a break and they sat down, dabbing their foreheads with napkins.

Jordan sipped her drink and watched the crowd. "How do you keep yourself inside that non-dress with all those moves?"

Brie licked her lips, her mouth very inviting. "Remember. My little secret."

"Not too little," Jordan said and then bit her lip.

"I didn't know you'd noticed." Brie's smile was both surprised and amused.

Jordan looked away. The swimming suit, the softball banquet, and now…little shards of memories of Brie swept across her mind, leaving her helpless in front of her own desire. Almost with relief, she saw someone from her softball team at the bar. "Hey, there's my catcher and her girlfriend." She gestured at the bar.

Brie squinted a little. "Which ones?"

"The little blonde and the tall lady. Whoops, the ones that are lip-locked right now."

"Would you like to say something to them or just hide up here?"

"They'll faint, I promise. Can you put up with all the questions?"

"Bring 'em on." Jordan walked down the steps and fluidly threaded through the dancing women, moving toward the bar. "Be ashamed, O'Malley," Brie said. *It hasn't even been two months and I'm mentally ripping her clothes off! The day in the restaurant when I first met Niki was…minutes. Is this the same thing?* She pondered that for a moment. *It's more than just getting naked with her. It's the same feeling, the knowing.* Brie clenched a little at the thought of Niki and jerked her attention back to Jordan.

The couple did look shocked to see her. Jordan turned and pointed at Brie. The three of them made their way up the stairs. After introductions and everyone was sitting, Shelly and Terry gave Jordan and Brie slightly amazed looks.

"When did this happen?" Shelly stared frankly at Jordan. "The last I knew, some guy from the diamond next to us was trying desperately to get your home phone number."

"Long story." Jordan laughed.

Terry spoke to Brie. "That was a nice piece you and Dannie did for Niki at the banquet." Terry never took her eyes off Brie as she spoke to Jordan. "Is this the date we dared you to ask for, Carter?"

"No, this is the second time we've been out."

"The hell you say." Terry blinked at Brie as if she were unreal.

"Take it easy, Terry," Jordan said. "Brie, this is one of our pitchers. They're calculating as hell."

"Seriously," Shelly said, elbowing her girlfriend. "When did this happen?"

"Not too long ago, actually," Jordan said and cleared her throat.

Brie teased her. "Yes, tell them, Jordan." She slid her hand obviously inside Jordan's shirt, caressing her tight stomach.

"Uh, well, Brie and I sort of met in the park, the big one by our ball diamonds, McKittrick Park. Things just kind of went from there." Jordan floundered, squirming under Brie's fingers. Her stomach had gathered into one big knot.

"So, you two are…" Shelly frowned, confused.

"Honey," Brie said, helping Jordan out, "did you order?"

"No," Jordan answered. "Have you girls eaten?" she asked Shelly.

"We're on our way to a party," Terry said and stood. Terry looked openly at Brie's dress and raised her eyebrows at Jordan.

"That went well," Jordan said once Shelly and Terry had left.

Brie took Jordan's hand and rubbed it. "When you see them again, you can explain."

"This is like running with scissors." Jordan groaned. They both laughed as they looked through the menu.

"I've eaten here a lot," Brie said, "but I've never had the house special."

"What is it?" Jordan said and scanned the menu again.

"Lobster. Are you game?"

"Let's do it. I haven't eaten that in years."

A slow dance began and Jordan led Brie to the dance floor, anxious to be close. She closed her eyes as Brie's body moved against hers. This and kisses had been on her mind all day

"This feels good," Brie said into her ear, her breath tickling Jordan's skin.

"Good," Jordan echoed, holding her a little tighter. She bit her lip as her entire body tightened with need. Brie pushed into her and Jordan held back a groan. The sensation was indescribable. The music went into something fast and they walked back to the booth, fingers interlaced.

Jordan pulled Brie close in the booth, not wanting to lose the intimacy of their dance. "Do you see anyone you know?" she asked.

"I haven't been looking. I've been looking at you."

Jordan never hesitated. She kissed her. Brie gave a little start of surprise but leaned in and returned the kiss. Brie's hands suddenly were on her and ran up her ribs, holding on hard. The sound of plates on their table startled them both as their food arrived. They grinned at one another, faces flushed. Both stared at the huge meal in front of them.

Later, Jordan admitted, "I'm too full to dance," and pushed her plate away. "Let's take a walk along the river. How about it?"

It was a cool but clear night and they walked along the Milwaukee River for a while.

Brie put her arm through Jordan's, staying close. "It was nice to see where you work. That was fun."

Jordan stopped and leaned on the wooden railing with her elbows, her back to the water.

A boat full of noisy partygoers cruised by. "Thanks for coming over. I'm kind of proud of that place. Bix almost fell over when you walked up. I talk to Bix, ask her advice and...things."

Brie leaned on the railing, next to her. "You should ask me."

"Yes, I should." She turned to face Brie.

"Well? Here I am." Brie opened her arms and grinned. "Ask

away." When Brie opened her arms, she looked carefree and young. Jordan grinned at her. *Carefree* was perfect.

"That day we crashed and met again at Urgent Care. What were you thinking?" Jordan said.

"How cute you were. Val had said some *cute woman* had crashed into me and I saw that she was right. I know you've heard this before, but you are adorable."

"No, I'm not—"

Brie placed a finger on her lips. "Yes, you are, Jordan Carter. You're gorgeous. You were the first woman I've looked at since Niki. I mean, really looked at."

"Thank you," Jordan said and looked down, turned on and revved up. *I've never had a woman flirt with me before like this. How do men stand it? It's so powerful.* Her heart pounded. The years in the bars, man after man, flashed across her mind. She understood all of that. But this beautiful, intelligent, genuine woman before her touched a new place inside her. "You said your life would confuse me. I don't think so, Brie." She smiled. "But I admit, it's new."

Brie put her arm through Jordan's again. "Did Bix explain why lesbians don't date straight women?"

"Wouldn't it just be a matter of preference?"

Brie nodded. "Sometimes, but usually straight women are just curious and then drop the person. Or maybe they just don't care for it, once they find out what it's really like."

"I'd never do that." Jordan opened Brie's coat and lightly brushed against her body, hands around her waist. She heard Brie pull in a quick breath. "What's the *it* you're talking about?"

"Take me back to the house and I'll show you," Brie teased but her voice was low. She gave a little shiver.

"You're cold," Jordan said.

"I said I wouldn't be if you held me," Brie murmured and leaned against Jordan.

"Let's go home."

❖

"Come to the kitchen with me," Brie said as she hung her coat in her closet. "I've been brewing something that we used to make and I'd like you to try it."

Jordan followed her and settled down at the big kitchen table as Brie placed a pitcher of sangria and two glasses on the table. "Take a taste and then decide."

"Oh, sangria," Jordan said after she'd tasted the drink. "A little tart and a little sweet." She poured them each a glass.

"Pretty much." Brie took a drink. "Actually, we usually kept some on hand all summer, into fall. We tried just about everything in this, had some fun with it." Brie took Jordan's hand. "I want to show you something." She led Jordan down the hallway. For a wild moment, Jordan thought she was taking her to the bedroom, but instead, they stopped at Brie's office. Brie turned the lights on over her desk and held up several inches' worth of paper. "See?"

"What is it?"

"I've been writing all week, the first decent work in over two years. I'm supposed to have a trillion more words by next month. That'll never happen, but I'm going to give it a shot."

"The meeting with your editor in New Mexico?"

Brie nodded. "I may save my contract."

One of Pete's books was open beside the papers. "Those books helped?"

"Good information," Brie said and showed her the old letters in the file box.

"Oh, they're fragile," Jordan said, taking care with the old papers and leaning closer to read some of the words. "This is amazing. I can't believe you can concoct a story from these."

"And I can't believe you can carve something like you have from blocks of wood."

"Brie, I've been carving this week, just as you've been writing."

"That's great news. The big carving?"

Jordan nodded. "Something else too." She was almost finished with Brie's owl.

Brie turned the lights off. "Let's sit in the living room, on the couch."

They both took their shoes off and set their glasses on the coffee table, resting their feet beside the glasses. Brie leaned against her shoulder. Jordan took her hand, rubbing it.

"The reason I talk to Bix is because she lived through those two years with me, after Pete was killed. She's just making sure I don't go off the deep end again."

"Are you?" Brie asked and tucked her legs under her. She rubbed Jordan's neck under her hair.

"No, but I learned something in those two years. Sex is the easiest thing in the world. It's everywhere. I tried everything, looking for a feeling, I guess."

"Everything?"

"Almost," Jordan said and frowned. "And I don't want you to think I'm one of those women you described earlier. Those *just curious* women."

"All right, if you're not just curious, why are you sitting here?" She turned Jordan's face to her with her fingers.

"Because I want to kiss you again."

"Oh," Brie said and immediately kissed her. "Like that?"

"Exactly." Jordan pulled her into her lap.

Brie held her face for a moment. "This time, I'm not going to stop until you tell me to," she said, kissing an ear slowly and carefully. Jordan held her breath as the tongue traced the front of her throat and then tiny kisses moved up to her lips, capturing them. "Sex is only one way you express your feelings, show your love," Brie whispered against her mouth, tenderly biting the lower lip in between words. "But it's nice."

"Brie, my body doesn't always tell the truth."

"Mine does," Brie said, her words barely audible as she pushed into Jordan.

"Maybe I've just challenged mine too often."

"Maybe you just haven't had the right person touch it," Brie whispered as she kissed her jaw. "Tend it." A kiss caressed her eyes. "Love it." And she kissed her mouth. She took Jordan's hands, kissed the palms, and placed them on her chest, just above her breasts.

Jordan could feel Brie's wild heartbeat as she moved her hands quickly into the easy-access dress. Jordan closed her eyes, her fingers touching soft skin across the ribs, a firm belly and hips. Finally, for the first time in her life, she touched a woman's breasts, fingers memorizing their firm shape and hard nipples as Brie gasped into her mouth. A surge of heat lodged directly between her legs. She felt Brie fumbling with the buttons on her shirt and held very still. She wanted this. She wanted Brie. But somewhere in her sexual fog she could hear a phone ringing.

"Let it go," she said against Brie's mouth.

"No," Brie said, raising up. "It's your phone."

"What?" Befuddled, Jordan opened her eyes as Brie reached behind her and handed her the phone. Jordan answered and listened, then said, "I'll be there soon, Mom. Thanks for calling."

She closed her phone. "Jenna's vomiting, really hard."

"Do you want me to come with you?"

"No, I don't think you'd better. Are you going to be up for a while?"

Brie said, "Of course. Will you call me?"

"Brie, I'm sorry," Jordan said.

Brie held up a hand. "Stop. Let's make a deal now. Kids come first, always." She smiled, but Jordan saw her hands shake as her fingers closed the button of her shirt.

Driving toward her house minutes later, Jordan groaned. She was worried about Jenna and tried to control the desire that still wrapped itself around her body. The need Brie created was familiar, but everything about it was ramped up. She drove onto the freeway and eased into faster traffic. Suddenly she remembered. Brie had said *love*.

When she got home, Jenna was sound asleep. Her mother had given her the medicine Jordan always kept on hand for upset stomachs, and it had worked. She sat beside her sleeping daughter's bed and called Brie.

"Tonight was special," Jordan said.

"To be continued," Brie said softly.

CHAPTER NINETEEN

So far, the afternoon had been quiet at Omni. Brie rummaged in her pack and found the note cards she wanted. She'd had some ideas for the book and wanted to get them down before she forgot them. Through the first two books she'd had a relationship developing between the two main characters, and this book would resolve that as well as end the series. She scribbled the words *hands touching her skin* and stopped, mid-word, staring at the note card.

Last night, when Jordan touched me. Brie took a quick breath. Not here. Not now. But, of course, her body completely disobeyed her. She could still feel Jordan's hands and fingers on her hips, cross her belly, cruise her ribs. Breasts. She peeked across the room at her EMS partner, Sean, thankfully engrossed in his magazine, just as her nipples hardened and she gave a tiny groan.

A wad of paper hit the side of her head and she jumped. "What the...?" she squeaked. Sean looked out of the windows, innocent. "That's about the most exciting thing that's happened around here all afternoon." She lobbed the paper back at him.

"I took my girl to the steakhouse across from the Ice House last night and saw you, getting out of a silver car." He grinned. "Looking mighty fine, Ms. O'Malley."

She raised her eyebrows. "You like?"

"I like." He chuckled. "How do you stay inside those dresses?"

Brie grinned. "A woman's secret, my man."

"Well, that woman with you looked like she'd like to know the same thing."

"Really? That's nice to know. Does that mean I was successful?"

Sean nodded. "Definitely. It's good to see you smile again, Brie." "The feeling's even better, believe me." Brie smiled just as dispatch squawked and they both stood.

"Let's go, oh blond one. Vet's already on her way," Sean said and grabbed his jacket. Brie tossed her cards in her backpack and followed him.

❖

Brie left the lights on but cut the siren when she parked the ambulance at an angle to Vet's. Sean was already out as Brie grabbed an equipment bag. The beach spread out before her, sending her heart rate up until she realized it wasn't the same place that she and Niki had always used. The scent of October off Lake Michigan brushed by her and Brie heard Sean yell, "Two. There's two."

The smell of scorched metal burned her nose as she checked the little silver convertible.

"I smell hot metal," she said to Sean.

"I think they shot the car up some," he said, kneeling on the sand on the passenger side. Brie got her first look at one of the victims. A young woman in a white blouse and dark pants lay on the sand, arm over her face, dark hair lifting in the light breeze. Brie sank down beside Sean staring at the woman, who was pale and cyanotic. He gently lifted an eyelid, checking pupils. "NR," Sean said and shook his head. Brie brushed the hair back from the pale face and saw the bullet holes. Gulls cried above Brie, catching the sunlight as she looked up at them.

She lifted Niki gently off the car, holding her to her body, crooning softly. Going to her knees, she laid her carefully on the sand and covered her with the plaid blanket that was always in the backseat. Niki's long black lashes lay across her tanned cheeks and Brie kissed them, tasting salt. The mouth was relaxed as if she were sleeping, just as it had been for over thirteen years. She kissed it tenderly. "I'll be right back, baby," she whispered and turned to crawl across the sand and up the bank of dirt. She was immune to the pain, nor did she notice her blood-soaked dress. The birds wheeled above her, crying out.

"Brie!" Vet said, shaking her shoulder.

"What!" Brie looked up at her.

"Let her go," Vet went to her knees, talking firmly.

Horrified, Brie saw that she was holding the young woman and she was soaked in blood.

"Stand up," Vet said. "The M.E. needs to do her job." Sean helped her up and they sat on the back bumper of the ambulance. "We've got to go. The man may make it," Vet said and looked at Sean. "Take care of her, okay?"

Sean nodded and put an arm around her. "C'mon, Brie. We're going too. They'll take hours here."

They drove quietly through the streets, lights and sirens off. "Sean," Brie said. "I should go to the hospital and see Dr. Wolfe."

He never said a word, only nodded and changed directions. Brie was a little frightened. She couldn't remember a thing before Vet had spoken to her.

❖

It was almost nine that night and Jordan was upset. Brie wasn't home and was two hours overdue. She had called both of her phones at least four times, but no Brie. Jenna was asleep and she had just finished reading to Tyler. "This is wrong," she said, flipping her phone open as she walked down the hallway. Just as she was about to dial, her phone rang.

"Jordan? It's Vet. You know, Vet and Peg."

"I was just dialing Brie."

"I'm at Urgent Care with Brie. I have a situation with her. Could you come over?"

"Is it Brie? Is she all right?" Jordan said.

"We had a bad call and…and I think it would help her if you came."

"Be there in twenty at the most," Jordan said and ran toward her mother's door.

❖

Brie kept her eyes down. Something was wrong. A tall redhead kept trying to talk with her, but she didn't like her pushy attitude.

She decided to wait for Dr. Wolfe. He was Niki's doctor too. A cute dark-haired woman was kneeling in front of her and Brie regarded her curiously. She was familiar.

"Hello." Brie smiled politely.

"Hi," Jordan said. "Did you forget to call me?"

"Was I supposed to?"

"You said you would."

"I'm sorry." Brie frowned. "I was supposed to call you?" That smile was terrific. She looked at the hands on her knees. Niki shouldn't see someone's hands on her. She scooted back a bit.

"Jenna and Tyler said to tell you hello."

"Jenna and Tyler?" Brie answered, concentrating on the words. Her eyes widened with sudden understanding. "Oh, Jen and Ty. Are they all right?"

Jordan got up and sat beside Brie, an arm securely around her. "They're at home, with Mom. We were waiting for you to call us."

Everything blurred until Brie met Jordan's gray eyes. Her mind cleared and the tears came then.

Peg, still dressed in scrubs, came down the hallway with a doctor.

"Who got hurt?" Brie asked, wiping her eyes.

"Honey, it's all right. Dr. Porter's going to look at you."

"All right, Peg," Brie said quietly. Why was Jordan there?

Dr. Porter opened an exam room door. "Dr. Wolfe is on his way back from out of town, but I just spoke with him. He wants me to look you over."

"Can Jordan come in with me?"

"Sure," he said and motioned for her to sit on the exam table. He wrapped a cuff on her arm and asked her to describe what she remembered. He took some notes and showed her that her vitals were normal. Brie answered carefully but felt as if she was fading in and out. "I think you're good to go," he said after asking a few more questions. He looked at Jordan. "Are you able to stay with her?"

"Of course," Jordan said. She helped Brie into her jacket.

"Brie, when you get home, take one of these pills with food. It'll help you focus and you'll sleep better. Dr. Wolfe will call you in about an hour."

Jordan tucked the small envelope into her shirt pocket. Dr. Porter held her back for a moment. "Dr. Wolfe is calling her therapist." Jordan nodded and followed Brie.

"Can you stay the night with her?" Peg asked. "Otherwise, I'm going to call her family."

"I'll stay all night, but I think you should call her family. I'm good to go. Mom has my kids."

Jordan wrapped an arm securely around Brie. "I'll call you, Vet." They walked toward the doors. Jordan hummed absently.

Brie laughed, startling Jordan. "You really can't carry a tune."

"Shut up." Jordan grinned. "My poor kids. They put their hands over their ears at their birthday parties." She opened the car door for Brie. "I didn't even realize I was humming."

The bathroom door was open while Brie showered. She peeked out of the curtain as the water rolled over her. Jordan was sitting on the floor in the hallway. Brie dried off and slipped into her old sweats and T-shirt.

"Want to tell me what happened out there?" Jordan said.

Brie rubbed her hair with the towel and curled down next to Jordan on the floor. She shook her head. "I remember driving up to the accident scene. Was that woman really dead?"

"Vet said she was when you got there."

Brie's head sank and a single drop of water ran down her nose, onto the floor. Jordan reached for the towel and got to her knees, rubbing Brie's wet hair. Brie wrapped her arms around Jordan, pushed her face into her body, shaking with hard, silent sobs.

"Hang on, baby," Jordan said and pulled Brie into her lap, held her face against her until Brie quit crying. Gently, she kissed Brie's wet, salty eyes.

"This is crap." Brie sniffed and wiped her nose with her T-shirt. "I told you my life would confuse you. We've even sort of knocked each other down again." Brie tried to smile.

"I have ulterior motives," Jordan said and wiped Brie's face again. "I think we've been on a collision course since day one."

Brie hiccupped a laugh, mixed with more tears.

"What do you mean, your life will confuse me? Do you think I don't know what this feels like?"

"No, one of the first things I knew about you was that you'd understand. I just don't want you to have to go through it again." Brie wiped her eyes. "I've already forgotten what I remembered this afternoon. Worse, I can't hear her anymore."

"Who? Who can't you hear?"

"Niki. I've lost her voice. I could hear it this morning but it's gone now." She hit her head lightly with her hand.

"Here, I know how to fix that." Jordan helped Brie to her feet and took her into Niki's office. "Come on, I'll hold you." She settled them into Niki's big desk chair, hit the remote button, and Niki spoke, talking about their anniversary. Brie stiffened and sat up.

"Okay, stop it," Brie said. "I've got it. I can hear it again."

"Are you sure? I'll sit here with you, all night if you want."

Brie relaxed back into Jordan and took her hands. She kissed the ends of her fingers. "No, it's all I needed. Thank you."

"Why not skip this one and go on to the rest?"

"Why not just skip them all?" Brie said and stood. "I'm hungry."

"Hungry is good."

"You should be with Jenna and Tyler. Give me the pill and go home, if you want."

"No, Mom knows how to reach me."

"How is Jenna feeling today?"

"She's fine. Whatever it was went away. That happens with kids."

They were fixing ham sandwiches when Dr. Wolfe called. Brie talked to him while Jordan finished the sandwiches. When she hung up, the food was on the table.

"Want some pickles?" Brie asked as she took the milk out of the refrigerator. She demolished the first sandwich and leaned back with a sigh. "I have a situation here," she said and held her hands up, making quote marks in the air. "Now I've officially *remembered*."

Jordan nodded and took the packet of pills out of her pocket. "So it appears." She handed her a pill.

"About time," Brie said and took the pill. "Little do they know that I've already forgotten what I remembered. They'd probably put me back in the hospital. Christ, what's happening to me?"

"Vet said you thought it was Niki today."

"Dr. Wolfe and my therapist have both warned me. Did you go through anything like this?"

"No. Nothing like this. There was nothing for me to remember."

Brie looked into space, working on a second sandwich. "It's what I said. I don't want you to have to go through this all over again."

"I'm the perfect person to be with you. I get it."

Brie made a face. "So you say, but I still don't think it's fair to you." She finished the sandwich and pushed the plate away. "Maybe if I distract my mind it'll come back to me. How about a movie?"

"What?"

"I have tons of movies. Want to watch one?"

Jordan started to laugh. "I haven't seen anything but kids' movies in so long that I wouldn't even know where to begin. What do you have?"

"Let's finish here and I'll show you." Brie imitated an old-movie gangster. "Come with me, pal, I'll catch you up in no time."

The phone rang again and Brie talked with her therapist for quite a while as Jordan cleaned the kitchen. Just as Brie hung up, her mother called. Jordan washed up in the bathroom and turned on the low light in Brie's bedroom. When she came back, Brie had the movie ready. Brie curled into her lap. When the movie finished, she was sound asleep. Jordan lifted her carefully and took her to bed. She crawled in beside her and rubbed her shoulders, arms, and hands. Satisfied that Brie was soundly asleep, she carefully moved away and out of bed.

Jordan stripped down to her underwear and T-shirt and stretched out in the dark, next to Brie. Part of her was afraid to fall asleep in case Brie needed her, so she listened to the sounds of the house. A branch scratched at the window. These were the sounds Brie heard at night. She turned her head and watched her sleep. She was so aware of this woman. Every move and breath Brie took registered somewhere in Jordan's mind and body.

CHAPTER TWENTY

The warm body against Jordan woke her the next morning. A hand held her stomach tightly; breasts pushed into her back. Breasts? Disoriented, Jordan squinted at the room. Her shirt was up, skin against skin, but her body's memory was miles ahead of her, totally alert. Totally turned on. Brie mumbled something and the hand was gone. They both sat up, staring at each other, until Brie's breath hitched, breaking the spell.

"I'm sorry," Brie whispered. She adjusted Jordan's T-shirt and then her own.

"C'mere," Jordan said, pulling Brie back into her. "I'll hold you. I want to hold you." She tried to shift her body into a lower gear but took a deep breath as Brie snuggled into her.

"I woke up in the middle of the night, remembering." Brie sounded shaky. "I remembered Niki on the sand, what I did. But I've lost it. Again. All I can remember is sand and blood. Thank God you were here. I'd have left. I thought I heard Niki talking last night."

"Could you understand what she said?"

"She was talking about the card she'd given me on the way to the beach that day. It had airplane tickets for a vacation and she had written something that I can't remember, except that it made me laugh. We were drinking…something." Brie rolled to the edge of the bed and sat up. "This sucks."

"Yes," Jordan said to Brie's back as she left the bedroom, then popped back into the doorway.

"Want to take a shower while I'm getting dressed?"

Jordan reached for her clothes. "Deal. I'd better call home as well."

After she'd showered, Jordan walked toward the kitchen, talking on the phone to her mother and then to John. She explained that she would not be in today and they talked business as she checked the refrigerator.

"Do you want to try my special eggs?" she called to Brie.

"I was just going to offer cereal," Brie answered and laughed. "Eggs. Yum."

Jordan loved the smell of the chopped green onions and the other spices she used for this breakfast. This felt good, making breakfast in Brie's kitchen. Finally, they sat across from each other and Brie closed her eyes after the first bite.

"This is delicious," she said. "No wonder Pete married you."

"Pete married me because I was pregnant."

"I'd marry you for these eggs."

Jordan snickered. "That's a first."

Brie reached for her vitamin and the pills the doctor had given her the night before. She held them up for Jordan. "When I got out of the hospital, I was taking so many pills that I had to count them out on a daily basis. Thank God I'm past that."

"I just drank anything I could get my hands on." Jordan got up with their plates. "You don't need all those pills anymore and I don't need alcohol. We're going to be great." She began to rinse their dishes.

"Jordan, leave everything. I'm fine. The only thing I have to do is pack for the New Mexico trip, do some writing on my book." She finished her orange juice.

At the sink, Jordan turned to look at Brie. Her color was good and her eyes were clear. She finished her coffee and put the cup in the sink. "Is there anything else you'd like me to do?"

"Yes. Have a good day." Brie got up from the table and hugged Jordan hard. "I'd never have made it through yesterday and last night without you. I have an appointment with the therapist this afternoon and I'll call you when I can."

"Okay, but if you need anything, I'll be here or anywhere in a heartbeat."

In the driveway, halfway to her car, Jordan stopped. When was

Brie leaving for New Mexico? She turned, expecting to see her standing at the door, but it was closed.

❖

Jordan walked up the long walk to her house. She stopped to check her flowers, then settled into a patio chair. The leaves were beginning to fall. She'd have to put away the outdoor furniture soon. The kids loved to rake leaves and take care of the flowers. Maybe this weekend… Her mind idly rambled, finding its way back to last night and this morning.

"Jordan?" Her mother's voice startled her. "How is Brie? How did it go last night?"

"I was coming over to talk with you," Jordan answered and they began to walk across the backyard. Sunlight caught the gazebo's shiny dome, making her think of the carving in the studio. A shadow of something shuffled through her mind. Brie and the statue.

"You didn't answer me," her mother said.

"Sorry, Mom. I'm distracted. What's your day like?"

"Nothing more than thinking about dinner. After you called this morning, I assumed you'd gone to work. Just happened to see you go by."

"Do you have coffee?"

They sat at the kitchen table and talked. Jordan told her about Brie's sudden memory and how she had lost it again. Her mother's face creased in a frown. "This is going to be a very hard thing for her, Jordan. Sudden memory, even in the instance of a normal death, can have terrible repercussions."

"That's what I'm afraid of. She looks good but feels fragile." Jordan fiddled with her cup and finally plunged in. "Mom, Brie and Niki lived together, as more than friends. I thought you might have a problem with this." Jordan raised her eyebrows, waiting for her mother to react.

"Tyler and Jenna like Brie. I do too, and I loved her books."

"But the Church…" Jordan couldn't finish, searching her mother's eyes.

"Jordan," her mother began and then stopped. "Let's talk about us.

I loved your father with every piece of myself, just as you did Pete. I simply couldn't handle it when he died."

"Don't apologize. I was horrible after Pete." Jordan made a derisive noise. "Is that really why you turned to the Church? You couldn't handle it?"

Her mother nodded. "I've been meaning to tell you what a good job you've done with Jenna and Tyler, through all this with Pete and those hard years afterward. You've come out of this very nicely."

"You knew?"

"Of course I knew you were in the bars. I don't live on an island."

"I saw Dr. Bauer last week. I'm okay, Mom." Jordan gauged her mother's expression. "Mom, about Brie. I'm interested in her. Obviously, she's still struggling with Niki but, if it should happen, would you...be angry? We'd be back to where we were, before these last few months?"

"Interested in her?" Her mother's face was careful, reflecting no opinion or judgment. "You mean, as in the way Brie lived with that woman?"

"Yes. I've always been honest with you about Pete. The rest of those men were just...I'm not sure what they were."

"Men love you, Jordan. I'm surprised."

"I'm surprised too," Jordan said and got up for more coffee. "Mom, you can't say that I didn't try with every man that you had over for dinner. It isn't men, it's everyone. I know you've noticed that I've dropped all my friends. No one moved me, interested me. Until Brie."

Her mother's mouth was set in a firm line but she nodded at Jordan's words. "I noticed. When your dad died, it was as if someone pulled the carpeting out from under me. I lost my way, I admit it. And the Church had all those nice rules, in place, something to guide me." She paused. "Are you sure this isn't that? Trying to find something to guide you?"

"I'm sure. I went through men like Kleenex after Pete, and I can honestly say that I never met one that truly interested me."

"Give me some time," her mother said. "Let me think about it. Please?"

Jordan smiled a little. "Of course, but I warn you, I'm going to try to change your mind." She started to leave but looked back. "Would you like some help with dinner? Otherwise, I'm going to work in the studio."

"No, I'm fine. I'm trying a new recipe, something I brought back from Ireland." Her mother hugged her. "Jordan, all those years we missed together. Give me this chance to make up some of those moments."

CHAPTER TWENTY-ONE

The minute Jordan left, Brie finished her packing for the trip to New Mexico and then checked her computer. Her e-tickets for the trip to New Mexico tomorrow night were confirmed. She checked the clock and saw that she had time for another cup of coffee before she had to see her therapist.

She found her glasses and toggled over to her book file on the computer. The cursor on her computer blinked while Brie examined the scene and the character she'd last written for her Civil War fiction. "Facile, lithe body, dark brown eyes with gorgeous lashes, and curly black hair." Brie smiled at the image in her head. Niki's twin, right down to the quick temper. Niki had teased her mercilessly about some of the decisions Brie's main character in the story had made. But Brie had also written the smart, clever side of Niki. The tenderness and love too. Although she hadn't set out to write it that way, the books had somehow become her love story to Niki.

However, some of the scenes had been written to rile Niki up, and it had worked. Brie laughed a little, remembering. She reached for the second book. She knew the page by heart.

That day, when Niki had first read this scene, dinner was ready when Brie came home. She'd tossed her briefcase in her office and changed into shorts and a Brewers T-shirt. Barefoot, she walked into the kitchen just as Niki came in from the deck.

Brie had kissed her but Niki had stiffened. "What's the matter?" Brie had asked, feeling the resistance.

Niki pointed to Brie's book beside her plate. "I was cooking and reading your book," she said. "What were you thinking of? That character has—" She had stopped and Brie saw that Niki was not angry, just ticked off.

"Has what?" Brie had asked, confused. She had glanced at the book, saw where the book mark was placed and knew immediately.

Niki finally finished her statement. "No couth."

"Couth?" Brie asked innocently. In fact, Niki was dead-on. They'd had an argument as Brie had been writing the book, and she'd replicated the argument in the book.

"Brie," Niki had said as she began to put the food on the table. "Do you have to put our private life in your books?"

At that moment, Brie had felt a small pang of remorse. A small pang. "I'm sorry, baby. But you have to admit, it added quite a bit of zing and a lot of people thought it was funny."

"Me? Furious as usual. Barefoot. Running out of the house after someone in my underwear and sweatshirt when it was snowing? That was funny?"

"It was to some people, as well as the dialogue." Brie bit back a grin. "But it wasn't a sweatshirt and underwear. It was a long nightgown and she wore her father's boots."

"Who cares? I know what you meant."

"Still," Brie had said, shaking her fork at Niki.

"I never called you a *troll*."

Brie had merely raised her eyebrows.

"Did I?"

"You did, but who cares? Remember later that night? You can call me anything you want if you promise to keep on *apologizing* like you did then…and not so long ago."

Brie closed the book and laughed, recalling that particular moment. And just as quickly, she was crying. Christ! She missed Niki. She missed their life.

Sad and restless, she got up and went down the hall to Niki's office. She looked at the open desk drawer. It was almost empty and she pulled out the remaining files. It was Niki's research on their house, the cottage. Brie put the files into a new box. Niki had worked hard on the research. For that matter, Brie had too. She'd put in quite a few hours at school, pursuing something Niki had asked for. The drawer was empty so she closed it slowly, feeling as if she was putting Niki's life away.

She looked up at the wall, the discs. Had everything in her life revolved around Niki? No, just the important parts, she thought sadly. She didn't want to lose Niki, ever. The moment she'd just recalled, with Niki and the book over dinner, was crystal clear in her mind. Why couldn't she remember those few minutes on the beach? If the human mind truly stored everything, where was the shooting? Or yesterday?

The remote control was on the desk, where Jordan had left it. She examined it nervously, put it back on the desk, then picked it up again. Could she find it, that memory? She'd spent time at the beach where they were shot and nothing had happened. She lived here, in their house, but nothing had released the things she suspected had been in her mind yesterday. Worse, it felt as if the shooting had just happened, all over again. That and a brief memory of blood on sand.

Once again, she looked at the discs. She rubbed her wet eyes. She hadn't cried like this in weeks. What if she did know something the police could use, even if it wouldn't bring Niki back? *Did you feel any pain, Niki? Or see me get shot? Were you ever conscious in the hospital when I wasn't?*

She gripped the desk. "All right," she said. "I'll see the therapist and then come home and do this."

❖

Jordan stood before the workbench in her studio. She'd played a little kickball with the kids and cleaned the studio after the afternoon's work. The little owl was about done. She held it up, turning it slowly in her hands. All it needed was a little color.

The almost dusk was robbing the room of light and Jordan turned the overhead lights on. She could hear the kids still playing in the yard. Mom wanted them in to dinner soon. She turned back to the large, elegant carving. Brie's suggestion of just having one foot emerge was worth considering, and she examined the base of the statue, running her fingers lightly over the wood.

Some subtle color should be added to shadow the woman's clothing. She'd already added one shallow dimple this afternoon, but color on the face? The eyes? The mouth?

Her camera was on the workbench and she went through the photos one by one until she came to the picture she was looking for. It was Brie, sitting on the pier at the lake in an unguarded moment, the wind catching her hair. She looked so relaxed. Jordan compared this image to last night. Brie had been completely wrecked at the hospital and later.

She turned back to the carving. Perhaps if she put just a hint of color into the eyes? Jordan looked back at the photo. Blue eyes, the color of stained glass in the rain.

❖

Brie woke with a gasp. It was dark. Her arm was numb and she rolled to her back. She shook her arm and rubbed it until it tingled. "What the— Where?" she said hoarsely. She stretched hard, like an animal, and tried to get her bearings. The kitchen lights were on, leaving a thin triangle of light on the wall.

Her hand hit the remote on the floor beside her. She'd been lying on the floor, listening to Niki's discs, and had fallen asleep. She licked her dry mouth and made a face. It tasted like burnt rubber. She grabbed the edge of the desk, got herself up, then picked up the remote. It was the winter before they were shot. Niki was talking about the house and the flowers for spring. Brie remembered it and shut the system off.

Her arm was still tingling and she shook herself. "Damn." She headed to the kitchen for something to drink. She peered into the refrigerator. There was orange juice. Or sangria? No, better stick with orange juice. She was already fuzzy-headed.

She looked inside the pharmacy bag on the table. Packets of pills? Right, samples that the therapist had wanted her to try. All the pills in the world wouldn't bring her memory back. Even the therapist admitted that. She'd also admitted that this kind of recall was commonly triggered by an event. Brie massaged her temples and wondered how rude she'd been. She distinctly remembered asking furiously, *For what purpose? I can stay in therapy until I'm a hundred years old. What good does all of this do?*

Brie stood and finished the orange juice. *Two years of this and I'm still looking at a blank wall. Until yesterday.* "Except for blood on the sand. Let's not forget the damned blood on the sand." This was like walking around with a bomb.

She turned off the kitchen lights and went to her bedroom. She took two pillows and the comforter off the bed, opened the closet, and tossed them inside.

Later, after brushing her teeth and washing her face, she lay on the pillows on the closet floor and pulled the blankets over her. Expecting the faint scent of Niki to comfort her, she closed her eyes but a few minutes later, she was still not asleep.

There was a new scent. She sat up and touched the clothes above her. Fleece? It was Jordan's jacket. That smell was the distinctively hers, wood and spicy shampoo.

"No," she said. She pulled Jordan's coat off the hanger and threw it into the bedroom. Arms over her face, she thought about Niki's voice today, the things she'd said. The flowers she'd found. That she'd never seen them bloom or smelled their sweet fragrance made Brie begin to cry once again. She closed the closet door and tried to find the scent that was Niki, but there was nothing. She stood and felt the clothing. Nothing. The clothing she was holding could have belonged to anyone. Just like Niki's desk, the cottage was slowly emptying of Niki.

Her heart began to pound. Not just Niki but even Jordan's scent was gone as well. If she'd lost Niki, she could lose Jordan, just as quick. She licked her lips again as panic began to inch inside. She sank back to the floor. She couldn't stand the thought of losing Jordan as well. Just as her scent had disappeared, so could Jordan. Niki had.

Brie rolled over onto her stomach and buried her face in the pillow. Her mind raced as she fought the rising fear. The only thing to do was to end the relationship with Jordan. Before something happened.

CHAPTER TWENTY-TWO

A stiff autumn wind blew around Thomas Teller's house. Jordan could hear it as she worked in the upstairs dressing room. She zipped her jacket and adjusted her tool belt. Thomas had chosen the marbled top for the counter in his dressing room, and Jordan liked the color. She ran her fingers around the edges, checking it out. Smooth and perfect. She unplugged the router and set it on the floor. It was a good day.

John had met her when she came to work this morning, waving a paper in her face, making her laugh. They had been successful in their bid for the Willis Foundation's newest project and they had spent some time in their office, looking it over.

Voices drifted up from the yard, drawing her to the window. There were puddles in the yard from last night's rain and people were carefully avoiding them on their way to lunch. She laid her tool belt on the counter. As she went down the steps she thought of Brie. She hadn't called last night, but Brie had said she would call when she was ready. Still, if Brie didn't call today, she'd call or go over to the house. Wait until she told her this news.

She hopped the puddles, playing a little as she walked toward the trailer. Maybe she could talk John into going to lunch with her, celebrate their new contract. "John," she called out as she walked into their office, but pulled up short. Thomas Teller was sitting in front of John's desk.

"Excuse me, Thomas. I didn't know you were here. Great news about our bid. Thank you and thank the Willis Foundation." She smiled and shook his hand.

"Jordan, wait, I came to talk with you," he said. "Have you eaten?"

"No, I was just on my way to lunch." She looked at them both. "Is something wrong?"

"Not at all. Would you and John take a little drive with me and then have lunch?"

They drove in John's Lexus to an area just north of the central part of Milwaukee, winding through ramshackle homes with broken windows and porches. Many were empty.

"Grant Willis's father bought this area in nineteen thirty-eight, when he was just starting out," Thomas explained. "Of course, it looked very different then. He didn't want what we now call tract homes, but he did want affordable housing. It'd be a Milwaukee version of Habitat for Humanity."

Jordan scanned the street. "Would the families work on each home, like Habitat?"

He nodded. "I wanted to show you this because we need someone to head up the project. The foundation's board has authorized me to offer you that position."

Jordan's heart pounded. "Me? I don't have the experience. Shouldn't this be someone like…" She looked at her uncle.

John grinned. "You have to get your feet wet sometime, honey."

She simply looked at both men. It was a gigantic offer and would test her to the limits. "You'd be there, right behind me?" she said to John. He nodded.

"Jordan, don't doubt your skill or your talent. What we want is your vision. Yes, you're shy on experience, but with John behind you, you can do it," Thomas said.

"I'd be honored," Jordan said.

Thomas pointed at a cement slab where kids were shooting hoops. "You'd probably want to start about here. The entire area is shaped like an oblong."

"Are the plans in place?" Jordan asked, her brain beginning to function.

"Yes, Grant's plans and then Niki's revisions are available, but it will be your decision if you take the offer and work for the foundation."

Jordan sat quietly and tried to absorb everything. Finally, she looked at John. "You promise to help?"

"Of course," he said.

"Can I have my crew from work? Bix and the girls?"

"Just let me know," John answered and they grinned at each other. "Actually, you're going to need all of us. This is huge."

❖

Brie's night had been filled with restless dreams, scattered bits and pieces of Niki, their life. Then she dreamed of Jordan, alone, in her studio, before finally waking. If there was time today, she'd find Jordan, talk to her in person. She shook her head, feeling guilty. This was her fault. Jordan was just recovering, and this put her at risk.

After a hurried breakfast, Brie finished packing for her flight. She ran off a disc of her manuscript for her editor and put her bag and laptop in the car.

She started a pot of coffee and went into Niki's office. The handful of discs that she'd already listened to were on the desk. She reached for one labeled "Christmas–New Year." Thirteen Christmases with Niki and they'd all been different. Niki had a childlike enthusiasm for the season. She loved the decorations, the music.

Christmas music flooded the room and she turned the volume down. Tears pushed at her eyes as she remembered Niki, sitting here, working, listening to this music. She found the remote and fast-forwarded past the music. It picked up in the middle of a sentence.

"...thank you for this Christmas. I've had a strange fall. For some reason, I can't stop thinking about my family. I've missed them terribly. You've been so busy with your paper, your presentation, but that's all right and I mean that."

Brie stopped the recording. "What?" She stared at the wall in front of her. Niki had been in trouble but hadn't told her? How had she missed that? All she could remember were the hours she'd put in on that damned position paper, the one she'd wanted published.

While she was doing the research, she'd found old clippings and commercial transactions about Niki's family, extending back into the late eighteen hundreds, when they'd first arrived in Milwaukee. She'd had a TA and a grad student help her assemble a book of every piece of information she could find. They'd bound it and put a photo of Grant Willis's family on the front, the last one they'd had taken. Brie had snapped the photo herself years earlier.

"God," Brie whispered. They had been sitting on the floor, the night before Christmas, trading a gift apiece. The rest of their gifts would be opened the next morning at her mother's. Niki had opened the gift and looked up, stunned. She had simply let it drop and scrambled over to Brie's lap, crying. At that moment, Brie had thought it was the wrong gift, and no matter how much she had begged, Niki would not explain the tears. About a month later she realized that she saw the book everywhere in the house, lying open. Or Niki would be sitting, reading it.

Brie got up for coffee and brought it back to the office. She mulled that autumn over in her mind before she began the disc again.

"The book you did for me, this Christmas, is probably the best thing you've ever given me. Except yourself, of course. I miss my family so much. It doesn't bring them back, but it reminds me. Thank you. I'm going to try to leave some things around Milwaukee that may be a reminder of the family as well. It looks as if our family will end here, with me, but it was a good run while we ran."

There was a pause but Brie could hear Niki breathing, so she let it continue. Niki laughed, the one she always saved just for Brie, as personal as a kiss. *"I'm writing this down and someday, I'll put it in a card for you. Let's see, you are my blue-eyed model with a red-hot heart and glory hallelujah body. Remember that I loved you from the moment I saw you, that day. That beautiful day."* It was the writing on the card that Niki had given her for their anniversary.

And that did it. The disc ended but Brie never heard another breath or word. She was back at the beach, seeing everything. She could feel her heart thunder in her chest. Niki's skin was warm as she laid her on the sand. Something red. Whose blood was that? She looked around wildly and heard the bike leave but didn't see it. The smell of exhaust lingered thickly in the air. Niki's eyes never opened as Brie told her to wait. She'd be right back. She felt the dirt as she climbed the bank to the pavement. An old pickup stopped and an older man got out. He ran to where she lay on the cement. His face shone with fear as she held her hand up to stop him. And then, darkness. The EMS people were above her but it went dark again.

❖

After the long lunch with Thomas and John, Jordan came home early. The house was empty but there was a note from her mother saying she had taken the kids to dinner at Richard's home. Thomas had given Jordan four boxes of information and blueprints from Grant and Niki Willis, and she hauled them into her office.

Still excited, she began to go through the smallest box first. There were letters that were over fifty years old. She could hardly wait to show them to Brie. She would love the historical content, the language that was used. She stopped. Brie sat on the board of the Willis Foundation. She had to be aware of this, didn't she?

She looked at the time. It was too early to call Brie. She wouldn't be home from school yet. Tonight, no matter what else was going on, she'd call her and thank her. This was such good news. Everything felt so good. She did a little dance into the kitchen, laughing. While the kids were gone tonight, she might have time to work in the studio.

They had set up an appointment with the foundation board tomorrow, late afternoon. She'd have time to take Brie out afterward. No, wait, Brie was going to New Mexico. Jordan reached for the phone. She wouldn't have left without calling, would she?

❖

The phone rang and Brie raised her head from the desk and looked around Niki's office. It was almost dark. What time was it? She got up in a hurry but stopped, light-headed and dizzy. Didn't she have to fly out tonight? Brie made herself go back to the kitchen and check her purse for the flight information, then the calendar. She checked the phone and saw Jordan's name. She stood there, indecisive. There was time if she hurried.

At least she wasn't in pain like before, she thought as the hot water cascaded across her in the shower. Her body had healed. But mentally, she was as befuddled as when she got out of the hospital. Suddenly, she was crying again. Why hadn't they just killed both of them? She was next to dead anyway. Or why hadn't they spared Niki and taken her? Worse, how could she have possibly almost gotten involved with Jordan? She loved Niki with her entire being. Brie rubbed her aching head, trying to find one clear thought. "Niki?" she said outloud and the word echoed in her head.

She considered the things she might say to Jordan as she went around the house, making sure it was locked up.

It was raining as she left her home. Her mind just would not stay focused. She swerved around a large puddle. Jordan's place was dark and her heart dropped. Brie pulled into the driveway to turn around but then saw lights in the studio. She found a pad of paper and wrote down some information, then ran to the studio through the rain.

Jordan was sitting on the floor, working on the base of the carving when Brie opened the door.

"Hey, I was just calling you." Jordan's face lit up and she smiled her beautiful smile, holding up her phone. "You're not home. You're here," she said, laughing. "Brie, I've had the best day."

Heart pounding, Brie held her hand up. "Don't get up," she said. "I couldn't leave without seeing you. I have to fly out tonight, to New Mexico, and I only have a few minutes." She walked over to where Jordan sat and looked at the carving. "Jordan, she's lovely," she said, looking at the statue. The words were echoing in her head again.

"Here," she said. "This is where I'll be and when I'll be home. If you ever want to talk to me again." She handed Jordan the information she'd just written down. Going to her knees to look into Jordan's face, she said, "Jordan, I can't do this. I'm truly sorry. I don't know if you'll ever forgive me but, if you do, please come and talk with me." Jordan's eyes went empty. Blank. Brie rose and turned to leave.

"Wait." Jordan stood. "What can't you do?"

"You," Brie said but didn't turn around.

"Me?" Jordan sounded strangled. "Why?"

Brie's head dropped, her eyes stinging, but she didn't turn and kept on walking. She drove away but had to stop down the street because she was crying too hard to see the road.

❖

Brie walked out of the Santa Fe airport in a crowd and saw her editor almost immediately. Karen Forbes was an extraordinary woman, and Santa Fe was an extraordinary place. Even the air was sharper and sweeter. Brie gasped as Karen hugged her and squeezed the air out of her.

"My Lord, you've melted. I'm taking you to food, hungry or not. Don't argue with me," Karen said. They went to a lovely restaurant and Brie ate more than she'd eaten in three days and drank enough wine to relax every muscle in her body.

"You're thin and you look exhausted. What's going on?"

Brie sighed. "Do you want the good news or the bad news first?"

"The good, of course."

"Okay. My professional life, my teaching, my academic work is great. I had two offers from West Coast colleges for next year. And I'm writing on the book like crazy. I've written over thirty thousand words in the last five weeks, and I think it's pretty good."

Karen grinned and leaned back into the booth. "That's good, you're right. The bad?"

"My personal life. It's like the Taliban. Dark and shadowy. Shifting. And definitely dangerous."

Karen laughed a little at Brie's words but stopped smiling as Brie talked about the months since Karen had last seen her.

"You don't have to listen to this. We can stop right now. I'm thoroughly sick of myself."

"Are you all right?"

Brie took a deep breath. "What is *all right* these days?"

Karen got up, gathering their things. "Let's get you to the lodge."

Brie handed Karen a large manila envelope. "Here's the manuscript, and there's a disc in there. You can get started without me if I sleep late."

CHAPTER TWENTY-THREE

People came and went as Jordan waited for Dr. Bauer at the clinic. Still numb after Brie's announcement the previous night, she stared at the floor until the nurse called her. Last night had been mostly sleepless after Brie's appearance in her studio.

As Jordan entered Dr. Bauer's office, she saw him look at her clothes. She looked down at what she was wearing. She couldn't remember and was relieved to see the pearl gray suit with a silver shell.

"You look nice," he said. "Very businesslike."

"Thank you. I have an appointment after I see you."

"An appointment?"

"Yes, with the Willis Foundation. Are you familiar with them?"

"Of course. They're a huge economic force in this area."

"They have a new project that they're about to undertake and my company, Kelly Construction, received the bid. They've asked me to lead the project."

"What an honor. Congratulations."

"I'm so excited that I'm about to fall off the planet."

He leaned back and regarded her. "You may be falling off the planet, but where's the sparkle?"

Jordan took a deep breath. "I'm certain that you remember our conversation about Brie O'Malley and her murdered lover?"

"I remember."

"Her lover was Niki Willis."

"Willis? As in the foundation?"

Jordan nodded.

"How long ago was that?"

"Two years and a few months."

"How's she doing?"

"Off and on, but better than when I first met her. Right now she's struggling."

He fiddled with his pen. "As I said, then, it's an important shared experience."

Jordan nodded. "The day of my last appointment with you, Brie and I ended up in a meadow at Kaker's Point, kissing my mind into oblivion. And several times since then. It was…stunning." She glanced at him. "I even told Mom, just to see if she'd speak to me again."

"How'd she take it?"

"Mom's thinking about it, but it's probably a moot point." Jordan took a deep breath. "Brie had to leave town on business and stopped by my studio last night. She said it just wasn't possible for this—for us—to continue."

"What?" He leaned forward. "She started this and then…? How are you?"

"*We* started this. And I'm sad. Shocked. Brie has never been able to recall the shooting, and the other day it suddenly all came back to her. I don't think she's in very good shape right now."

"Sudden recall can blast the mind. But still…"

"This is normal?"

"Normal? I don't use that word very often. Usually, when this recall happens, it's devastating."

"What happens next?"

He shrugged. "It's unpredictable. I can tell you to stop drinking or stop giving your body away like you did because it's unhealthy for you, both physically and emotionally. But I can't advise you here, at least at this point. She's not my patient and I have no idea where she is in the grieving process. Except to say, it happens and it's usually traumatic. Sometimes the grieving person will go backward in the process. You know about anger. Fear."

"Fear? Well, I'm certainly *traumatized*, no matter what she is. Also angry. And hurt." Jordan looked at him.

"It's common to exhibit fear when entering a new relationship, no matter what the age. You were the exception."

"You've always said my anger was a normal reaction."

"It's part of the grieving, but then what did you do?"

"I stopped caring." Jordan shifted in her chair and stared at her hands. "Was that acceptance?"

"Maybe," he said. "That's where I see you now. Finally accepting. Moving forward. Do you think it will complicate things, the fact that it's Brie's dead lover's foundation?"

"No. I think this will make her happy." She knew that much was true. It would make Brie happy, no matter what happened between them. "It's ironic that I'll be working and carrying out Niki's vision."

"Brie may come out of it and she may not." He looked at the clock and stood. "I'm out of time. Do you want to schedule another appointment?"

"No, I don't think so. If I need you, I'll call. Is that a good way to leave this?"

He leaned across the desk and shook her hand. "It's been a pleasure, Jordan. Our problems to solve were Pete and the anger. I think we were successful. Go get 'em. Do a good job on that project."

A light mist began as she drove to the Willis Foundation on Wisconsin Avenue. She sat in the car for a moment, thinking about the doctor's words. *Sometimes the grieving person will go backwards in the grieving process.* With a deep breath she reached for her briefcase and tried to put Brie out of her mind. She had to prepare herself for the meeting.

❖

After the first day's work, both Karen and Brie finished with a meal and a beer in the lodge's dining room.

"Let's not talk about the book," Brie said.

"Okay," Karen agreed with a healthy drink of beer. "How are you doing otherwise?"

"You mean my Taliban life?" Brie said with sarcasm. "I slept solidly last night, and focusing on the book all day helped."

Karen nodded. "Do you know what I noticed?"

"What?"

"You wrote those first chapters before you were shot, over two years ago. Then, this morning, I looked at the chapters that you've written recently."

Brie smiled tiredly. "We agreed not to talk about the book."

"I'm going someplace with this. Hang on. What I'm trying to say is that I was braced for a very sad story, some of the trauma of what you've been through, leaking onto the pages."

"Really?"

"Really. It's not there, so far. Of course, this was done before that moment on the beach the other day. Right?"

Brie nodded. "I'd never even thought about that."

"So, something has been working, going right during the last months."

"Oh," Brie said and frowned. "Discipline?"

"Sure." Karen made a face at her. "Okay, no more book talk."

After Karen had left, Brie got ready for bed. She parted the drapes. The stars were silver and soft in the black sky. Of all the traveling she and Niki had done in their life, she'd never seen a sky like New Mexico's. The stars gleamed and sparkled and reminded her of Jordan's eyes the first night they'd danced together.

She turned away quickly and saw her phone on the bedside table. She'd intentionally left it turned off all day long. There was a message and she dialed in her access code.

"Brie," Jordan's warm voice said, only softer and more serious than she'd ever heard it. "I just have one question. You told me that lesbians don't date straight women because straight women are usually just curious and then dump them." There was a pause. "What do you call it when lesbians dump the straight women?"

Brie pulled in a quick breath as the words stopped and the message ended. She saved it on her phone, standing absolutely still. Jordan hadn't sounded angry. It had sounded exactly like something she would have said when they were holding each other. Like that last night in her own living room, when Jenna had gotten sick and Jordan had to go. Jordan had said, "I'm not one of those curious women you were talking about earlier."

Brie undressed and got into bed, skipping the shower. She cried herself to sleep.

❖

Jordan hid the last screw in the wood and blew the dust away. She stood and looked around at Thomas Teller's new kitchen. "Almost done," she said and braced herself on the counter, stretching her stiff back.

She stared at the floor thinking of a rain-drenched Brie standing in her studio doorway, her damp hair darkened to the color of ripe wheat.

"Looks great," Bix said behind her, startling her. "You do fine work, kid. Did you choose the wood?"

"Well, yes and no. I met with the client's wife and we worked it out." Jordan sat on a sawhorse and picked up her thermos. She offered it to Bix as well and poured them both coffee.

"Our next project for the Willis Foundation sounds exciting. Aren't you about jumping out of your skin?"

Jordan nodded. "I've been looking at the plans that Grant and Niki Willis were playing with. In fact, I've already had a meeting with the foundation. Yesterday."

"All this good news, but you look like hell, if you don't mind me saying so," Bix said. "Where's Brie?"

"In New Mexico, with her book person."

Bix laid her hard hat on the floor. "What's going on?"

"It's complicated." Without warning, tears stung Jordan's eyes. "Brie stopped by my studio, the night she left, said she couldn't do this." Jordan cleared her throat. "When I asked her what she couldn't do, she said 'you' and left."

Bix stared at her. "What? She said that?"

Jordan reached into the back pocket of her jeans and handed Bix the paper with the information on it that Brie had given her.

"This is odd. She says good-bye, tells you it won't work, and then gives you her address, the room number, the telephone number...look, even the dates and flight numbers. You called her, right?"

"I left a message on her phone, but I didn't talk with her," Jordan said.

Bix nodded and handed her the paper. "It's just strange, that's all." She picked up her hat, asked a question about work, and left.

Jordan sat on the sawhorse, thinking about what Bix had said. Why *had* Brie cut the relationship off but given her all this information?

That night, she bent and unlaced her boots at the back door so she could kick them off as she went into the house. The kitchen smelled good as she stepped inside, and she grinned at her kids. Both of them yelled "Mom" as she made her way to the table. Her mother sat down with them and Jordan looked at her family, suddenly feeling very lucky. When she came home, someone said her name and usually there was the aroma of food in the house.

Later, she cleaned the kitchen alone and listened to the kids play a game in Tyler's room. She had made coffee and took a cup to the window. It was dark so early now. The night was clear and the stars were beginning to come out over the lake. When Brie came home at night, her house was quiet. She thought of Brie turning on the lights to a dark and empty house.

None of this made sense to her. What had happened since she'd walked out the door that morning? And why hadn't Brie called her back? Had the stress of that day at Omni driven her over the edge? What had Dr. Bauer said? *Sudden recall can blast the mind. Devastating.*

She turned away from the window quickly. Her mother was standing there, watching her.

"What's wrong, Jordan?" she asked. "You look absolutely miserable."

Jordan poured herself another cup of coffee and got her mother one as well. They sat at the table and Jordan put the piece of paper that Brie had given her between them. "Mom, I think I need to take a trip."

❖

The next night, Jordan drove her rental car up an enormous hill to the Eagle's Lair Lodge on the outskirts of Santa Fe and parked. "Number five," she said and got out of the car. The huge stone and wood building looked to be built into a mountain, something she'd never seen. She stood for a moment, looking at the structure, then reached back into the car for her coat.

Her boots clattered on the stone walkway as she got to the right number, but the windows were dark. She could see that each unit was a suite. *Private, spacious* were the words that came to mind as she walked back to her car. Maybe she should try Brie's cell phone? No, considering that Brie hadn't called her back, she'd probably better wait in the car. See her face-to-face. She walked back to her car and pulled into a parking space in front of Brie's suite.

Jordan stretched out on the front seat of the car, tired and worn out. Sleep had been scarce since Brie had been gone. She sat up and reached for her bag in the backseat to use as a pillow, then curled up once again on the front seat. Santa Fe and the mountains were a new experience. She laughed a little. Everything in her life right now was a new experience. She stared at the huge stars through the windshield. They were so big and soft. The wind rocked the car gently just as she fell asleep.

CHAPTER TWENTY-FOUR

Karen shoved herself back from the table and closed her laptop. "Enough," she said. "We've been at this almost eight hours." She looked across the desk at Brie. "Hungry? I am. Let's go into town and see what's happening at Mama's Chili and have a meal, some beers. Go take a shower and change clothes. I'll be back in an hour." She popped back into the doorway. "And be prepared to tell me about that woman you've been talking about for the last two days." Then she was gone.

"What?" Brie said to the silence. She'd been unaware she'd been talking about Jordan as Karen had tossed in questions about Milwaukee. She shook her head at her confused mind and turned off her computer. At least she'd been able to focus on the writing. *I may just have a book here*, she thought and left for a shower.

Later, as Karen opened the door to the packed club, the loud music reminded Brie of the first club she'd taken Jordan to, with Vet and Peg. For a moment she missed Jordan fiercely.

❖

Voices going by the car woke Jordan, and she sat up. Brie was going into the recessed entryway of her suite with some tall woman. She rubbed her eyes and then her cold hands. They went inside and she sat there for a moment. The woman was probably her editor. Should she wait until she left? Or just go pound on the door?

"Safety in numbers," she muttered and turned on the inside lights of the car, checking her hair. She looked down at her wrinkled clothes.

Her old pea coat had kept her warm but it looked a bit worn. "She's probably going to kick me out anyway. What's the difference?"

Squaring her shoulders, she walked to the door and knocked. When Brie answered, her eyes widened. "Jordan?"

"You didn't call me back."

"No. Oh, what? I'm sorry, come inside. It's chilly."

The tall woman still had her coat on and was starting a fire in the fireplace. She gave Jordan a warm smile and held her hand out. "Karen Forbes, Brie's editor."

"Jordan Carter." Jordan said and shook Karen's hand, glad to see a smile in the room. Brie seemed frozen, still at the door. Karen reached past both of them and shut the door, making a face at Brie.

"Do you drink?" Karen said. "How about a beer?"

"I'd love one," Jordan answered and looked at Brie. She wasn't frowning. But she wasn't smiling either. When Karen left for the kitchen, Jordan said, "Is this all right?"

Brie shook herself a little. "Of course it is. I'm just shocked to see you. I'm sorry, Jordan. Oh, for God's sake, give me your coat." She took the coat and laid her hand on Jordan's cheek. "You look so cold. Come over here, sit by the fire." She tugged Jordan to the chair closest to the fire, then sat on the couch. Karen brought two beers out, handed them each one, and went to the door.

"Thanks for dinner, Brie. You know how to reach me. We'll finish those two chapters tomorrow." Karen gave Jordan an encouraging smile. "I have someplace to be. Nice to meet you, Jordan. I've heard a lot about you." The door closed firmly behind her.

"I'll go somewhere else, if this is a bad idea," Jordan said and took a drink.

Brie did frown then. "Somewhere else? You must be kidding. Fly all the way out here and go to a motel? I don't think so." She looked at her. "You did fly?"

Jordan nodded. She felt a bit dizzy and her stomach suddenly grumbled. "I'm sorry," she said and stood. She was so tense that every muscle ached.

Brie stood too. "Have you eaten?"

"Of course, I…" Jordan began. It'd been over eight hours since she'd had food.

Brie started for the kitchen. "There's roast beef in the refrigerator. It'll make a great sandwich."

"Wait a minute, Brie." Brie turned. "We're going to talk first." Jordan sat back down in the chair. "Sit down."

Brie went back to the couch and sat but wouldn't look at Jordan. The silence stretched out between them. Jordan thought Brie looked tired, her eyes more distant than they had the first day they'd met. She remembered what they'd looked like the last time she'd kissed her and swallowed hard.

"Would you at least answer my question? The one I left on your phone?"

"I don't know what to say," Brie answered in such a soft voice that Jordan had to lean forward to hear. And then, silence.

"I think I understand," Jordan said carefully. Her stomach growled again and she looked at the floor. All of her courage disappeared and she felt flat, defeated. "I'll go. I saw a place to eat on the way in today and a motel. Brie, it's okay. I only wanted to know why. Nothing's changed as far as I'm concerned, and I wanted to tell you that. I think you need more time to think about this." When Brie didn't answer again, Jordan put her coat on, opened the door, and left.

The cold air was sharp against her lungs. Jordan fumbled with the car key, swore at it and at the situation. Tears stung her eyes, making it hard to see the ignition. Something suddenly pounded on the window.

"Wait," Brie said. "This is silly, Jordan. Don't go."

Jordan looked at Brie's anxious face through the window. She nodded and turned the car off.

"Bring your bags in," Brie said. "While I'm making a sandwich, you can take a shower, relax a little. We can sit in front of the fire and—"

Jordan put her finger on Brie's mouth to quiet her. "Okay," she said. She took a deep, calming breath. *Patience*, she told herself. If she didn't let Brie tell whatever there was to tell, she might never find out. This was why she'd come all the way down here.

After a shower, Jordan put on sweats and a rust-colored T-shirt. She set her bags by the door and turned. Brie was sitting on the floor, leaning against the couch, her white V-neck sweater and gold hoop earrings shinning in the firelight. Jordan noted again how beautiful she was, and her heart hurt for a moment.

"Sit with me?" Brie asked and patted the floor beside her. They stretched their feet toward the fire.

"Have you eaten?" Jordan asked and picked up the sandwich.

"That roast beef is from our lunch. Karen took me out to dinner."

"I didn't mean to arrive like the cavalry," Jordan said. "I should have called."

"You did call," Brie said.

"But you didn't," Jordan said and took another bite of the sandwich.

"I haven't changed my mind, Jordan. I still feel as if this is the right decision."

"Okay," Jordan said, acknowledging Brie's feelings, but she changed the subject, playing for a little more time. "How's the book coming?"

"Good. We've worked on it." Brie took a drink of her beer and stared at the fire. "Would it help if I said I'm sorry?"

Jordan didn't answer. Instead, she finished her sandwich and pushed the plate away. "What would help would be an explanation."

"I honestly don't know."

Jordan saw that she had tears in her eyes. "Okay, let's start with the morning I left your house. After we woke up together."

Brie nodded. "I didn't know any of this was going to happen, that day. I read my writing on the computer and remembered a moment with Niki. I'm sure, after the first book, you realize that the main character is her?"

"Actually, I didn't," Jordan said. "I didn't know her, Brie."

"Isn't that funny? I thought everyone would know."

"All right, so the book's character is Niki and you were thinking about it."

"I was desperate to recall the shooting. Remembering that book made me so sad. I went into her office and ended up listening to her recordings, the discs." Brie pulled her knees up and wrapped her arms about them. "I also had an appointment with my therapist that day and fought with her. I came back home and listened to more of Niki. I ended up sleeping in the closet that night and thought about you, a lot.

The next day, the day I left, I listened to more of the recordings and remembered the shooting. Everything, and I still remember. I decided that this is unfair to you...if I still love Niki? And I do."

Jordan shivered, realizing she'd just heard some of the answer. Most of what she needed to know was in Brie's words. "Give me your feet," she said. "Lean against that chair." Brie moved and Jordan began to rub her feet. Brie gave a little groan of pleasure.

"Remember Emma's question, what Niki would have wanted for you?" Jordan said.

Brie nodded. "She would have wanted me to be happy."

"Then, whether it's me...or whoever...are you going to continue to run away from someone who makes you happy?" She continued rubbing Brie's feet and watched her begin to relax. "I know that no amount of wishing or love is going to bring Pete back. God knows I tried hard enough to find him, or at least human comfort." She stopped and looked at Brie. "And just for you to know, I would find you really strange if you didn't still love Niki. Why shouldn't you?"

"You make it sound so simple." Brie took a deep breath.

Jordan smiled at Brie. "Would you expect me to suddenly forget Pete?"

"No."

"My point exactly. So, then I come along. You caught me at a really unguarded moment, Brie. And you're a woman, the last place I'd look."

"I've never lied to you, Jordan." Brie shifted and took her feet away, then put them back. "That really feels good."

"It does to me too." Jordan smiled and began to rub her feet again. "I was angry and hurt, but I didn't doubt your feelings."

Brie looked up quickly. "You didn't?"

"Why did you tell me where you'd be? Why did you tell me that we—you and I—were not possible?"

"Because I wanted to tell you I was leaving and where to find me if you wanted to talk." Brie paused. "I cared too much to hurt you." Her face was a mixture of bewilderment and understanding.

"What you're going through is hard and hurtful. Most of all, confusing. I know because I've gone through it too. If I'm willing to risk it all, are you?"

Brie covered her face with her hands. "I care."

Jordan pushed Brie to the floor gently and kissed her. When she raised up, Brie's eyes were still closed. "Do that again," Brie said.

Jordan did and this time she started at the collarbone, worked her way up the neck, skimmed the jaw, and finally, found her mouth.

Jordan propped herself on an elbow, ran her hands through the shining hair below her. "See, it's still there."

"Come here. I've missed you." Brie said, but she had a small smile on her face. Jordan almost groaned when Brie held her tightly. "Sit up," Brie whispered against Jordan's ear. The next few seconds were magic to Jordan. Brie had her sweater and bra off in a second and sat before her, naked from the waist up.

"Your turn," Brie said. Jordan could not move, so Brie took the T-shirt off her and tossed it on the couch. "Drooling," she murmured and pushed Jordan to the floor again. She stretched out very lightly across Jordan's skin, barely brushing her but igniting her to the tips of her fingers. The only sound was their heavy breathing.

"Follow me," Brie said, taking Jordan's hand. She hopped, trying to get out of her sweats, and by the time she got to the bedroom, every hair on her body rose as she saw the naked body in front of her. "Here we are," Brie said softly and moved Jordan onto the bed.

It wasn't anything like Jordan thought it would be, but somehow more than she had hoped. A thrill settled between her legs. Brie kissed her stomach, up her ribs to the neck, the hollow of her throat, glanced off an ear, and finally landed securely on her lips. Every time Brie kissed her, Jordan needed more and instinctively lifted into Brie. They groaned. Fingers slipped between her legs, teasing the inside of her thighs. "Brie," Jordan gasped helplessly.

"Shh, just enjoy. Remember, I said you only needed the right person to"—and she touched her carefully—"touch you...tend you. Ah, you're wet. This *is* right. I told you so." Brie opened her, slowly, gently. Jordan tried to breathe, every piece of her begging for Brie's hands. She floated for a moment as a warm mouth covered her breast and enclosed her nipple. She pushed upward for more as a thumb teased her clit and she came unexpectedly and hard.

They collapsed back into the pillows, their ragged breathing the only sound. When Brie started to pull out, Jordan caught her hand. "No. Stay." Her body was still throbbing. "Don't you dare move." Jordan captured Brie's mouth, tasting her lips, then her smooth cheeks and jaw. Neither said a word until Jordan whispered, "More," and impaled herself on the fingers again.

Brie put two more fingers inside the slick heat and skimmed herself across the now sweaty body beside her. She ran her tongue around the hard nipple, heard Jordan groan, and stroked harder. Tightening muscles warned her and she grazed the nipple with her teeth, then bit lightly. That did it and Jordan raised up. Brie held her, feeling the powerful orgasm trap her fingers. When the tremors stopped she took her hand away and they stretched against each other.

Jordan tried to breathe, her eyes closed. Finally she whispered, "That was a land speed record for me."

Brie kissed her, aware of her own aching desire lurking just beneath her skin. "Hold me," she said, wanting the arms around her that always made her feel safe.

Jordan's eyes were still closed. "I could stand a lot more of that," she said, settling Brie under her own body. "More."

Brie moved Jordan's hand between her own legs and bit her lip as Jordan's fingers tentatively explored her. She stared into eyes full of smoldering heat.

"God. You're wet," Jordan said. "This is sexy."

"I want you right…there," Brie said but felt Jordan hesitate, and she spread her legs to encourage her. She pulled Jordan's mouth down to hers for a long, passionate kiss and pushed against her fingers until they were deep inside. Every nerve in her body snapped as Jordan's warm lips moved up her stomach to her breasts. She shoved her hands in Jordan's hair, said her name as the orgasm pulled her into the familiar haze. She held on to Jordan with everything she was worth.

"Wow," Jordan exhaled.

When she had enough breath to talk, Brie whispered, "I was afraid."

Jordan wiped the tears from the corners of Brie's eyes. "Afraid?"

"What if something happens…to you?"

"Is that what *this* is about?" She stared into Brie's eyes. "Let's get every day we can. I don't want to miss a single moment."

"I mean it. It makes me shake just to think of it."

"Wait," Jordan said. "Think of how we met. That was chance. The same random moment that you're afraid of. Look at us now."

Brie gave her a slightly dazed smile. "Yes. *Look at us.*" She threw her arms around Jordan, holding her hard.

Jordan tucked Brie's trembling body against her. They held each other until they fell asleep. Somewhere in the darkness of the night they both woke at the same time, turning to each other, and went at each other like a couple of kids. Finally, sweating and breathing hard, they lay side by side, staring at each other.

"I love this, lying here, naked with you. You'll never know how much I've looked at your body, the different ways. Here, let me show you something." Jordan straddled Brie, her hands flat on Brie's hips, thumb to thumb. "This area, from just above the tattoo to here, on your thigh. This is what I sketched. I love it. And if you'd ever told me I'd love a woman's breasts, I'd have laughed in your face." She cupped the beautiful breasts under her. "Yum."

Brie laughed at Jordan's kidlike gleefulness and pulled her down into a heap on the bed. Still playful but worn out, they fell asleep again, tangled together.

The next morning, Brie looked across the bed and ran her fingers through the dark hair. Lifting the covers, she surveyed the body. She hadn't touched another woman's body in over sixteen years. She paused as she traced between the firm breasts. Jordan certainly had been creative. Jordan jerked and her eyes flew open. Brie smiled at the well-kissed lips and the satisfied eyes.

Gray eyes blinked above a very sexy smile. "Come here. I can't move."

Brie covered Jordan with her body, then propped herself on her elbows over her. She brushed the hair out of Jordan's eyes and pulled the covers over their heads.

❖

Jordan set her coffee cup down, half listening to the voices from the little office next to the kitchen. Karen had come in that morning, ruffled Brie's still-damp hair, smiled at both of them, and gone into the office without a comment.

She smiled. Never had she been so teased or satisfied. No one had taken her to the heights Brie had. Ever. She poured more coffee and watched a small bird in the tree beside the window. She had thought her life was over, but here she was, beginning again. They'd made love, not just had sex, last night.

"Jordan, did you order breakfast for Karen?" Brie called and triggered a quick memory of her crying out her name last night.

"Yes," Jordan said, shifting in her chair as her body responded to the memory. Someone knocked at the door. "It's here, Brie."

They talked about Brie's book while they ate. Karen was congenial over coffee afterward. She asked about Jordan's kids, her husband, and her business. Jordan was surprised to discover that Karen had begun her professional career as a carpenter with her father, going to college at night. They talked about carving a bit as well.

Brie let them talk as she put notes into her laptop, interrupting occasionally with questions for Karen. The tapping of the keys stopped for a moment and Jordan looked up to see Brie's eyes on her, warm and happy. Jordan lost the thread of the conversation and turned back to Karen's wide smile.

"Okay, you two," Karen said, stuffing papers into her briefcase. She hugged Brie and shook hands with Jordan, handing her a business card. "Just in case." She grinned as she left.

"One more cup of coffee?" Jordan asked.

Brie sat down across from her, a question on her face.

"Thomas Teller talked to me about Niki's foundation. The new project."

Brie's face lit up. "Does it make you happy?"

"I'm hanging on the moon. That and last night and sitting here now, with you. I'll begin on the project when Thomas's house is finished. I've already been looking over the plans at home and had a meeting with them while you were gone. Brie, you're welcome to be any part of this that you want." She reached for Brie's hand.

"I hope so," Brie said with a sexy smile.

"You should have seen how excited the kids were when I showed them where I was going to fly," Jordan said with a laugh. "They like you so much, Brie."

"I like them," Brie said. "Their mother too." She took their cups to the sink. "I have something I want to buy them, if you'll let me. It's on the way out of town, toward the airport." She glanced at her watch.

"We'd better pack if we're going to do that and get to the airport on time." Brie started to leave but turned back and settled into Jordan's lap. "You promise? Every day? Every single moment?"

Jordan took her face in her hands and searched the solemn blue eyes, saw the glance of fear. "I promise."

CHAPTER TWENTY-FIVE

When they got home, the Milwaukee airport was bathed in unusually mild November air. The world felt easy and comfortable. Jordan laced Brie's fingers in her own. "I can't get enough of you," Jordan said and bumped Brie gently with her hip.

"I'll miss you tonight," Brie said with a slow, inviting smile. She bumped Jordan back and they both staggered a little. "I feel a little drunk."

Jordan pulled Brie to her. "Tonight? I hadn't even thought that far. I think I've lost my mind."

"It's safe, I've got it," Brie teased gently.

"Maybe you could stay the night? Remember, we have your gifts. You'll have a hard time getting away from the kids. A sleepover?"

❖

Jenna and Tyler were thrilled with the gifts but especially the cowboy boots Brie had bought them, just as Jordan had predicted. Brie and Jordan made spaghetti for dinner because both kids loved the meal. Jordan's mother joined them and they talked about New Mexico. Jenna kept interrupting with questions about cowboys and Indians until Brie promised to tell her all that she had seen after dinner was over. Brie took the kids after the meal, promising lots of stories about the Southwest. Jordan and her mother cleared the dinner dishes. After they were done and her mother had left, Jordan stopped at Jenna's bedroom. Brie was just pulling the covers up over a sleeping Jenna.

"Asleep?" Jordan asked.

"She loved the stories," Brie said.

Jordan frowned. "What's wrong with her bed?" She stepped inside and pulled the covers back. Jenna was still wearing her cowboy boots. "Brie," she whispered and took the boots off carefully.

Brie smiled at her impishly. "What's one night? And they're perfectly clean. C'mon, meanie."

"I'm not mean. It's not good for her feet. Jeez, I'm just being a mom. Sometimes I have to remind them that I'm the adult in the house." Jordan shook her head. "Will you make a fire while I take out the whip so I can beat our son before he goes to sleep?" she said and left.

"Our son?" Brie repeated to herself.

Later, they collapsed on the couch in front of the fire. "My God," Brie said. "How do you do this every night?"

Jordan pulled her into her lap. "You'll get used to it. See, the trick is the whip. You have to know how to beat them without leaving a mark."

Brie giggled at that thought. They both sighed and let the fire warm them. Brie snuggled into Jordan and closed her eyes, almost asleep.

"Brie, do you remember the first time you were here?" Jordan's voice startled Brie.

"How could I forget? I'd had such a hangover that morning and Emma saved my life."

"I was isolated then," Jordan said. "I'd cut myself off from everything. You came along and it was…I could breathe again. Even if I hadn't fallen in love with you, that's what you've done for me."

"Love?" Brie felt slightly dizzy for a moment as she kissed Jordan hard. "I swear I never thought another person in the world would say that word to me ever again. Or that I'd ever say it to anyone else."

The firelight glinted off the gray in Jordan's eyes. "You haven't said it yet."

"Love."

"And?"

"More love."

"Brie," Jordan said as her hands trailed up across Brie's stomach to alert breasts, already waiting for Jordan's touch, "let's go to bed."

"What's wrong with…here? The couch?"

"Kids. That's what's wrong with here." Jordan grinned and shoved them both upright. "However, we do get to shower together."

"Okay," Brie said good-naturedly. "I can take your clothes off just as fast there as I can here."

❖

"My God," Brie gasped.

"You're incredibly inspiring," Jordan said, worn out but happy. She kissed Brie's stomach and crawled up her body, collapsing beside her. "Where'd you get that tattoo?"

"I lost a bet with Niki."

"You like to bet, don't you? Do you feel like telling me?"

"Sure. This one's easy. We loved football and, that week, I had to go out of town for school. Niki was normally pretty sloppy about football stats, so when she called me and wanted a bet on the Packers, I thought, no problem. The bet was a tattoo, anywhere."

"And?"

"I lost. I'd been busy, hadn't noticed that our ace receiver was out for a couple of weeks. For once I wasn't paying attention."

"Oh, I like Niki's style."

"Oh yeah? Want to bet? You lost the last one."

"Did you choose the naked lady?"

"No, she did."

"You can have it taken off, you know. But I hope you won't. I like it."

"You would." Brie looked at Jordan's eyes. "Here, let me hold you. You're worn out." It didn't take long and Jordan was sound asleep. Brie looked out the window at the oak tree and the almost-orange moon behind it. What a wild few days this had been, but she no longer felt as if she was carrying a bomb around inside herself. She smiled in the dark, thinking of her therapist. That woman probably would forgive her for last week. The therapist had told her to be patient with herself. Amen, Brie's tired mind repeated as she turned over and snuggled against Jordan, falling into sleep.

"Move over, sweetie." Niki nudged her.

"Where are your clothes?"

"You took them off earlier."

"I don't think so," Brie said and ran her hands through the curly hair. "Miss you."

Niki nodded. "I know. Me too." She braced herself on her elbow, looking at Jordan.

"She's a good person, Brie."

"It was natural, just like you."

"Yeah." Niki laid back down and rubbed Brie's stomach. "I miss your laugh. Your skin. The way you finish a kiss...I'm sorry this has been so hard. Promise me something, Brie."

"Anything."

"Treat her as good as you did me."

"I just loved you, Niki."

"And you love her. Be happy, baby." She kissed Brie thoroughly. Brie remembered the mouth instantly and...

Jordan wrapped an arm tightly around Brie, pulled her very close. Brie woke up, confused and disoriented for a moment. She took a deep breath and closed her eyes, holding Jordan's hand.

❖

The next morning, Jordan fixed breakfast for the kids and let Brie sleep. She got the kids out the door in time for the school bus and then sat at the kitchen table. Brie appeared in the kitchen, hair standing up. Her T-shirt was on backward and inside out.

"Coffee?" Jordan offered, laughing at Brie's T-shirt. "You're batting five hundred."

"What?" Brie said, her voice still full of sleep.

"Your T-shirt."

Brie looked down and then fiddled with the collar. "Oh." She took her shirt off.

Jordan inhaled deeply at the sight of Brie in only a skimpy pair of panties in her kitchen. It was a wonderful morning. "How about some waffles?" she asked as Brie took her first drink of coffee.

"Yum," Brie said and put the shirt back on, yawning.

Jordan bent and kissed her on her way to the stove. "I have a surprise for you today," she said. "But you have to wear more than a T-shirt and underwear."

"At least I'm wearing underwear."

Jordan gave her a warning look.

They walked to the studio together later, each carrying a fresh cup of coffee.

Jordan opened the curtains to the windows and the overhead skylights.

"I've never seen your studio in the daytime," Brie said, turning slowly. "What an unusual light. It's almost blue."

Jordan turned and held out a carving. "For you."

"Oh," Brie said. "It's Charlie."

"Does it look like him?"

"Yeah." She began to laugh. "You'll never know how much. Thank you, thank you, thank you." Brie kissed her and hugged her tight.

"I also wanted to show you what I've done to our lady."

"Our lady?"

"It is, Brie. It's ours."

Brie walked around the tall, slender statue in the center. "I can see more of the details in daylight. The rosy wood with green highlights, here and there, and the subtle colors you've added. You've lightened the eyes and…a subtle dimple?" She grinned at Jordan. "She seems taller, determined," Brie said and swallowed hard. It was beautiful, almost ethereal.

Jordan leaned against the workbench, staring at the statue, her dark brown cargo pants almost the same color as her hair. She wore a light gray polo shirt that matched her eyes. There was that coiled energy again, Brie thought, watching Jordan lose herself in the wood.

"I have something to ask you," Brie said. She leaned on the bench, beside Jordan. "We could convert Niki's office into another bedroom for one of the kids so they'd each have their own bedroom. And we can both use my office. There's plenty of room for another desk in there. What do you think?"

"Your place? What?" Jordan frowned, coming back to Brie. Then it dawned on her what Brie was asking. "The cottage?" Jordan said. "Brie, I'd love it…but Niki?"

"It would make Niki happy. I know that for a fact. Not only that, but she'd love the thought of kids there."

Jordan put her hands on Brie's face. "You're going to make me swoon."

"Does that mean…you'll marry me?" Brie joked.

"Of course. I never said no, did I?"

"Yippee," Brie crooned, hugging Jordan.

"But you have to explain all of this to the kids."

"Wait a minute." Brie stepped back with an anxious look.

"Don't be silly. We'll do it together, when they ask—and they will. I'll show you how to make the answer match the question. No hurry." Jordan wrapped her arms around Brie.

"I love you," they both said at once.

CHAPTER TWENTY-SIX

The following summer

Light jazz filled the air as Tyler held the door for Brie and Jenna. Brie grinned at him in his first tuxedo, a little self-conscious but proud. She saw him straighten. *Just like his mother*, she thought. "C'mon," he grumbled. "I can't hold this big door forever."

"Tyler," Jenna complained. Jenna was wearing her first long dress, and even though she was thrilled, she had told Brie she was afraid she'd trip over it.

"Kids." Brie's voice had a hint of a warning. "Let's do this right. It's for your mother. Let's be as good as we can." They stood together and looked at Emma's gallery. It was packed, and Brie squinted a little and wondered if she was going to need her glasses.

Tonight, they would dedicate two things: the Willis Foundation's newest project, Century, and Jordan's carving. After tonight, the carving would be displayed at Emma's gallery, and then, when the family center at Century was complete, it would be moved there.

Brie tried to see the carving over the crowd. Emma wouldn't let her in during the final days, so she had no idea what was going to be shown tonight. She had simply handed everything over to Emma. She and Jordan had chosen the photos, but Brie had not a clue what Emma had done with it all. Dannie Brown had worked with Emma on the presentation, so Brie knew it would be good, whatever it was.

Emma was suddenly beside them. "You're late," she said.

"And you're nervous." Brie smiled. "You always want everyone early. Actually, Em, we're right on time." She took a flute of champagne from a passing waiter. "Can we get the kids a soda?"

"Root beer," Jenna said with a little tug on Brie's arm.

"Root beer, Emma," Brie said as they followed her through the crowd.

"Brie," Jordan's mother said as she walked toward her. "Let me take the kids. My sons are here with their families and we'll keep watch over them." She turned and pointed to a group of tables. The kids, seeing their cousins, immediately went toward them. Brie held up a hand in relief. "Thanks, Charlotte. Emma's getting them some root beer. Is Jordan here?"

"No," Jordan's mother said and frowned slightly. Brie just patted her arm. "Don't worry. She'll be here soon." She turned and almost bumped into Thomas Teller.

"Thomas," she said. "This is lovely. What a way to kick the project off."

He grabbed her hand. "You have to come and see how Emma and Dannie did this. It's just wonderful. I am so proud of this, and look at the people."

Brie nodded and followed him toward the inner gallery.

"Where's Jordan?" he said over his shoulder.

"Getting dressed, I'm sure" was all Brie said. She giggled a little. Jordan was getting dressed at John and Nancy's with Nancy's help. It had taken them weeks to get her to agree to wear a floor-length dress, but finally she'd agreed. And only then if Brie agreed to wear the outfit she'd worn to the softball banquet.

They stepped into the center section of the gallery, and even Brie took a small gulp. It was brilliant. Dannie Brown waved as she saw Brie. The podium was designed as a lily, something Brie had never seen. She walked around it and looked up at Dannie, who stood tall and handsome in the middle of the flower. She too wore a tux.

"You look like an exclamation point," Brie teased.

"Thanks for that," Dannie grumbled and bent to make a connection for the microphone. Her black hair tumbled across her forehead as she stood and pointed at the cameras. "Actually, wouldn't Niki have loved this?"

Brie nodded but swallowed hard as she saw the walls. They had set up a continuous film of the Willis family that slowly moved around the walls of the inner gallery. They had used the book that Brie had made for Niki. The film moved slowly and Dannie said it took about twenty minutes to go full cycle. It began with Niki's great-grandparents and ended with Grant and Niki. Then just Niki.

Brie and Jordan had worked hard on the shots of Niki and made sure Niki was smiling in every single picture. Brie's favorite was Niki hanging off a yardarm of her father's yacht, their first summer together. It was goofy but it always made Brie laugh. Niki was trying to swing herself out into the water. She had ended with a resounding belly flop that had knocked her unconscious. Dannie had gone in the water after her.

An arm went around her waist and she jumped, startled. Jordan stood there with champagne.

"Hi, baby," she said against her ear, and Brie's entire body lit up.

"Let me see you," Brie said and was immediately dazzled. The dress, though simple, was perfect. A straight design to the floor with delicate straps and lace sleeves. It made her elegant and tall, just as Brie had thought. And although she hadn't chosen the color, it struck Brie as odd that it was almost the same yellow as Niki had worn that first day. She hugged her. "You're beautiful. Did anyone remember to tell you that?"

"Not since you." Jordan smiled self-consciously. "Let's get this going." She looked up and gave Dannie a nod.

The crowd turned and Brie finally got a clear look at the statue, standing silently below a soft light. Little shimmers of gold dust fell from the ceiling around it. In her opinion, the lovely shoulders belonged to Jordan. She bit her lip and looked at the torso. Jordan claimed it was her beneath the clothing. The face could have been any woman that had survived. It was one of a kind, and she swore it was taller every time she saw it. As the crowd turned to Dannie and Thomas, she saw that it *was* taller. It was sitting on a graceful dais, as if the woman were stepping up from water with reeds around her. One bare foot was visible.

Dannie began the presentation and Jordan put her arm around Brie once again. Brie sighed, leaning into her. Jordan's arms were home.

About the Author

Born and raised in the Midwest, C.P. Rowlands attended college in Iowa and lived in the Southwest and on the West Coast before returning to Wisconsin. She is an artist in addition to having worked in radio, sales, and various other jobs. She has two children, two grandchildren, a partner of nineteen years, and a dog and a cat. All in all, it's a happy life.

Books Available From Bold Strokes Books

Magic of the Heart by C.J. Harte. CEO Susan Hettinger and wild, impulsive rock star M.J. Carson couldn't be more different if they tried—but opposites attract in ways neither woman can resist. (978-1-60282-131-6)

Ambereye by Gill McKnight. Jolie Garoul is falling in love with her assistant. The big problem is, Jolie is a werewolf. (978-1-60282-132-3)

Collision Course by C.P. Rowlands. Tragedy leaves Brie O'Malley and Jordan Carter fearful and alone. Can they find the courage to take a second chance on love? (978-1-60282-133-0)

Mephisto Aria by Justine Saracen. Opera singer Katherina Marov's destiny may be to repeat the mistakes of her father when she becomes involved in a dangerous love affair. (978-1-60282-134-7)

Battle Scars by Meghan O'Brien. Returning Iraq war veteran Ray McKenna struggles with the battle scars that can only be healed by love. (978-1-60282-129-3)

Chaps by Jove Belle. Eden Metcalf wants nothing more than to flee from her troubled past and travel the open road—until she runs into rancher Brandi Cornwell. (978-1-60282-127-9)

Lightbearer by John Caruso. Lucifer dares to question the premise of creation itself and reveals that sin may be all that stands between us and living hell. (978-1-60282-130-9)

The Seeker by Ronica Black. FBI profiler Kennedy Scott battles ghosts from her past, deadly obsession, and the evil that haunts her. (978-1-60282-128-6)

Power Play by Julie Cannon. Businesswomen Tate Monroe and Victoria Sosa are at odds in the boardroom, but not in the bedroom. (978-1-60282-125-5)

The Remarkable Journey of Miss Tranby Quirke by Elizabeth Ridley. When love enters Tranby's life in the form of a beautiful nineteen-year-old student, Lysette McDonald, she embarks on the most remarkable journey of all. (978-1-60282-126-2)

Returning Tides by Radclyffe. Insurance investigator Ashley Walker faces more than a dangerous opponent when she returns to the town, and the woman, she left behind. (978-1-60282-123-1)

Veritas by Anne Laughlin. When the hallowed halls of academia become the stage for murder, newly appointed Dean Beth Ellis's search for the truth leads her to unexpected discoveries about her own heart. (978-1-60282-124-8)

The Pleasure Planner by Larkin Rose. Pleasure purveyor Bree Hendricks treats love like a commodity until Logan Delaney makes Bree the client in her own game. (978-1-60282-121-7)

everafter by Nell Stark and Trinity Tam. Valentine Darrow is bitten by a vampire on her way to propose to her lover Alexa Newland, and their lives and love are placed in mortal jeopardy. (978-1-60282-119-4)

Summer Winds by Andrews & Austin. When Maggie Turner hires a ranch hand to help work her thousand acres, she never expects to be attracted to the very young, very female Cash Tate. (978-1-60282-120-0)

Beggar of Love by Lee Lynch. Jefferson is the lover every woman wants to be—or to have. A revealing saga of lesbian sexuality. (978-1-60282-122-4)

The Seduction of Moxie by Colette Moody. When 1930s Broadway actress Violet London meets speakeasy singer Moxie Valette, she is instantly attracted and her Hollywood trip takes an unexpected turn. (978-1-60282-114-9)

Goldenseal by Gill McKnight. When Amy Fortune returns to her childhood home, she discovers something sinister in the air—but is former lover Leone Garoul stalking her or protecting her? (978-1-60282-115-6)

Romantic Interludes 2: Secrets edited by Radclyffe and Stacia Seaman. An anthology of sensual lesbian love stories: passion, surprises, and secret desires. (978-1-60282-116-3)

Femme Noir by Clara Nipper. Nora Delaney meets her match in Max Abbott, a sex-crazed dame who may or may not have the information Nora needs to solve a murder—but can she contain her lust for Max long enough to find out? (978-1-60282-117-0)

The Reluctant Daughter by Lesléa Newman. Heartwarming, heartbreaking, and ultimately triumphant—the story every daughter recognizes of the lifelong struggle for our mothers to really see us. (978-1-60282-118-7)

Erosistible by Gill McKnight. When Win Martin arrives at a luxurious Greek hotel for a much-anticipated week of sun and sex with her new girlfriend, she is stunned to find her ex-girlfriend, Benny, is the proprietor. Aeros Ebook. (978-1-60282-134-7)

Looking Glass Lives by Felice Picano. Cousins Roger and Alistair become lifelong friends and discover their sexuality amidst the backdrop of twentieth-century gay culture. (978-1-60282-089-0)

Breaking the Ice by Kim Baldwin. Nothing is easy about life above the Arctic Circle—except, perhaps, falling in love. At least that's what pilot Bryson Faulkner hopes when she meets Karla Edwards. (978-1-60282-087-6)

It Should Be a Crime by Carsen Taite. Two women fulfill their mutual desire with a night of passion, neither expecting more until law professor Morgan Bradley and student Parker Casey meet again…in the classroom. (978-1-60282-086-9)

Rough Trade edited by Todd Gregory. Top male erotica writers pen their own hot, sexy versions of the term "rough trade," producing some of the hottest, nastiest, and most dangerous fiction ever published. (978-1-60282-092-0)

The High Priest and the Idol by Jane Fletcher. Jemeryl and Tevi's relationship is put to the test when the Guardian sends Jemeryl on a mission that puts her not only in harm's way, but back into the sights of a previous lover. (978-1-60282-085-2)

Point of Ignition by Erin Dutton. Amid a blaze that threatens to consume them both, firefighter Kate Chambers and property owner Alexi Clark redefine love and trust. (978-1-60282-084-5)

Secrets in the Stone by Radclyffe. Reclusive sculptor Rooke Tyler suddenly finds herself the object of two very different women's affections, and choosing between them will change her life forever. (978-1-60282-083-8)

Dark Garden by Jennifer Fulton. Vienna Blake and Mason Cavender are sworn enemies—who can't resist each other. Something has to give. (978-1-60282-036-4)

Late in the Season by Felice Picano. Set on Fire Island, this is the story of an unlikely pair of friends—a gay composer in his late thirties and an eighteen-year-old schoolgirl. (978-1-60282-082-1)

Punishment with Kisses by Diane Anderson-Minshall. Will Megan find the answers she seeks about her sister Ashley's murder or will her growing relationship with one of Ash's exes blind her to the real truth? (978-1-60282-081-4)

September Canvas by Gun Brooke. When Deanna Moore meets TV personality Faythe she is reluctantly attracted to her, but will Faythe side with the people spreading rumors about Deanna? (978-1-60282-080-7)

No Leavin' Love by Larkin Rose. Beautiful, successful Mercedes Miller thinks she can resume her affair with ranch foreman Sydney Campbell, but the rules have changed. (978-1-60282-079-1)

Between the Lines by Bobbi Marolt. When romance writer Gail Prescott meets actress Tannen Albright, she develops feelings that she usually only experiences through her characters. (978-1-60282-078-4)

Blue Skies by Ali Vali. Commander Berkley Levine leads an elite group of pilots on missions ordered by her ex-lover Captain Aidan Sullivan and everything is on the line—including love. (978-1-60282-077-7)

The Lure by Felice Picano. When Noel Cummings is recruited by the police to go undercover to find a killer, his life will never be the same. (978-1-60282-076-0)